The One-Week Wife

by B...

Fr...

We all kn... wedding that didn't happen between a certain Eastwick heiress and her well-moneyed fiancé. We all assumed the jilted groom was crushed beyond consolation. Well…he couldn't have been too despondent. Someone – who shall remain nameless – has stated this unmarried man proceeded to go on his honeymoon, not with the bride (of course not – she's marrying someone else) but with his own wedding planner. Come to think of it, wasn't that wedding planner a good friend of the bride?

We're not implying that anything improper went on behind those honeymoon suite doors. But if one working-class woman were to spend an entire week at a luxury resort with one very handsome, wealthy man…maybe friendship wasn't the first thing on her mind.

From the "People Are Talking"
Column of the
Eastwick Gazette

The Bought-and-Paid-for Wife
by Bronwyn Jameson

ᎽᏉᎷᏨᏮ

From the "People Are Talking" Column of the
Eastwick Gazette

Always the subject of many luncheon discussions, Mrs Vanessa Thorpe is back on top of the gossip list this week with the sudden appearance of the widow's stepson, Australian businessman Tristan Thorpe. Everyone wondered if Vanessa's marriage to her much older husband was for love... or money. And it seems the late Mr Thorpe's estranged son is convinced it was for the latter. He's held his father's will in probate for over two years – seems he'll do anything to keep his stepmother from receiving her inheritance.

Vanessa and Tristan have never crossed paths until this week. And perhaps that was for a very good reason. Because if the sparks flying between them now had been as evident when Vanessa was still married...no doubt *both* parties would have been left out of the will!

Available in August 2007 from Mills & Boon Desire

The Honour-Bound Promise
by Peggy Moreland
&
Bedded Then *Wed*
by Heidi Betts

 logo

Secret Lives of Society Wives
The One-Week Wife
by Patricia Kay
&
The Bought-and-Paid-for Wife
by Bronwyn Jameson

logo

The Pregnancy Negotiation
by Kristi Gold
&
Marriage of Revenge
by Sheri WhiteFeather

The One-Week Wife
PATRICIA KAY

The Bought-and-Paid-for Wife
BRONWYN JAMESON

MILLS & BOON®

Desire™

First published in Great Britain 2007
Harlequin Mills & Boon Limited,
Eton House, 18-24 Paradise Road, Richmond, Surrey TW9 1SR

The publisher acknowledges the copyright holders of the
individual works as follows:

The One-Week Wife © Harlequin Books S.A. 2006
The Bought-and-Paid-for Wife © Harlequin Books S.A. 2006

Special thanks and acknowledgement are given to Patricia Kay and
Bronwyn Jameson for their contribution to the SECRET LIVES OF
SOCIETY WIVES mini-series.

ISBN: 978 0 263 85026 0

51-0807

Printed and bound in Spain
by Litografia Rosés S.A., Barcelona

THE ONE-WEEK WIFE

by
Patricia Kay

Dear Reader,

This is my first Mills & Boon® Desire™ novel, and I couldn't have picked a story that was more fun to write than *The One-Week Wife*. I fell in love with Reed and Felicity from the first page, and I hope you will, too. They are nothing alike, yet they complement one another perfectly. Of course, they don't realise it immediately. Nor does the course of true love run smooth, but since this is a romance, we know they'll work it out in the end.

That's what I love about romances. No matter how many conflicts and obstacles the hero and heroine have standing in the way of their love, we know they will always win out in the end. And knowing doesn't take away from the satisfaction of the book, either. In fact, I think it enhances it. We don't have to worry that something horrible and sad will happen in the end, so we can relax and just enjoy the journey.

I hope you enjoy this journey as much as I've enjoyed bringing it to you.

Warmly,

Patricia Kay

PATRICIA KAY,

formerly writing as Trisha Alexander, is the *USA TODAY* bestselling author of more than thirty contemporary romances. She lives in Houston, Texas. To learn more about her, visit her website at www.patriciakay.com.

Don't miss any of the drama.
Collect all six titles in

SECRET LIVES OF SOCIETY WIVES

One

Felicity Farnsworth stopped her Toyota Highlander just outside the entrance to Rosedale Farms and took a deep breath to calm her jittery nerves. She dreaded her upcoming encounter with Reed Kelly. But she'd put the meeting off long enough. Now, even if she'd wanted to, she could no longer do so. Not since Madeline Newhouse had insisted her daughter Portia's wedding photos simply *had* to be taken at Rosedale.

Felicity was a wedding planner, the owner of Weddings By Felicity, the most successful event-planning business in Fairfield County, Connecticut. Her weddings were all spectacular, and the Newhouse wedding promised to be the most spectacular of all, for Portia was the adored only daughter of Alex Newhouse, the famous actor. And he had decreed that no expense should be spared when it came to his beautiful daughter's wedding.

So if Madeline wanted Portia's wedding photos taken at Rosedale, Felicity had to make that happen. Otherwise, she would be risking her hard-won success. And forfeiting the chance to be recommended by Madeline to her wide circle of free-spending friends.

Felicity took another deep, steadying breath, released the brake and drove slowly through the arched portal leading into Rosedale. Yet no matter how she cautioned herself to remain calm, her heartbeat picked up speed the closer she got to the main building, which housed Reed's office.

Reed.

Felicity hadn't seen him since her best friend Emma Dearborn had broken her engagement to him, throwing him over for Garrett Keating. How was Reed taking the breakup? Was he devastated? Maybe he wouldn't want to see Felicity or anyone else associated with Emma. Maybe he hated *all* the Debs who were in Emma's close circle of friends. If he did, Felicity certainly wouldn't blame him.

Yet as uneasy as she was about seeing Reed, Felicity couldn't deny an underlying flicker of excitement. It was so ironic that the only man to interest her since her miserable ex of a husband had betrayed her and robbed her blind was Reed. That interest had sparked while Felicity was planning his wedding to Emma, and no matter how Felicity had fought it, telling herself Reed was off-limits, it had refused to go away.

But Reed was no longer her best friend's fiancé.

In fact, Reed was now available.

No, I'm not going there. Not, not, not...

After her divorce, Felicity had made a promise to herself. She'd vowed to spend her time and energy rebuilding her life and her fortune. Period. Because obviously she had rotten judgment when it came to men. What she'd thought was love on her ex's part had been opportunism, nothing more. He'd used her, and Felicity had no intention of ever being used again.

So no matter how attracted to him you are, put sexy, available Reed Kelly out of your mind and stay focused on your goals—goals that do not *include marriage or any other kind of permanent commitment to a man.*

Arriving at the main building, Felicity pulled in and parked. Then she briskly climbed out of her truck, put on her game face and walked up the three shallow concrete steps into Reed's domain.

"Oh, hi, Ms. Farnsworth."

Felicity smiled at the pretty young girl who sat working at a computer in Reed's office. She recognized her as one of his nieces, but wasn't sure which one she was. "Hi. Is Reed around?"

The girl—who looked to be about fifteen or sixteen—nodded. "He's out back in the stables. Want me to go get him?"

"No, that's okay. I'll walk back there." Felicity

preferred to see Reed alone. Especially if his reaction to her visit was anywhere close to what she feared.

Heading back to the stables, Felicity was grateful that the walkway was paved. The last thing she wanted was to ruin her Jimmy Choo mules, which had eaten up a big chunk of her disposable income last month. Shoes were Felicity's big weakness—some might even say her obsession. Currently she owned more than eighty pairs, and she still kept buying new ones.

Sometimes she felt guilty over the amount of money she spent on shoes, but she didn't allow those feelings to last long. After all, she worked hard. The cash she spent was hers, earned by that hard work. It wasn't as if she was spending some man's money.

No, it was the other way around. Sam spent all my *money,* she thought bitterly. She wondered how long it would take to get over the fact she'd been stupid enough to let her husband dip his hands into her inheritance from her parents.

"Felicity!"

Felicity blinked. She'd been so lost in her thoughts she hadn't even seen the approach of Max Weldon, Reed's trainer and assistant manager. A former jockey, Max topped out at five foot one and a hundred pounds, but his deep voice belied his size.

She smiled. "Hi, Max." Max and her father had been very good friends, even though Max was closer to Felicity's age than to her father's.

Max's brown eyes gazed up at her with fondness.

"Been a while since I've seen you. What're you doing out here? You in the market for a horse?"

Felicity shook her head. "I don't have the time to ride anymore. No, I've got to see Reed about a business proposition." From the curious expression on Max's face, she knew he was dying to know what kind of business proposition she could possibly have that would interest Reed, but he was too polite to ask.

"Well, he's in the stables," Max said.

"Thanks. Tell Paulette I said hi." Paulette was Max's wife.

"Will do."

They said goodbye, then headed in opposite directions.

Nearing the stables, Felicity heard a soft whinny, then the unmistakable low voice of a man.

Reed.

Pulse quickening, she left the brightly sunlit walkway and entered the shaded interior of the main stables. Assorted smells—molasses and oats, cured hay and wood shavings, and that particular scent of the saddle soap Reed and his workers used to wash the horses—assaulted Felicity's senses as she walked inside. Although she had once been an avid horsewoman, she hadn't ridden in many years. Her ex had considered riding and everything connected to the sport to be a waste of time and money, and for a long time, what Sam had wanted Sam had gotten. But today, once again among the familiar sounds and smells, she remembered with an ache of nostalgia all the reasons she'd loved horses and riding so much.

Reed stood a few dozen yards away, talking softly to a beautiful black gelding with a classically chiseled head. Felicity's breath caught at the picture. She wasn't sure which was more gorgeous…the horse…or Reed.

Feasting her eyes on Reed's six-foot-two frame, his thick brown hair and his tanned, muscled, athletic body clothed in a white knit shirt and coffee-colored riding breeches, she couldn't help thinking Emma was crazy. She'd told Felicity that once she'd seen Garrett again she'd finally realized she didn't love Reed the way she should. But how any woman could *not* love—or at least lust after—Reed Kelly was a mystery to Felicity.

In her opinion, Reed was the perfect man, if such a thing actually existed. For not only was he gorgeous, he was sexy, lots of fun and *nice*. Warm, generous and kindhearted, he was the type of man both men and women liked. Added to all that, he loved horses.

If he'd been mine…

But he hadn't been hers. And he never would be. Because she was no longer in the market….

Felicity didn't finish the thought, because just then Reed turned. The stable was dim, and her eyes hadn't fully adjusted from the July sun outside, so Felicity couldn't quite make out his expression.

"Hello, Felicity," he said quietly.

He didn't sound mad. That was promising.

"H-hello, Reed." Damn. She hated that slight wobble in her voice. She prided herself on always being calm, cool and collected. Some people even called her the Ice Princess, a name she had actively cultivated, for it helped her when she was dealing with the megarich, as she often did. *Never let 'em see you sweat. Always give the impression you're in perfect control.* That had become her mantra.

"What brings you here? Did you come to gloat?" *Oops. Maybe he was mad.*

"Gloat?" she said innocently. "About what?"

Instead of answering, he stroked the gelding one more time, then strode toward her.

Felicity had to force herself not to back up, even though that nervousness she'd managed to quell earlier was back in spades.

"Is everyone talking about me? Feeling sorry for me?" he said sharply.

Now she could see his eyes. She had never known that blue eyes could actually blaze. Her heart beat faster. "No, of course not." But they were. After all, Emma and Reed's breakup was one of the juiciest pieces of gossip to hit Eastwick in months. And Eastwick thrived on gossip. Especially that witch Delia Forrester, who seemed to think she might become the new Bunny Talbot now that the "Eastwick Social Diary" gossip maven was dead.

Reed's jaw hardened. "Don't lie to me, Felicity. I know everybody in the entire damned county is gossiping about me. Hell, I can hear them now. 'There must be something wrong with Reed Kelly if Emma Dearborn has thrown him over.'"

"Oh, Reed." Felicity's heart melted at the realization that he wasn't mad. He was hurt. Unable to help herself, she reached over and laid her hand on his arm. He flinched, but he didn't pull away. Wanting to comfort him, she moved closer, sliding her arms around his waist and hugging him. "I'm so sorry," she said softly. "About everything that's happened."

For a moment he stood stiffly, and Felicity was afraid she'd crossed an uncrossable line. Then his arms encircled her, and he rested his chin on the top of her head. Felicity closed her eyes. Being held like this, even if it was only a hug between casual friends, felt so good. It had been a long time since she'd been embraced by a man she respected. Especially a man as attractive as Reed.

She sighed and, drawing back slightly, looked up, wishing she knew what else she could say to make him feel better. "Reed…" she began.

He looked down.

When their gazes met, something electric and undeniable sizzled between them. And then, in an action Felicity knew she'd never forget, his head came down and his mouth captured hers.

Shock waves radiated through Felicity as his tongue delved. She moaned when his hands dropped lower to cup her bottom, pulling her even closer so that she could feel his arousal. Her insides had turned liquid, her entire body on fire with need.

Reed…Reed…

Her mind spun with the realization that one of her fantasies was actually taking place. For even during Emma's engagement to Reed, there had been times Felicity couldn't stop herself from wondering what it would be like to be Emma. To be kissed by Reed. To have him touch her. To make love with him…

Suddenly, penetrating the haze of desire consuming Felicity, she heard the sound of someone's footsteps outside. Reed must have heard them, too, for he immediately released her, and she staggered backward.

For just a moment they stared at one another. Then Felicity, knowing her face was flaming, sputtered, "I—I have to go. Here. This is what I came to give you." Reaching into her handbag, she grabbed the check she'd prepared earlier and thrust it at him. It was a refund of the deposit he'd given her months ago when he and Emma had asked her to handle the arrangements for their wedding.

Too embarrassed to wait for his response, she spun about and, as fast as she could manage on her four-inch heels, she fled the stable.

Hell's bells!

What had he been *thinking?*

You weren't thinking. At least, not with your brain.

Huffing out a breath, Reed swore at himself. Jesus. That had to have been the stupidest thing he'd ever done. He'd practically attacked Felicity. Why?

Was he that horny? Or was he somehow trying to get back at Emma for making him a laughingstock?

He gritted his teeth.

That's what galled him.

That's what *really* galled him.

On some level he'd always known that something was missing in his relationship with Emma. She was sweet and lovely and exactly the kind of woman any man would be proud to have as his wife. But if he'd been honest with himself, he'd have admitted that there were no sparks between them, which didn't bode well for their future.

In fact—and he couldn't have admitted this to anyone—they had never been intimate. Emma had been reluctant, wanting to wait until they were married, and Reed had respected her feelings.

So when she'd broken their engagement because of another man, he'd been more embarrassed than hurt. But afterward he had wondered if her reluctance to engage in sex before their marriage had more to do with a lack of desire than it did with wanting to remain chaste, as he'd thought.

Now he questioned everything about their relationship, especially his own judgment. His ego was sorely bruised, and the fact that everyone in their circle knew exactly what had caused the breakup made the situation ten times worse.

Although Reed came from a big, gregarious family and really liked people, he was a very private person where his feelings were concerned. If he could have licked his wounds alone, he could have dealt with being jilted. As it was, he felt raw and exposed.

And stupid. Don't forget stupid.

"Hey, boss, everything okay in here?"

Reed tried for a normal smile. "Everything's fine, Max. Why?"

His assistant frowned. "I just saw Felicity rushing out of here. Thought maybe you'd had some kind of argument or something."

"No, uh, she had an appointment, I think."

Max nodded, but the speculative look remained in his eyes, and Reed wondered if he suspected what had *really* happened between them. "Which reminds me, there are some phone calls I need to make," Reed added.

Walking out of the stable, Reed put on his sunglasses and headed for the office. In the distance he glimpsed the taillights of a silver SUV heading away from the farm. Felicity's vehicle, he realized ruefully. Getting away from him as fast as she could.

And yet…

She certainly hadn't shoved him away when he'd kissed her. In fact, he thought, she had responded rather enthusiastically. Just remembering that response and how good her slender curves and warm body had felt in his arms, he could feel himself growing hard again.

Maybe Felicity was just what he needed right now. If they were to get together, the gossips would have something new to talk about, and they'd stop feeling sorry for him. The idea was appealing, but after a moment or two he pushed it away. He couldn't do that to Felicity. It simply wouldn't be fair to use her that way. Especially when he knew, from comments Emma had made, that Felicity had been badly hurt by her former husband's betrayal.

Belatedly he looked at the check she had shoved into his hand. A twenty-thousand-dollar refund of the deposit he'd given her when he and Emma had first begun planning their wedding.

That was generous of her. As it was, he'd lost the thousands he'd paid for the honeymoon he wouldn't be taking. Not to mention the cost of the expensive diamond Emma had returned to him—a ring that he was sure the jeweler wouldn't take back, or if he did, would give Reed only a fraction of what he'd paid for it.

He hoped Felicity wasn't out any money because of the canceled wedding. Surely she would have deducted any expenses she'd incurred before making out the check. He made a mental note to ask her about that.

Reaching his office, he walked inside and smiled at his brother Daniel's daughter, Colleen, who promptly handed him three pink telephone slips.

"Julianne Foster, Dr. Finnerty and Gram called," Colleen said. "Gram just wanted to know if you're coming to dinner tonight."

"Thanks, honey." Reed looked at his watch. It was after one. "Shouldn't you be heading home by now?" Colleen was working half days for him this summer.

"I just wanted to finish up the newsletter," she said as Reed headed into his office. "Then I'll be off."

Reed sent a monthly newsletter to his clients, who numbered in the hundreds—some living as far away as Texas, for Reed's thoroughbred horses were renowned and commanded top prices. Rosedale Farms was a full-service facility providing the highest-quality care and environment for all boarding, foaling and bloodstock management needs. It sat on six hundred acres of rolling hills and pastures in a gorgeous setting that was the envy of many other horse breeders. Reed was justifiably proud of the farm named after his paternal grandmother, Rose Moran Kelly, who, along with her husband, Aloysius, had owned and run a successful horse-breeding farm in their native Ireland, and he hoped to pass it down to his children.

Children. At the rate he was going, he'd never have any. Too bad he couldn't just arrange a marriage the way they had in the old country. Make it a strictly business proposition and pick a wife who wanted children the way he did. Of course, he wouldn't want just anyone. She'd have to be smart, attractive and agreeable. Unwanted came the thought *Someone like Felicity.*

He grimaced. Oh, sure. As if Felicity would be interested. She'd made her feelings about marriage known to anyone who would listen. She'd been burned once and had no intention of being burned again. He and Emma had often talked about Felicity's attitude, because Emma really cared about her best friend and wanted her to be happy.

"She told me," Emma had said, "that from now on she's devoting herself to her career and only her career. When I tried to tell her she could have both a successful career and a successful marriage—all it would take is the right man—she said she was happy for me if I felt that way, but marriage was not for her."

Remembering that conversation, Reed told himself to put Felicity out of his mind. She was not a candidate to be Mrs. Reed Kelly.

Determinedly clearing his thoughts of everything but work, he sat down at his desk and picked up his phone to return the calls.

Felicity couldn't stop thinking about what had happened between her and Reed. Dear heaven, what had she been *thinking?* Why had she permitted that kiss? And permitting it, why had she responded like a bitch in heat?

You know why. You've been lusting after Reed for a long time....

And now he knew it. Or if he didn't exactly know it, he sure as hell suspected it.

Damn.

Her face burned just thinking about her wanton, out-of-control behavior. She couldn't imagine what Reed was thinking. How could she ever face him again?

And Max. Why, she'd nearly run him down when she'd rushed out of the stables that way. She could just imagine what he'd been thinking. She'd muttered an apology and some nonsense about being late for an appointment and avoided his eyes. *Oh, God...*

She was still mentally berating herself when she got back to her office. Trying to regroup and forget what had happened out at Rosedale Farms—so Reed had kissed her, so what?—she entered her office.

Rita Dixon, her diminutive assistant, looked up from her desk. Her brown eyes sparkled with the boundless energy that made her such a valuable employee. "So how'd it go? Did he agree?"

Felicity froze. Oh, my God. She had completely forgotten her main reason for going out to Rosedale. Sure, she'd intended to return Reed's deposit, but her most important goal was to get him to agree to allow Portia Newhouse's wedding photos to be taken there.

And she'd forgotten to ask him! Thinking fast, she said, "He's going to get back to me."

"Oh, fudge," Rita said. "I was sure you could persuade him. Should I call Bo? He'll be disappointed, but maybe he'll have another idea that Madame Newhouse will go for." Bo Harrison was the photographer Felicity always used unless her clients specified someone else.

"Don't call him yet. I mean, Reed didn't say *no.*"

Rita shrugged. "Okay. I guess if anyone can get a yes out of him, it's you."

Felicity told herself she hadn't really lied to Rita in implying that Reed was thinking about allowing the use of Rosedale for the photos. Her mind whirled as she escaped into the relative privacy of the War Room—so named because it was used to plan the strategy for their large events.

Now what? she thought, trying not to panic.

But she knew the answer.

She would have to get over her embarrassment, pick up the phone and call Reed.

Now.

TWO

Reed had the phone in his hand. He'd just finished talking with Jack Finnerty, who wanted to buy a broodmare, and was about to call his mother to say that, yes, he'd be there for dinner tonight, when the phone rang.

Glancing at the caller ID, he saw Weddings By Felicity. He hesitated only a moment before pressing the talk button.

"Reed Kelly."

"Reed? This is Felicity."

"Hey. I'm glad you called. Beat me to the punch. I'd planned to call you later to thank you for returning my deposit." Would she say anything about what had happened between them earlier?

"You're welcome."

"You gave me too much, though. You must have had *some* expenses connected with our canceled wedding."

"My expenses were negligible. You don't owe me anything. However, I do need a favor." Her voice was crisp and businesslike.

He finally realized she wasn't going to mention the episode in the stables. Good. That made things easier. They could both pretend it hadn't happened.

"What do you need?" he said, equally businesslike.

"I'm handling Portia Newhouse's wedding, and she and her mother have set their heart on having her photos taken at Rosedale Farms. Would you consider that? They're willing to pay whatever you would want to charge."

Normally, Reed would have refused this kind of request. But he did owe Felicity, and there was something to be said for creating goodwill with the New-houses.

"What are we talking about?" he asked. "I don't want tons of people tramping about, and absolutely no TV cameras or paparazzi."

"No, of course not. It would only be the wedding party, the parents and immediate family, my photographer and his assistant, and me and my assistant."

Reed thought for a minute, finally saying, "That sounds okay." He made a swift calculation. "The fee will be five thousand dollars. Will they go for that?"

"They'll be happy to pay it. Thank you, Reed. Portia will be thrilled."

"When's the wedding taking place?"

"In three weeks. Um, one more thing. Bo—that's my photographer—and I will need to stop by as soon as possible to scout out different locations. Is that okay?"

"Sure. You can come out tomorrow, if you like."

"Great. I'll call Bo to see what his schedule is like. Ten o'clock tomorrow morning would be best for me. Would that work?"

Reed looked at his calendar. Nothing urgent was penciled in for the morning. "That'll be fine. We can meet at my office."

Thanking him again, she hung up.

Reed didn't immediately call his mother. Instead, he sat there and thought about the conversation with Felicity. He knew creating goodwill with the Newhouses wasn't the only reason he'd agreed to Felicity's request.

The truth was, despite all the reasons he'd told himself she was not for him, he wanted to see Felicity again.

"Dinner was wonderful, Mom."

"Thank you, darlin'." Maeve Kelly beamed at Shannon, one of Reed's two older sisters. "There's nothing I enjoy more than feeding my family."

Wednesday-night dinner at his mother's was a weekly ritual in Reed's family. Not everyone could always attend. Shannon was a nurse anesthetist and her husband, John, was a lawyer with a busy practice.

The same was true of Reed's other sister, Bridget, and her husband.

If everyone in the family, including brothers Daniel and Aidan, their spouses and children, came to dinner, the total count was twenty-three. Tonight only Reed, Shannon and her family, and Daniel and his family were there, making a total of eleven.

Normally, Reed enjoyed these gatherings. With everyone's busy schedules, he didn't get to see much of his siblings and their families, even though they all lived in Eastwick or its environs. So he made an effort to attend the Wednesday dinners. Today, however, he'd just as soon have skipped it, because everyone, but most especially Shannon, had been giving him furtive looks filled with pity. He knew they all thought he was miserable over the breakup with Emma, but he also knew if he made a big deal of denying his misery, they'd think he was protesting too much.

Once again he realized the best thing he could do to stop all the gossip in Eastwick and the unwanted pity of his family would be to start seeing someone else…and fast.

Felicity.

Jeez! No matter how he tried, he couldn't get the sexy blonde out of his mind. Nor could he stop thinking about the way she'd looked earlier. He knew some people thought Felicity had ruined her hair when she'd chopped it all off after her divorce, but he liked the short, spiky style. In his opinion, she looked sexier than the other Debs, the tight-knit group of friends that she ran around with. They tended toward more conservative styles, whereas Felicity looked as if she could have been one of the trendy actresses on television.

Today she'd worn some kind of sparkly butterfly clip in her hair and one of her trademark short black dresses that showed off her rather remarkable legs.

He grinned, thinking of those legs and the completely inappropriate shoes she'd had on, all pointy toes and spike heels. She definitely hadn't looked as if she belonged in the stables, but she'd certainly gotten him thinking in terms of throwing her into the hayloft.

"Hey, Reed, you doing okay?"

He turned to Shannon, who had scooted over next to him now that her two teenage girls, along with Daniel's kids, had begun clearing the table.

"I'm fine. Why?"

Shannon, who had the Kelly blue eyes and dark hair, shrugged. "You know…" She lowered her voice, although no one else at the table was paying any attention to them.

Reed stifled a sigh. "Trust me. I'm fine."

She looked as if she wanted to say something else, but instead bit her lip. Her eyes held concern.

Reed reached over and squeezed her hand. "Thanks for worrying about me, Shannon, but I'm really okay. In fact, I'm relieved."

"Well, I think the whole thing stinks. What's wrong with that woman, anyway?"

"There's nothing wrong with Emma. She was just more honest than I was. Our breakup is for the best."

"You're not just saying that? You've been awfully distracted today."

He shook his head. "No, I'm not just saying that." Shrugging, he added, "There was always something missing between us. I felt it, but I didn't want to face it. I'm glad Emma did."

Now Shannon gave him a real smile. "You know, I never thought she was right for you, either."

He couldn't help grinning. Her loyalty warmed him. He could always count on his family.

"What's going on over there?" Daniel said.

"Who wants to know?" Shannon said cheekily, winking at Reed.

After a few more lighthearted remarks, Daniel's wife, Anna Lisa, turned to Shannon and said, "Hey, guess who I saw coming out of Goldman's Deli this afternoon."

"Have no idea," Shannon said.

"Alex Newhouse."

"Really?"

Alex Newhouse sightings were rare in Eastwick, for even when he was home and between films, he usually stuck close to his gated estate, especially during the height of tourist season.

"Yes. You should have seen the tourists gawking at him." Anna Lisa giggled. "Of course, I wasn't much better. God, the man's gorgeous! Those eyes…" She sighed. "Did you know Felicity Farnsworth is doing his daughter's wedding?"

Shannon nodded. "I'd heard."

"Wouldn't you *kill* for an invitation?"

"I know *I* would," Reed's mother said. "I've loved Alex Newhouse from the moment I first saw him in a movie."

"He *is* magnetic," Shannon agreed.

Reed wondered if he should mention the fact that the Newhouse wedding pictures were going to be taken at Rosedale. And that Alex would be in them. Best not to, he decided. The Newhouse family wouldn't want an audience, especially at a photo shoot that was costing them five grand.

"Felicity's done quite well for herself, hasn't she?" Anna Lisa said.

"Surprisingly so," Shannon said.

Daniel stifled a yawn, clearly bored with this talk of weddings. "Reed, want to go catch the rest of the ball game?"

What Reed really wanted to do was stay and hear what the women had to say about Felicity, but he couldn't think of any way to do that, so he reluctantly pushed his chair back.

"Why do you say surprisingly so?" Anna Lisa asked.

Yeah, Reed thought, stalling by pretending something was in his shoe. *Why do you?*

"Oh, you know," Shannon said. "She was born with a silver spoon in her mouth. I just didn't think she'd have that kind of drive."

"She strikes me as a woman who, once she sets her sights on something, will work like crazy to accomplish it," Anna Lisa said. "I give her credit for picking herself up after that horrible divorce of hers and making something of her life."

"It's too bad she doesn't have better taste in friends," Reed's mother said, shooting him a dark look.

Reed knew an exit line when he heard one.

But even after he and Daniel were settled in the family room in front of the big-screen TV their father had bought less than four months before his fatal heart attack, Reed's mind was only marginally on the Red Sox game. Most of it remained centered on Felicity, his ex-fiancée's best friend. And the more he thought about her, the more he wanted to pursue what they'd started earlier today.

Damn!

Why couldn't he get the woman out of his mind?

Maybe his subconscious was trying to tell him something. Maybe, instead of trying to forget about Felicity, he should be figuring out how to get her into his bed. Because, obviously, he wasn't going to be able to move on with his life until he did.

When Felicity arrived at her office Thursday morning, she wasn't surprised to see Bo Harrison already there, ready and waiting. Bo, with his dyed platinum hair, diamond earrings and all-black "uniform," looked like the creative artist he was. His photographs were works of art, and he was in high demand despite his outrageous prices.

"Good morning," he said, smiling.

"Good morning, Bo."

"Ready to roll?"

"As soon as I get my coffee I will be." She'd barely uttered the words before Rita emerged from their little kitchen and handed Felicity an insulated cup. Felicity grinned. "You're an angel, Rita."

Today her assistant wore a bright yellow dress and matching yellow heels with peekaboo toes. She, too, was a shoe junkie, although unlike Felicity, Rita bought her shoes on sale at discount stores instead of designer shops.

"You look nice today," Felicity said.

"So do you," Rita countered, eyeing Felicity's frothy multicolored sundress, a far cry from her normal work attire of either black or taupe—colors that would never take attention away from her brides or their attendants.

"Thanks," Felicity said. "I have a Debs Club luncheon later."

"I saw it on your calendar," Rita said. "What time will you be back here?"

"Probably not until three. Why? Is there something urgent that I've forgotten?"

"No." Rita smiled. "I just like to keep track."

"If anything changes, I'll call you. Or if something *does* come up, you call me on my cell."

"Okay. Have fun today, you two."

Five minutes later, Bo and Felicity were on their

way. Felicity had declined Bo's offer of a ride, since she would go straight to the club from Rosedale.

As they neared the entrance to the horse farm, her heart beat a little faster. Even though she'd spoken to Reed on the phone after that kiss—and both had pretended it hadn't happened—it would be different seeing him in person. Meeting his gaze, remembering how his body had responded to hers, and hers to his. But no matter how awkward the situation, Felicity was determined to be her normal cool, efficient self today.

Because the last thing she wanted was for Reed to think that kiss had been important to her or that she attached any significance to it. Better for him to think her behavior yesterday had been a temporary aberration, a momentary lapse of good judgment.

Reed stood outside the office building as Felicity and Bo drove in. They both parked, then walked over to greet him.

"Good morning," Felicity said crisply.

"Good morning," he answered.

Damn, he looked good. Once again he wore close-fitting breeches, but today they were topped with an open-necked blue shirt the same vibrant shade as his eyes.

Felicity's heart clutched when those eyes met hers. It took every ounce of her willpower and self-control not to look away. Instead, she said in a voice admirably even, "Reed, this is my photographer, Bo Harrison. Bo, Reed Kelly, the owner of Rosedale."

"Bo," Reed said, extending his right hand. "Nice to meet you."

"Thank you, Mr. Kelly. I appreciate the opportunity to work here."

Reed smiled. "Where did you want to start?"

"Maybe you could just give us a tour of the place," Felicity suggested. "Give Bo an idea of what's here?"

Reed gave her a dubious look. "Are you planning to walk around in *those* shoes?"

"And risk my Blahniks? Are you crazy?" Felicity grinned. She'd shopped far and wide for the perfect complement to her shimmery sundress in shades of turquoise, violet and gold. "I brought some others."

She reached into her tote and extracted a pair of New Balance cross trainers, exchanging them for her strappy gold sandals.

Soon they were off, Reed leading the way and explaining what each area's function was. Felicity was glad they'd decided on a morning tour, for already the sun was getting uncomfortably warm. As they walked, she couldn't help being impressed with the scope of Rosedale. It was truly beautiful, and far more comprehensive than Felicity had imagined from Emma's sketchy description the one time they'd discussed what Reed did for a living.

Come to think of it, Emma hadn't talked about Reed much at all during their engagement, other than to say they'd been there or done that. The omission should have been Felicity's first clue that all was not well between them.

Had Reed sensed Emma's misgivings? Because surely she'd had them for a while, even if she hadn't been able to articulate them or share them with Felicity. Wondering how long it would take him to get over Emma, Felicity shot Reed a furtive look.

And caught him looking at *her* with the oddest expression on his face.

Startled when their eyes met, she could feel her face coloring and quickly looked away, pretending to be interested in the quarantine and layup facility he had just pointed out.

What had he been thinking just now?

She swallowed. Damn, she wished she had been capable of restraining her baser instincts yesterday.

For the remainder of their tour she studiously avoided looking at Reed. He unnerved her, and she didn't like the feeling, even as she liked *him* far more than was good for her.

Telling herself any future interaction with Reed that didn't involve business would complicate her life in ways she absolutely did not need, Felicity thanked him when the tour was over, said goodbye to both him and Bo, and drove away from Rosedale without looking back.

Reed stood outside and watched the departure of Bo and Felicity. An idea had struck him this morning, one that, on the surface, seemed outrageous.

And yet…was it *that* outrageous?

He didn't have to be a rocket scientist to see that

Felicity was as attracted to him as he was to her. Just the way her gaze darted away every time it met his—well, maybe not *every* time—would have told him she felt the same things he did.

So what if she had no interest in marriage and he did? All he wanted right now was something new. A brief liaison, one that would satisfy both of them and be a hell of a lot of fun in the process.

Sex with no strings.

He grinned.

Sex with no strings. They'd both get something they wanted and wouldn't have to worry about any messy entanglements or hurt feelings afterward.

And if he presented his proposition to her on that basis, she might just say yes.

Three

Felicity headed straight for the powder room when she reached the club. She felt overheated by her excursion to Rosedale. Or maybe the heat had been caused by her impossible-to-deny attraction to Reed.

God, he was sexy.

Just looking at him made her feel weak in the knees.

Well, no matter what had caused this unwelcome heat, she needed to put herself together again before facing the Debs, some of whom were way too perceptive. Of course, no one had to know where she'd been earlier today. In fact, she absolutely did *not* want them to know, because the last subject she wanted to discuss, in front of Emma or anyone else, was Reed.

After repairing her makeup and repositioning her

violet rhinestone butterfly hair clip, Felicity felt ready to make her appearance.

Walking past the Emerald Room's malachite bar, she waved to Harry, the bartender, who waved back, and headed straight for the table where she and the other Debs always sat.

Sure enough, two of them were already there—Emma, wearing a powder-blue dress that set off her silky black hair and violet eyes, and Lily Miller Cartwright, who was now seven months pregnant and radiant in a yellow maternity dress that hugged her rounded belly.

Felicity used the few moments before her friends noticed her approach to study them. She couldn't help feeling a twinge of envy at the happiness evident on both faces. A happiness caused by being deeply in love and knowing they were loved back.

But I don't want to be married. I don't even want a long-term commitment. So why am I envious because they've both found their soul mates?

Just then, Lily turned and saw her. "Felicity!" she exclaimed, giving her a beaming smile.

"Hi, Fee," said a quieter Emma.

As Felicity leaned down to kiss first Lily, then Emma, she wondered at Emma's more restrained greeting. Was it possible she suspected something about Felicity's whereabouts today? Her inappropriate feelings for Reed? Was she even now wondering if Felicity had harbored those feelings all along, even when Emma and Reed had been engaged?

Oh, don't be ridiculous! How could she possibly suspect anything? That's just your guilty conscience bothering you.

Besides, Felicity thought, even if Emma *did* suspect something, why would she care now? She hadn't wanted Reed. She'd wanted Garrett. And Felicity had absolutely no interest in Garrett Keating. But even after telling herself this, she still felt uncomfortable. After the debacle with Sam, she hated deception of any kind, even when it was rooted in an omission rather than an outright lie.

Telling herself to chill, Felicity sat next to Emma and when their waiter approached, ordered a glass of her favorite German Riesling, then joined in the conversation, which centered around an upcoming baby shower for Lily.

"It's being hosted by Jack's cousin Jennifer," Lily said happily. She absently pushed an errant strand of curly auburn hair under her yellow headband. With her blue eyes and bright coloring, she could have been the model for a Botticelli painting.

"I hope we're all going to be invited," Felicity said brightly.

Lily gave her a look of incredulity. "Of course you are! How could you even *think* I wouldn't want all the Debs Club there?"

Just then, Vanessa Thorpe and Abby Talbot, the last two members of their group who were joining today's lunch, arrived together. Both young women were immaculately turned out—Vanessa in the same shade of green as her eyes and Abby in white, which set off her beautiful tan and long blond hair. Felicity hadn't seen much of Abby since her mother's funeral earlier in the summer, and she wondered how Abby was doing.

Kisses, hugs and compliments flew while the newcomers settled themselves and ordered glasses of wine. Once they'd had a chance to briefly study the menu—they met here for lunch so often they'd practically memorized it—the five women ordered. Mostly they stuck to salads, fish, or chicken, although Lily—laughing—said she didn't care, she was going to have pasta today. "After the baby comes, I'll have to say goodbye to carbs. Might as well enjoy myself while I can."

"Knowing you, you'll be back into a size four before that kid's a month old," Vanessa said.

"I've never worn a size four in my life," Lily said.

"Well, six, then."

"Eight's more like it."

"Listen to her," Vanessa said.

"Oh, she's just trying to make the rest of us feel better," Abby quipped.

"Like *you're* fat or something," Vanessa shot back.

Felicity sat back and enjoyed the banter. She loved these get-togethers with the Debs. They were all terrific women and had become loyal friends who had supported and encouraged her through her problems with Sam.

Even Abby had been loyal, although that mother of hers had had a field day writing about Sam's desertion and the loss of Felicity's inheritance. Felicity had long wondered how a mother and daughter could be so different, for Abby rarely gossiped. Maybe she'd had enough of it growing up with Bunny.

After their orders had been placed, the conversation turned to Emma's relationship with Garrett, or more accurately, the breakup with Reed.

"How's Reed taking the news?" Vanessa asked.

Emma shrugged. "I haven't seen him or spoken to him since I broke the engagement," she confessed.

Vanessa grimaced. "Poor Reed. He's probably brokenhearted."

"I hope not," Emma said. She bit her lip.

Emma was tenderhearted, and Felicity knew she'd truly cared for Reed and wouldn't have wanted him to suffer.

"Have any of you seen him?" Emma asked, looking around the table.

The question unsettled Felicity. She didn't want to reveal that she'd seen him, because she was afraid that in talking about their meetings she might give away her feelings, yet she hated deceiving Emma. So she pushed back from the table. "Sorry, I've got to visit the ladies'. Now, don't talk about me when I'm not here to defend myself."

They all laughed.

She would stay away just long enough to let the conversation move to another subject. Unfortunately, when she entered the ladies' room, Felicity almost turned around and walked right out, because standing in front of the large mirror in the outer lounge area was Delia Forrester, one of Felicity's least favorite people.

"Felicity! Darling, it's been *too* long," Delia exclaimed. For some unknown reason, the woman had taken a shine to Felicity, almost as if she thought they were two of a kind.

Felicity forced herself to smile and say pleasantly, "Hello, Delia." Although she detested the woman, she saw no point in openly antagonizing her. "How are you?"

"I'm absolutely wonderful." Delia patted her dyed platinum pageboy, which was always perfectly coiffed.

Why was it people seemed to love platinum-blond so much? Didn't they realize the dyed version looked completely fake? Felicity looked in the mirror at her own natural platinum hair color with satisfaction.

"And what about you, dear? I know you must be run ragged these days, what with the Townsend wedding and the Newhouse wedding and the Dearborn-Kelly cancellation, not to mention all that committee work."

This last was said disparagingly, because Delia was not a part of any of the charities or club committees that the Debs were involved in. Felicity nastily wondered if that was because she knew the other women would not let her run roughshod over them as she was wont to do.

"I'm managing just fine," Felicity said. Her tone didn't invite further comment. Taking lip gloss out of her handbag, she applied a fresh coat.

Delia, however, was too obtuse to take the hint.

"I'm just shocked that your *supposed* friend Emma would do that to you."

Felicity frowned. "I'm not sure I know what you mean." She closed the tube of lip gloss and dropped it back into her handbag.

"Oh, come on, Felicity. Why, she just canceled her wedding out of the blue, now, didn't she? That tells me she doesn't care *who* she hurts. Frankly, I think it's horrible that she would let you lose money like that. But that's typical of your friends, isn't it? They're all independently wealthy, so they can't understand what it's like for someone like you."

"Delia, you don't know what you're talking about," Felicity snapped, suddenly not caring if she antagonized this stupid woman or not. "Emma would *never* purposely hurt anyone, least of all me. Breaking her engagement to Reed Kelly had nothing to do with me, and even if it had, I would not have wanted her to marry him if she didn't love him. And as far as my friends being independently wealthy, Lily's had *nothing* given to her. She's worked hard all her life. And Abby's an executive—she works like a dog. In fact, they *all* work. Emma has an art gallery and Vanessa…" Her voice trailed off. Why was she even talking to this despicable woman? "Never mind. I'm wasting my breath talking to you."

And with that, Felicity spun on her heel and walked out. She told herself to calm down, but she was still gritting her teeth and muttering under her breath when she got back to the table.

"What's wrong?" asked Emma.

Felicity rolled her eyes. "Delia Forrester. Need I say more?"

Everyone immediately groaned and agreed.

"You know," Abby said, "I sure would like to know what that woman did before she married Frank. My mother tried to find out, but as far as I know, she wasn't successful."

"Oh, I know what she did," Felicity said.

"You *do?*" This came from Lily.

"Yes." Felicity grinned. "She stirred her cauldron and concocted her brews."

For a moment there was silence. Then Vanessa snorted, and they all burst out laughing.

"Oh, you're bad," Emma said, but she was laughing, too.

"Well, she *is* a witch," Felicity pointed out.

"More like a bitch," Vanessa corrected.

"That, too," Felicity said.

The conversation stopped as their waiter approached with their food, and after that, the subject of Delia was dropped. For the next hour they talked about the blackmail letters that Lily's husband and Garrett's sister Caroline had received. Abby was convinced that the extortion attempts and the theft of her mother's journals were connected, and Felicity couldn't help thinking she was right, even though that might mean Abby's other theory—that her mother had been murdered—might also be right. Felicity shivered at the thought. Murder seemed so horrible, but Bunny had certainly inspired animosity among those people whose lives and secrets she'd written about.

When they'd exhausted that topic, the conversation turned to Vanessa's ongoing battle with her deceased husband's family over his will.

Emma, much more openly kindhearted than Felicity would ever be, reached over and clasped Vanessa's hand. "I'm sorry you're having to go through this, Van."

At times like this, Felicity couldn't help remembering how Sam's family—whom she had adored—had turned against her after the divorce. She, too, reached for Vanessa's hand. "Just remember. This will pass."

Her reward was a smile. "Thanks," Vanessa said softly. "To all of you." Raising her water glass, she said, "Here's to friendship."

After they toasted one another, the talk finally veered to lighter subjects, and before Felicity knew it, it was time to go.

Emma walked out with Felicity, and as they stood in the parking lot, she asked, "Is everything all right? You left the table so abruptly before." Her eyes were troubled. "Are you angry with me for some reason?"

"Why would you say that?" Felicity wished she could confide in Emma, but how could she? "Of course I'm not angry with you."

"I know you've always liked Reed. You probably think I treated him badly."

Felicity sighed. "Emma, you did the right thing.

Actually, I admire you for having the guts to tell him the truth." She smiled. "I'm glad for you and Garrett."

"You're not just saying that?"

"No," Felicity said softly. "I'm not just saying that."

Emma sighed in relief. "I'm so glad. I—I would've hated if this had impacted our friendship." She hesitated, then added, "Your friendship is very important to me—you know that, don't you?"

"Of course I do. Because I feel the same way."

Smiling at one another, they hugged, then said goodbye, promising to talk soon.

Driving home, Felicity vowed that in the future she would not do anything that would cause her to keep secrets from Emma again. Her friendship with Emma was too important to jeopardize, and even though Emma had broken up with Reed, she might still feel a sense of betrayal if Felicity were to start seeing him. She might even think Felicity had just been waiting for an opportunity to pounce. *I can't have that happen. I can't gamble with my friendship with Emma.*

So even though she felt regret, Felicity knew she had to put Reed Kelly out of her mind once and for all.

"Hey, Reed! Wait up."

Reed, who had been about to walk into the Eastwick hardware store, turned to see his lawyer and old friend, Jack Cartwright, approaching. "Hey, Jack. How're you doing?"

Jack grinned. "Great. How about you?"

"Great."

"No, I mean, how're you doing, *really?*"

Dammit. There was that look of pity Reed had come to despise. "Hell, Jack," he said irritably. "I'm fine. I wish everyone would quit *asking.*"

Because Jack really was a good friend, he didn't take offense at Reed's testy answer. Instead, he reached over and grasped Reed's arm, saying, "Sorry, man. I just…you know."

Reed sighed. "Yeah, I know." Determined to change the subject, he added, "How's Lily? Isn't she about due?"

Jack's expression softened. "She's got a couple of months yet."

Reed couldn't help feeling a pang of envy. Not only was Jack married to a beautiful woman he was crazy about, she was carrying his child.

They talked a while longer, then Jack said he had a three-o'clock appointment and had better hurry if he was going to make it. They promised to get together soon, and Reed went inside the store. He found the things he needed, then walked to the front of the store to pay for them. Mae Burrows, the wife of the owner, was working the counter. She rang up his purchases, told him what he owed, then said, "Reed, I just wanted to tell you how sorry I was to hear about you and Emma Dearborn splitting up."

Trying to keep his voice from showing his frustration, he said, "Thanks, Mae, but it was for the best."

"Well, that may be," she said, "but it still must hurt."

"Oh, no worse than having my nails pulled out one by one." At her expression, he chuckled. "Only kidding, Mae." Reaching over, he squeezed her hand. "Seriously, I appreciate your concern, but our breakup really is best for both of us." Taking his package, he waved goodbye and walked out before she could say anything else.

But her remarks, combined with Jack's sympathetic comments, only reinforced the idea that had been brewing now for more than twenty-four hours.

"People in this town need something new to talk about," he muttered. "And I know just what that something is."

So instead of heading straight back to the farm, he walked down the block to Georgia Lang's travel agency. He was in luck. Georgia was in, and she didn't have a customer. Peering at him over the glasses perched on her nose, she said with a slight frown, "Hello, Reed."

Reed knew she was worried he would want his money back on the paid-for honeymoon trip. "Hi, Georgia. I was wondering if you could take care of something for me. That honeymoon trip I paid for? I'd like you to change the reservation to next week."

She blinked. "Is the wedding back on?"

"Nope."

"Oh."

To her credit, she didn't question him further, although he knew she wanted to.

It took her only fifteen minutes to change his

booked reservation at the resort in Cozumel to one that would start the following Monday.

"What about the airline tickets?" she asked. "Want me to see if I can get a refund on one of them? Or at least a credit for a later trip somewhere?"

"Nope. I'll need two," he said.

Again her eyes were filled with curiosity, and he knew she was dying to know just who was going to take that trip next week. But he had no intention of telling her anything, and she was smart enough to understand she had no business asking.

As he left the agency with the tickets in hand, he was whistling.

Four

Felicity sighed and rubbed the bridge of her nose. She was tired. It had been a long day. A long, frustrating day. God, she was sick of Madeline Newhouse and her constant complaints and demands, and the wedding was still three weeks away. She'd almost had a meltdown today, wanting to say, "Dammit, Madeline, stop hassling me! Everything's under control. That's why you hired me, because I'm the best and you don't have to worry about anything, *remember?*"

But just in the nick of time, she'd stopped herself. Still, the urge had alarmed her. She'd never before been so close to losing control with a client.

I'm so tired. I wish...

But Felicity didn't know what she wished. Sighing, she reached for her laptop and logged on to her e-mail program. She'd just finished sending an inquiry to her printer to check on the status of an order when out of the corner of her eye she saw a red Dodge truck pull up front.

She frowned. Who? Then she blinked. That was Reed's truck!

What was *he* doing here? Her tiredness vanished. She whipped out her compact, checked her lipstick and hair, repositioned today's butterfly clip—this one made from seed pearls—then composed herself as she waited for him to come inside.

Her heart did one of those funny little flips when he entered. "Hello, Reed," she said as coolly as she could, even though the sight of him did things to her libido that should be illegal.

"Hey," he said with a big smile.

"What brings *you* here?" Why did he have to be so luscious? she thought distractedly. Even dressed as he was, in boots, faded jeans and a red T-shirt, he looked good enough to eat. "You haven't changed your mind about the Newhouse wedding pictures, have you?"

"No, nothing like that."

She expelled a breath. "Thank God. I don't think I could deal with having to tell Madeline Newhouse *that*."

"She giving you a hard time?"

"That's an understatement. The woman is a class-A pain in the you-know-what."

"You can say the word *ass*," he said with a grin. "I've heard the word before."

"But will you respect me in the morning?" Felicity countered.

He laughed and sat on the edge of her desk. His eyes met hers, his smile slowly fading, replaced with something else—an expression that made Felicity hold her breath. The moment stretched.

Because she had to do something, she picked up a paper clip and nervously began twisting it open. "What?" she finally said, completely unsettled by the look on his face. Thank God Rita wasn't here, because if her assistant were to see how rattled Felicity was, she'd immediately know something was in the air. And it wouldn't take her long to figure out what that something might be, either. Why, the hormone level in this room must be approaching liftoff.

"I've had an idea," Reed said in a slow, sexy drawl, with just the suggestion of a smile. His eyes were deep pools of blue.

Ohmigod. A woman could drown in those eyes. "Oh?" She put her hands in her lap to still their sudden trembling.

"You know," he continued casually, "I booked a week at the Grand Cozumel Resort for my honeymoon."

"Um, yes, Emma, um, mentioned it." Good grief, she sounded like a blubbering idiot. *Get a grip!*

"An unrefundable week."

Felicity couldn't think of anything to say, so she said nothing.

"Since I've already paid for it, I've decided not to waste it. I'm going to go to Cozumel. Leaving Monday morning."

Now she *really* didn't know what to say. What did he expect her to say?

"You should see the brochures, Felicity. I've reserved a suite at the Grand, which is a five-star resort. They have everything. It's on San Francisco Beach, just a five-minute boat ride from Palancar Reef. Have you ever heard of Palancar?"

"Um, no. Can't say that I have."

"The snorkeling there is second to none, I'm told. It's a beautiful place."

"I, um, hope you have a great time." She swallowed. Something about the way he was looking at her made her squirm.

"I'd have a much better time if I had someone to go with me," he said softly.

Felicity's heart lurched painfully. She wet her lips. She was unable to look away.

"How about it, Felicity?"

"H-how about what?"

"You know what."

She shook her head. "I—I don't."

Leaning closer, he whispered, "Come with me."

For a long moment there was no sound in the office except the ticking of the clock on the wall and the low hum of Felicity's computer.

Felicity opened her mouth to speak, but nothing came out. Finally she managed to pull herself together. "Reed, that's ridiculous. I can't come with you."

"Why not?"

"I—I just can't. It's impossible."

"Why is it impossible?"

"Well, for one thing, I have a job."

"How long has it been since you took a vacation?" he countered.

"That's beside the point."

"No, it's not. Don't you *deserve* a vacation?"

"Reed…be sensible. Even if I wanted to go, how could I? Don't you see every gossip in Eastwick would have a field day with this if they found out?"

He shrugged. "So what?"

"So *what?* I have a reputation to think of."

"Oh, come on, Felicity. You don't give a damn what other people think, and you know it."

That was true. She didn't. Ever since Sam had walked out on her, she had done exactly what she'd wanted to do, no matter what anyone thought. And she had to admit it was very tempting to say yes. But that was madness. She couldn't just abandon everything and take off with Reed. And why did he want her, anyway? Was this some crazy scheme to get back at Emma? Her best *friend,* Emma?

While these thoughts were swirling, he stood and walked around the desk to where she sat. Reaching down, he drew her up out of her chair. Before she could even think about resisting, he pulled her against him, tilted her head up and gave her a long, slow kiss.

Felicity melted against him. She was powerless to resist. Every molecule in her body was on fire with need, and she was oblivious to where they were or who might walk in on them. All she knew was that this man ignited something inside her, something she hadn't known she was capable of feeling.

When he finally let her up for air, his voice was husky as he said, "Come with me. There'll be no strings. Just sun, fun and the two of us together." He gave her a crooked smile. "What do you say?"

A week in Mexico with Reed. It sounded like heaven. *And no strings.* "I—"

He touched her lips with his fingertips. "You won't be sorry."

She shook her head.

"C'mon, Felicity. Don't say no."

"I have to," she cried. "What you're proposing— it's nuts." She pushed away from him, tried to calm her racing heart and the chaos in her brain. She took a deep breath. "I can't come with you, Reed," she said in a stronger voice. Looking up, she met his gaze evenly. "Thank you for the invitation, but I have to say no."

His smile disappeared. He shrugged, saying, "Well, I tried."

She knew it was unreasonable, but she felt oddly disappointed. *What? You thought he was going to beg you?*

He started toward the door, then stopped and came back to her desk. "Here," he said. "Just in case you change your mind."

A moment later he was gone.

Felicity didn't pick up the envelope he'd left on her desk until his truck was out of sight. Opening the flap, she withdrew an airline ticket for a first-class seat on a flight leaving this coming Monday morning from Westchester Airport and connecting with a flight at Kennedy. Her heart sped up as she stared at the ticket.

A week in Mexico.

With Reed.

I can't. It's madness to even think *about it.*

Maybe it was. But oh, wouldn't it be wonderful to go? To spend a week at a glorious resort?

With Reed.

Sun. Fun. *Sex.*

With Reed.

No strings, he'd said.

She wet her lips. Pictured the two of them on the beach. In the water. Kissing. Pictured him removing the top of her bikini.

Oh...

Felicity shook her head. What was she thinking? No, no, no. The whole idea was crazy. Impossible. Total and complete madness. Even though she'd told him she didn't care what anyone thought, she cared what *Emma* thought. She cared what the other Debs thought.

She shook her head.

I'm not going. And that's that.

She started to tear the ticket in two, then stopped. It would be wasteful to destroy the ticket. He could get a refund. She should mail it back to him. With a note. A sweet note. "Thank you for the lovely invitation, but I'm sure you understand why I can't go. I hope you have a wonderful time. Best, Felicity."

Yes. That's what she'd do.

She'd just gotten up and walked to the supply cabinet to get an envelope when the outer door opened.

"Boy, it's hot out there!" Rita, dabbing at her face with a tissue, walked to the display table and replaced the large books that contained samples of invitations and thank-you notes that she'd taken to show a new client. "I certainly will be glad when summer's over."

"You and me both," muttered Felicity.

Rita gave her a curious look. "What's wrong?"

Felicity shrugged. "Nothing. I'm just tired."

"Well, sweetie, it's no wonder, is it? When's the last time you had a vacation?"

Those were almost exactly the same words Reed had used. "I don't know."

"I do. It's been over two years."

Felicity bit her lip. She felt absurdly near tears. What was wrong with her, anyway?

"Felicity…" Rita touched her arm. "Are you okay? Did something happen while I was gone? Did that horrible Newhouse woman call here again?"

Felicity swallowed. The temptation to tell Rita everything was awfully strong. In many ways, Rita had been functioning as the mother Felicity no longer had. But she couldn't do that. If word of what Reed had proposed should ever get back to Emma…

Felicity hated the fact that she no longer felt comfortable confiding in Rita, but those blackmail notes some of her friends had received since the death of Bunny Talbot were disturbing, and lately Felicity couldn't help wondering if it was possible that Rita had had something to do with them. After all, Felicity had talked freely in front of Rita. Felicity didn't *really* think Rita had anything to do with the blackmail attempts—in fact, she felt guilty for even entertaining the thought—but if there was even the slightest chance Rita was involved, or even that she might inadvertently say something to someone else who might be involved… Well, better safe than sorry.

Sighing deeply, Felicity shook her head. "No, she didn't call. As I said, I'm just tired. You know what? Maybe I'll take the afternoon off."

"That's a great idea," Rita said. "Go home, have a long soak in the tub and a big glass of wine and order in a pizza or something. Doesn't that sound good?"

Felicity couldn't help smiling. Actually, it *did* sound good. Putting her arm around Rita, she gave her a shoulder hug. "Thanks, Rita. I feel better already."

Reed told himself he didn't care that Felicity had turned him down. At a resort like Grand Cozumel, there were bound to be dozens of beautiful women.

Besides, Monday was four days away.

Maybe, before then, he could figure out how to change Felicity's mind.

Felicity dreamed about Reed that night. In the dream they were lying in a soft bed in a sun-dappled room. Overhead a large fan whirred slowly, stirring the filmy netting that cocooned the bed. From somewhere outside the shuttered windows floated the lilting sounds of mariachi music. Reed whispered in her ear, his hands moving slowly over her body, touching, stroking, caressing…delving.

Felicity's body arched, and she gasped.

And woke up.

When she realized that she hadn't been in that bed with Reed, that the sensations he'd evoked hadn't really happened at all, that the whole thing was just a dream, she wanted to cry, the disappointment was so great.

Her entire body cried out for him. But he wasn't there. Instead, she was alone. Just as she'd been for three years. Three lonely years.

Three lonely years without sex…

That was her whole problem. She was frustrated and sex starved. A complete mess, in other words.

Maybe it's time to buy a BOB, she thought ruefully, remembering how her girlfriends had all laughed about "battery-operated boyfriends."

Turning her pillow to the cool side, she tried to get comfortable again. But it was no use. After thirty minutes of tossing this way and that, she knew she wouldn't get back to sleep. At three o'clock she finally gave up, got out of bed and walked out to her kitchen. She poured herself a glass of milk, added a large dollop of chocolate syrup—after all, if a girl didn't have sex, she might as well have sugar!—and, sitting at the kitchen table, allowed herself to once more consider what Reed had proposed.

Was his suggestion really so outlandish?

All he'd done was invite her to accompany him to a luxurious and beautiful resort where she would have a week of relaxing fun.

With no strings.

So as long as Emma never heard about it, what was wrong with that?

On Saturday morning, just before noon, Felicity was about to walk out the door of her office when a white van with Penny's Posies lettered in hot pink on the side pulled into the parking lot. She frowned. She wasn't expecting a delivery of anything. Had someone gotten an address mixed up or something?

A young man she didn't know got out of the truck. He was carrying a bouquet of some kind of red flowers in a clear glass vase. Was it Rita's birthday? But no, Rita's birthday was in December.

Felicity opened the door.

"Ms. Felicity Farnsworth?" the young man said.

"Yes?"

"These are for you, then." He handed her the vase

of flowers. Attached was a small box wrapped in red gilt paper.

Felicity closed the door and walked over to her desk. Who in the world had sent these? There was no card, just the box. Quickly she removed the box and tore off the gilt paper. Her mouth dropped open. It was a box of condoms. Taped to the top was a note.

> I think condoms are a suitable accompaniment to the passion flowers, don't you? I promise you we'll put them to good use if you change your mind.
> Reed.

Felicity couldn't help it. She burst out laughing. Oh, he was bad! Hurriedly she thrust the box of condoms and the note into her tote. She certainly didn't want anyone seeing them, and Rita would be back from her appointment at the First Presbyterian Church at any moment.

But even though the note and condoms were out of sight, for the rest of the day they were pretty much all Felicity thought about.

On Sunday evening Reed faced the fact that Felicity wasn't going to change her mind. Well, he'd tried, and even though he hadn't been able to persuade her to go with him, he was still going to Cozumel in the morning. He'd already called his mother to tell her he'd be away for a week—he purposely omitted telling her where he was going and allowed her to assume it was a horse-buying trip—he'd given Max a full set of instructions and he'd made the few phone calls that needed to be made to clients. Now his bag was packed, his tickets were in his carry-on and he was ready to go.

But early the next morning, as he climbed into his truck for the drive to Westchester Airport, he couldn't help feeling regret.

By the time Felicity made her decision, it was too late to join Reed on his flight to Cozumel. But the ticket agent at the airport was very accommodating, especially after Felicity offered to pay whatever it cost to get her a seat on the next available flight.

Throughout the short hop into Kennedy, she wondered what everyone would think if they knew where she was going and with whom. She'd told Rita and everyone else she'd booked a week at a spa and would be incommunicado for the duration.

"I'm not even turning my cell phone on while I'm away," she told Rita.

"Good!" said Rita. "When you get back is time enough to think about work again. Don't worry about a thing. Just have fun and get lots and lots of rest. And sun. I don't think you've been out in the sun once this summer."

Felicity felt guilty then, but she told herself she'd done what she had to do to protect herself. A guilty conscience was a small price to pay for the promise of the week ahead. She still couldn't believe she was actually going. Even after she boarded the puddle jumper that would take her to Kennedy and the flight to Mexico, she still felt as if this were all a dream and very soon she'd wake up, the same way she had when she'd dreamed Reed was making love to her.

It wasn't until she was settled in her roomy first-class seat on the second leg of her trip, a frosty piña colada in hand, that she finally allowed herself to believe she was actually going. That this was real. That tonight she would be with Reed.

And yet, even as the realization—and the excitement—settled in, she wondered if she were doing the right thing. Okay, so she didn't want any permanent commitments, at least not now, but she didn't want Reed to think she was cheap *or* easy. She certainly didn't want him to think she jumped into bed with just anyone.

He knows you don't. He's lived in Eastwick all his life....

Even so, it would probably be a good idea to make it clear up front that she'd taken him up on his offer of a week in Cozumel because she needed a vacation…not because she was sex starved.

She grinned.

Even if she was.

Reed had been right.

There were dozens of beautiful women at the Grand Cozumel Resort. And several of them were even now giving him the eye. One, a gorgeous brunette with a deep tan, wearing a clinging white dress with a plunging neckline, looked as though she'd happily desert her women friends if he were to approach her.

Reed thought about it.

It would be so easy to walk around to the other end of the bar and introduce himself, ask if she'd like to have dinner with him.

But he didn't really want to. And he knew why. As beautiful as she was, she wasn't Felicity.

Five

When the cab bringing Felicity from Cozumel airport to the resort pulled into the turnaround in front of the main building, Felicity took a deep breath before getting out.

"Welcome to the Grand Cozumel, señorita," said the young bellman who sprang forward to help her from the taxi.

"Thank you," Felicity said. She paid the cab driver, who eagerly accepted her dollars, then followed the bellman into the beautiful lobby. She had a quick impression of lush tropical plants and flowers, a cascading fountain and the illusion of being underwater as she walked to the check-in area.

A dapper man with a friendly smile said in perfect

English, "May I help you, señorita?" His name tag read Carlos Perez.

Felicity tried not to look as nervous as she felt. "Kelly," she said, having decided earlier to just brazen it out. "The reservation is under Reed Kelly."

Mr. Perez's smile expanded. "I beg your pardon, Señora Kelly. I did not realize…Mr. Kelly didn't explain that you would be arriving tonight."

Felicity blinked. Had Reed known she was coming, then? Had he somehow found out she'd changed the reservation?

Mr. Perez snapped his fingers, and instantly the same bellman who had brought in her bags was at the desk.

"Eduardo," Mr. Perez said, "please see Señora Kelly to her suite. It's 410. The Calypso."

Felicity opened her mouth to say she wasn't Mrs. Kelly, but it was too embarrassing. She'd hoped to just quietly find Reed's room. But maybe it would just be easier to allow the nice Mr. Perez and everyone else to think she and Reed were married. That way, at least, they wouldn't be giving her sly looks all week. Or maybe they didn't care. She'd been out of the dating/sex game so long, she had no idea how these things might work. Just thinking about how rusty she was, she had another attack of the jitters.

Oh, God. Was she making a huge mistake?

Well, it's too late now. You're here….

Thanking Mr. Perez, Felicity followed the bellman to the bank of elevators hidden behind a grove of palm trees growing right there in the lobby.

As the elevator made its smooth ascent, Felicity tried to will her heart to settle down, for the closer they got to the suite, the more unsettled it became.

Felicity wondered if Reed would be in his room. It was nearly seven o'clock. Maybe he was having dinner. She swallowed. A horrible thought suddenly struck her. What if he'd found someone else—another woman!—to have dinner with? What if he brought the woman back to his room?

Oh, no. What would she do? Was it too late to turn around and go home?

She was still debating when the bellman said, "Here we are, Señora Kelly. The Calypso." So saying, he knocked on the door.

Felicity barely had time to whisper a prayer when the door opened, framing Reed.

"Felicity?" he said, staring at her.

She swallowed. "Hello, Reed." Why didn't he smile? Her heart was now beating so hard, it scared her.

And then, just when she was ready to say she was sorry, she'd made a terrible mistake, he motioned the bellman in. While Reed took care of tipping the bellman, Felicity told herself it still wasn't too late. If he didn't accept her conditions— for she *did* have some—or if he acted as if he had changed his mind and didn't want her here, she could still leave. And she would.

When the door closed behind the bellman, Reed finally turned to her. Reaching for her hand, he drew her into his arms and, just before lowering his head to kiss her, he smiled and said, "What took you so long?"

How long they stood there kissing, Felicity couldn't have said. What she did know was that Reed caused her to feel things she'd never felt before—not even in the beginning with Sam.

Yet when Reed edged her toward the bed, Felicity—despite the flames of desire raging through her—still had enough of her wits about her to resist.

"Is something wrong?" he finally asked, drawing back to look at her. "Did I misinterpret something?"

Felicity, whose traitorous heart was trying to beat its way out of her chest, made her voice firm but pleasant, the same way she did for her clients. "Look, before we go any further, there's a condition you have to agree to. Otherwise, I'm turning around and going straight back to Eastwick."

"What condition?" he said warily.

"My presence here has to remain a secret. From *everyone*."

"You disappoint me, Felicity. I thought you were the original I-don't-give-a-damn girl. It's one of the things I admire most about you, that you don't put a lot of stock into what other people think."

"I *don't* normally give a damn about what most people think, but I do care about Emma, and I won't jeopardize our friendship."

"Why should Emma care? She's the one who dumped me, not vice versa."

Felicity inwardly cringed at the bitterness he didn't even try to disguise. He must still care about Emma. Her heart sank. If he was doing this only to get back at Emma, then Felicity wanted no part of it. But before she could give voice to any of those thoughts, Reed spoke again.

"I don't want you to go," he said softly. "I didn't ask you to come here to get even with Emma, if that's what you're thinking. I asked you here because I like you and because I think we have something going for us."

"You *do?*"

"I do. And I agree to your terms." He patted the space next to him again. "So why don't you come here? And we can quit wasting time."

Felicity shook her head. "There's…something else we need to settle first."

He raised his eyebrows.

"Um, don't you think it might be a good idea to get to know each other a little better before we leap into bed together?"

"I know everything I need to know about you," he replied in a sexy drawl. At the look on her face, he grimaced. "All right, you win. If the bed makes you nervous, I'll move." Getting up, he sat on the sofa and tugged at her to join him there.

But Felicity knew if she sat next to him, she'd soon find herself prone and completely unable to continue saying no. And she knew she was right about this. Even though he'd agreed to her terms of secrecy, it was important to say no for now. She and Reed might simply have a one-week fling, but she didn't ever want him to think of her as a woman who had no scruples. So she pulled her hand from his clasp and walked over to one of the two deeply cushioned chairs flanking a small table in front of the balcony doors. "Well, I barely know *you,* Reed."

"Yet you're here," he pointed out.

Oh, that sexy smile of his would be her undoing. "Yes, I am." *And I hope I won't live to regret it.*

"You can't pretend you didn't know what I was suggesting when I sent you those condoms." His smile grew mischievous. "You *did* receive them, didn't you?"

She tried to keep a straight face, but lost the battle. "I did. I even brought them with me."

"So what's the problem?"

Why did he have to look so good? In his lightweight linen pants and chest-hugging black T-shirt, he was the epitome of healthy male. Gorgeous, healthy male. Gorgeous, *sexy,* healthy male.

To distract herself from his hard-to-resist attributes, Felicity decided to tell him the truth. "Look, Reed, I know you said no strings. And I like that. I'm not in the market for a hus—" Hastily she corrected herself. "Long-term relationship and all that it entails. But I also don't believe in just jumping into bed with someone I hardly know, no matter how attracted to him I am."

"So you admit you're attracted to me?"

There was that smile again. "You know I am."

"And I'm definitely attracted to *you,*" he said.

Felicity swallowed at the expression in his eyes. It would be so very easy to forget her misgivings. "Still, along with getting to know something about a guy, a girl wants some foreplay."

"I do foreplay very well," he said huskily. "And if you'd come over here, I'd show you just how well."

"Not that kind. I'm talking romantic dinners, dancing, flirting…you know…things that will not only give us some time to get to know each other better, but will also increase the anticipation…and the pleasure," she added, playing her trump card.

"Increase the pleasure, huh?"

"Yes." She made herself meet his gaze squarely.

"So how long do you propose we wait? We've only got a week."

Felicity wanted to smile, but she restrained herself. "How about if we halve the week? Say three point five days?" she said crisply.

"That's far too long. How about twenty-four hours?" He looked at his watch. "That would be seven o'clock tomorrow night. We can get a lot of foreplay in before then."

She shook her head. "Twenty-four hours is too soon. How about three days?"

"One and a half." His blue eyes twinkled as they studied her.

Again she refused to lower her eyes or be embarrassed. This was a business negotiation. "Two and a half is more like it."

Now he shook *his* head. "Much too long. Why don't we say two days and, uh…" He looked at his watch again. "Two days and five hours. That'll make it midnight Wednesday that we, uh…connect."

"Connect." She fought another grin. "That's a good word."

"I thought so."

She gazed out the balcony doors and pretended to consider his offer. "Okay. Wednesday at midnight. It's a deal." Rising, she walked over to him and held out her hand.

Still grinning, he took it and they shook. "You drive a hard bargain, Ms. Felicity Farnsworth. In fact, I'd say we're going backward. From kissing to shaking hands."

"We'll go forward. I promise." Then she laughed. "As long as you do your part."

He stood. He was still holding her hand. "What does that mean? Do you intend to give me a grade on how well I do?"

"I hadn't thought about it, but that's a great idea. A report card on foreplay. We might even market that. I'll bet it would be very popular with women. I can see the Web site now—How Does Your Man Measure Up?"

"I was only kidding," he said dryly.

"I don't know. It's a great idea."

"You are really something, you know that? Not

just beautiful and sexy, but smart, too." Lifting her hand, he kissed her palm.

Her heart fluttered, but she told it to behave. Extracting her hand, she curtsied. "Thank you, kind sir. You're not so bad yourself."

"Now that we've settled everything to your satisfaction, how about dinner? Are you hungry?"

"Starving." She hadn't eaten in hours.

"Why don't we go down and get something to eat, then?"

"Do you mind waiting while I shower and change?"

"You look great just the way you are." He gave her white slacks and fitted green blouse an appreciative once-over.

"Thanks for the compliment, but I've been wearing these clothes all day. I'd like to put on something a bit more dressy."

"In that case, I'll change, too."

"How much time do I have?" she asked.

"As much as you need."

Smiling, she headed for the bedroom.

"Oh, and Felicity?" he said.

She turned. "Yes?"

He grinned. "Might be a good idea to lock the bathroom door."

Reed changed into charcoal slacks, an open-necked white silk shirt and a black linen jacket, then walked out to the sitting room to wait while Felicity finished getting ready for the evening. After fixing himself a weak rum drink—he wanted all his faculties tonight—he thought about the exchange that had taken place between them earlier.

He couldn't help smiling over the last negotiation. This week was going to be even more fun than he'd imagined.

He was standing out on the balcony, which overlooked the pool and the sea beyond. The sun had just begun to set, the water shimmering in red-gold splendor, when he heard a rustle behind him and turned.

For a moment he just stared. The vision standing a few feet away wore a form-fitting, strapless, hot-pink dress with a long slit up the front, exposing her gorgeous legs. Long crystal earrings dangled from her ears, and on her feet were a pair of impossibly high-heeled pink sandals the same shade as her dress. Clipped in her hair was another of her butterflies, this one studded with sequins.

Felicity inclined her head. "Well? Say something."

"You look spectacular."

"Thanks. You look very nice, too."

Reed put his glass down. "Shall we go?"

Linking her arm in his, she gazed up at him. "Let's."

God, she was beautiful. How was it he hadn't realized just *how* beautiful until recently?

When they approached the elevators, there were several other people waiting, so they didn't talk. It wasn't until they reached the lobby that Reed said, "The restaurant here is supposed to have great seafood. Or we could go somewhere else, if you like."

"Here's fine. I like seafood."

"Me, too."

When they entered the restaurant the pretty, dark-haired hostess smiled at them. "Would you like to sit indoors or out on the patio?"

Reed looked at Felicity.

"On the patio," she said.

Ten minutes later they were settled at a table with a view of the water. The sun had just dipped below the horizon, and the glow on the water's surface had softened to pale apricot tinged with violet. A gentle breeze caused the flames of the lighted candles on the tables to flicker and dance. At the far end of the patio, several guitar players and a keyboard player were warming up.

Reed smiled across at Felicity. It should be a crime to look as good as she did. "So what is it you want to know about me?"

"To the point, aren't you?" she teased.

"Why waste time?" he countered.

Leaning back in her chair, she said, "Tell me about your family."

Reed rolled his eyes. "Let's see. They're noisy. And bossy. Very, very bossy."

She grinned. "I can't believe you'd let anyone boss *you* around."

"I don't. But they still try. Especially my sisters."

"I've met your sister Shannon, but not the others."

"There's only one more. Bridget. And I have two

brothers—Daniel and Aidan. I'm the youngest of all of them."

"That's why they try to boss you around. The youngest always gets it."

"You say that like you've had some experience with it."

Her smile faded, her eyes growing wistful. "No." She shook her head. "I was an only child."

Reed couldn't imagine being an only child. Growing up, he'd often wished he was, because being the youngest in a large, gregarious family like his meant never having a moment's peace. His siblings were either teasing him, ignoring him, or bossing him around. He'd also had no privacy, and got stuck with his older brothers' hand-me-downs.

"You're lucky, you know," she said. "Being an only child, especially of parents who are totally wrapped up in one another, can be a very lonely existence. Sometimes I think that's why I jumped into marriage with my ex before I really had a chance to know him." She made a face. "Believe me, to know him was not to love him."

He'd wondered about her marriage. Emma had told him only that Felicity had really gotten a raw deal. "How long were you married?"

"Over seven years. By the time I'd divorced him, he'd wiped out my inheritance and cheated on me with countless other women." She said this matter-of-factly.

Reed couldn't imagine why any man would want another woman if he had Felicity. He started to say so, but just then their waiter approached to take their drink orders and tell them about the day's specials. When he'd gone, that moment had passed. Instead, Reed said, "Emma told me your parents were killed in a skiing accident."

Felicity nodded. "It was one of those freak things. They were on a lift, and the cable snapped. All five people riding on it were killed instantly."

"I'm sorry."

She sighed. "It was a long time ago. It happened when I was nineteen and in college."

"And you got married when you were...?"

"Twenty-four. I've been divorced for three years now."

"So..." Reed did a quick calculation. "You're about my age, right? Thirty-four or thirty-five?"

"Yes. I turned thirty-five in March. When's your birthday?"

"I'll be thirty-six the end of this month. The thirty-first."

"So you're a Leo. Leo the Lion." She cocked her head to study him. "You don't look like a lion type."

"Honey," he said in his best Groucho Marx imitation, "you should see me roar."

In answer, she just smiled.

Reed decided he'd like to keep a smile on her face at all times, because she didn't smile enough. A smile made her look softer and sweeter. That was a potent combination. Soft, sweet and...sexy.

"What?" she said.

"What, what?" he countered.

"Why do you have that look on your face?"

"I was just thinking how much I like you."

In the flickering candlelight her face bloomed with pleasure. The moment stretched, and for the first time since Felicity had come to the stables last week, Reed wasn't thinking about her body or sex or getting her into bed. Instead, he was thinking how much he enjoyed her company and how he really did want to get to know her better.

Just then, the waiter returned with their drinks, and for the next few minutes they were busy ordering their dinner. By the time the waiter left, the band had begun to play—something soft and romantic—and there were several couples on the dance floor. Felicity turned to watch them.

"Would you like to dance?" Reed asked.

"I'd love to."

Reed's parents had not been wealthy, but he and his siblings had all learned to dance. His mother had taught them; she'd been a dancer in her youth and she'd always said that as long as a young man was polite, knew which fork to use and could dance, he'd never lack for female companionship. Reed had hated the dancing when he was little. Now he was glad his mother had forced him to learn. When the number ended, they stayed on the floor. One dance became two, two became three.

Holding Felicity, feeling her body against his, moving slowly with her over the dance floor was almost as good as sex. "This is nice," he said, his lips brushing her hair. The scent of flowers filled his senses.

"Yes," she murmured. "You're a good dancer, Reed."

"So are you." He tightened his arms around her. "Why don't we forget about dinner? Just stay out here and dance all night?"

She chuckled. "It's a tempting offer, but I get cranky when I'm hungry."

The words were barely out of her mouth when Reed spied their waiter setting up a serving tray next to their table. Reluctantly Reed loosened his hold. "Looks like our food has arrived."

Dinner was delicious. In addition to seviche, they both had grilled red snapper that was served with fried plantains, fluffy rice and a tangy mango-lime relish. Reed enjoyed the food, but he enjoyed watching Felicity even more. She ate with enthusiasm, unlike so many women who only picked at their food or worse, pretended they didn't like it because they were afraid of gaining weight.

"What a wonderful dinner," she said, sitting back with a sigh after finishing.

"Yes," he said, laughing. "I'd say we did a pretty good job of cleaning our plates."

"I usually do."

"Good. I like a girl with a healthy appetite."

His comment hung in the air, and he knew they were both thinking of other appetites they might assuage later in the week.

While their waiter cleared their table before bringing dessert—Reed had ordered vanilla ice cream topped with caramelized pecans and Felicity had chosen flan, a specialty of the restaurant—they went back to the dance floor. This time the combo was playing some kind of salsa number and, laughing, they gamely tried it. By the time the dance was over, Felicity was fanning herself, and Reed was thinking about getting rid of his jacket.

"That was fun," Felicity said, dropping into her seat. "Do you do much dancing when you're at home?"

Reed shook his head. "I'm usually too busy." Which wasn't strictly true, but he felt a little funny admitting to Felicity that he'd never thought about taking Emma out dancing—because he'd only now realized that that, too, should have told him something about their relationship.

"Reed…"

His gaze met hers.

"Are you *really* over Emma?"

"Yes. The only thing that bugs me—and what I was thinking about now—is the fact I didn't see how wrong the two of us were for each other. It bothers me that I could have been so blind."

"So you're not unhappy that she broke the engagement? What you said before, about not using me to get back at her—did you mean it?"

"That thought never occurred to me." Uncomfortably he wondered if that were strictly true. After all, he *had* thought he'd give Eastwick's gossips something else to talk about by going off with Felicity. "I bear Emma no ill will. As I told my sister the other day, Emma did us both a favor."

Felicity studied him for a long moment, then seemed to make up her mind. "Good. I'm glad. Okay," she said brightly, "change of subject. Why is it we are just now getting to know each other when we both grew up in Eastwick?"

"I don't know. Our paths just didn't seem to cross. We went to different schools, for one thing."

"That's true. I was at Eastwick Academy and you…"

"Went to the local high school. My parents don't believe in wasting money on private schools."

"And then I went to Barnard," she said.

"And I was at U Conn."

"Then I worked in Manhattan for a couple of years."

"And I came home and started the business that eventually became Rosedale Farms."

"And I got married and went with Sam to Chicago."

"And now," he added softly, "here we are, finally getting to know each other."

The band had just struck up another lilting, romantic ballad. Reed held out his hand, and they got up. When he took her into his arms and they began to slowly move to the music, he thought how right she felt there. He drew her even closer, and she sighed.

Reed decided that waiting until Wednesday night at midnight might just be the hardest thing he'd ever have to do.

Six

No wonder some religions banned dancing. Felicity couldn't believe how much she was enjoying herself. Being held by Reed, moving with him to the music, felt so good. It had to be one of the top aphrodisiacs of all time. In fact, as a prelude to sex, she couldn't imagine anything better.

Oh, this was definitely foreplay, she thought ruefully. And it was such unbelievably great foreplay that she almost regretted saying they had to wait until Wednesday night before having sex.

"What are you thinking about?" he murmured against her hair.

"How nice this is," she murmured back. *And how much nicer it'll be Wednesday night, because if I'm any judge at all, you'll be a wonderful lover....*

Another woman might have expressed the thought aloud, but Felicity wasn't quite bold enough.

"It's going to get even nicer," he said.

Her breath hitched as he nuzzled her ear, letting the tip of his tongue lightly touch her lobe. "No fair," she said.

"What's not fair?" This time his lips brushed her temple and his right hand slid down her back to rest against the curve of her bottom, where it put gentle pressure to bring her even closer.

"Reed," she protested breathlessly. "Stop. People are staring at us."

"Who's staring? They're all too busy doing their own thing."

She pulled back, looked around and saw he was right. No one was looking at them. In fact, there were two other couples on the dance floor who were dancing even closer and more suggestively than she and Reed.

"Besides," he said, bringing her close again, "you're the one who wanted foreplay, remember?" He grinned. "Me? I'd just as soon go back to our room right now and try out that king-size bed."

Felicity swallowed. She'd just realized that even though they weren't going to have sex until Wednesday night, she'd still have to share his bed for two nights. Unless, of course, she made him sleep on the sofa in the other room. And even if she succeeded in convincing him, did she really want him so far away?

* * *

Felicity could have stayed out on the dance floor until the band quit for the night, but when she and Reed had finished their dessert and coffee, she could see there were several groups of people lined up near the hostess station, waiting for a patio table.

"I guess we should go," she said reluctantly.

Reed followed the direction of her gaze. "Yeah, I suppose we should. It wouldn't be nice to hog the table now that we're done with our dinner." He smiled mischievously. "We could go back to the suite and find some good music on the radio. Dance there."

She laughed. "Oh, no, you don't. I'm not sure I can trust you to stick to our agreement if we do that."

"Me?" he said in mock indignation. "Listen, sweetheart—" now he was imitating Humphrey Bogart "—if anyone can't be trusted, it's you. I know how much you want my body. I'm betting you'll be begging me to make love to you long before Wednesday at midnight."

Now she really laughed. "You just keep telling yourself that if it makes you feel better."

He tried to keep from laughing, but lost. Pretty soon they were both carrying on like fools, him saying he was on a mission to make her cry uncle, and her saying if anyone cried uncle, it would be him.

While waiting for their waiter to bring the check, Felicity thought about how much fun Reed was. She would never have dreamed, from the things Emma had said about him, that he had such a great sense of humor or that he loved to tease the way he did. She was also surprised at his gift of mimicry. "Are you an old movie buff or something?" she asked.

"Yeah, I am. Whenever I get the chance, I turn on that classic movie channel."

"I like old movies, too. Mostly, though, I like the musicals. I guess because they had such gorgeous costumes and were so feel-good. What're your favorites?"

"Me? I like comedies, especially the ones with Abbott and Costello or the Marx brothers. I also like the he-man movies. You know—Jimmy Cagney, Humphrey Bogart, Richard Widmark—all those tough-guy types."

"If you promise to behave yourself, we *could* go back to the suite and find an old movie to watch on TV."

"I don't know," he said slowly. "It might be too much for you—snuggling in the bed, watching love scenes together. You might be overcome and have to have me."

"Dream on, big guy." Now that he'd challenged her, she promised herself she would hold out until midnight Wednesday even if it *killed* her. But, oh, she did want him. He was certainly right about that. And the more he teased and played with her, the more appealing and sexy he was. And damn him! He knew it, too.

He grinned. "Are we declaring war? 'Cause you know what they say…"

When he looked at her that way, she found it hard to breathe.

"About fair means or foul…" His gaze pinned hers.

"No, we're not declaring war," she said as firmly as she could when everything in her felt as if it were melting into a puddle under that sizzling gaze of his. "We've already agreed to the terms of our contract."

"You're no fun."

Before Felicity could think of a snappy retort, the waiter approached with the bill. After Reed paid the check, he smiled across the table. "Ready?"

Felicity wasn't sure what she was ready for, but she rose and started to head toward the indoor entrance that would lead into the lobby of the hotel. Reed grabbed her hand to stop her. "Why don't we go walk on the beach for a while?"

"Oh, I'd love to." One of her happiest childhood memories was spending a month every summer on the Outer Banks with her parents. Poignantly, she remembered how they always took a walk along the beach at twilight. Her parents would be hand in hand while she skipped ahead and looked for seashells.

"You looked sad there for a minute," he commented as they headed toward the grounds. "Something wrong?"

She shook her head. "No. Just remembering my parents, that's all. They loved the beach."

"You miss them."

"I do." Even though they hadn't given her all the attention and love she'd craved, they'd been good people. Kind people. And they'd given her a good home.

"I understand. My dad passed away more than six years ago, but I still miss him like it was yesterday."

Felicity admired that about Reed. He wasn't embarrassed to show his love for his parents or his siblings, because even though he'd laughingly called them bossy and noisy, she had seen by the expression on his face that they were important to him. Once again, envy pierced her. She would give just about anything to have that kind of close-knit family.

As they went along the walkway leading to the beach, she could tell the resort had obviously spent a lot of money on flowers and plants. The grounds were gorgeous, with lush flowers and shrubs laced with coconut palms and giant ceibas. Flickering gaslights bordered the walkway, but even if they hadn't been there, the full moon would have lighted their way tonight.

Reed kept her hand in his, and Felicity thought about what a long time it had been since a man had held her hand like this. In fact, she couldn't remember Sam ever doing it. *Why did I fall in love with him?* she asked herself for about the thousandth time. *He wasn't even very nice.*

Reed, on the other hand, was just about the nicest man she'd ever met.

Where the walkway ended and the beach began, Felicity removed her shoes. Reed removed his, too, and rolled up his pant legs. Then, holding hands—and carrying their shoes in their free hands—they set off down the beach.

It was such a beautiful night. The full moon, the gentle surf, the balmy breeze, the cool sand under their feet, the distant murmur of voices mixed with the music of the combo at the restaurant, the rustling of nearby palm trees as they swayed—all stirred Felicity's senses. On a night like this, her troubles seemed so far away.

"It's lovely here," she said, although she wished she'd thought to bring a wrap for her shoulders.

"Yes," Reed agreed. "Lovely."

Something in his voice caused her to glance at his face, and when she did, she found him gazing at her. Warmth spread through her, even though a second earlier she'd started to feel a bit chilly.

Almost as if he'd divined her thoughts, he let go of her hand and put his arm around her instead.

In unspoken accord their steps slowed, then stopped. In the next moment his shoes fell to the sand and he encircled her with both arms, drawing her close.

For a long, silent moment broken only by the sounds of nature around them, they stared into one another's eyes. Felicity's heart thudded in her ears as she waited. When his lips finally claimed hers, she sighed. Her boneless fingers allowed her own shoes to fall, and her arms slid around his waist.

As her mouth opened under his, and their tongues began a dance of invitation and acceptance, all thought receded from Felicity's head. There was only sensation. Only Reed. His touch, his warmth, his scent, his strength and the pulsing need between them—a need that grew stronger and more insistent with every passing second.

How long they stood there kissing Felicity didn't know and didn't care. The only thing that mattered was the passion raging between them.

She wanted this man.

She wanted him more than she'd wanted anything in a long, long time.

And he wanted her.

Why in the world did she ever think she needed to wait?

"Whoo-hoo!"

Felicity and Reed sprang apart at the noisy laughter, and only then was she aware that some rowdy young men were approaching them. Face hot with embarrassment, she bent to retrieve her shoes, hoping the men would go on by quickly.

But no…one of them, a tall blonde who grinned widely, said, "Hey, man, I'd kiss her, too. She's hot."

"Yeah, wanna share?" another one called out.

"But I'd want more than kisses," another said. He punched one of the others, who punched him back.

Oh, God…

Were they drunk? Felicity hadn't felt frightened before, but now she did. She and Reed were too far from their hotel, she suddenly realized. Anything could happen.

But Reed only put his arm around her waist and gave her a reassuring squeeze. "Nice night, isn't it, fellas?" he said mildly.

For what seemed like hours but was in reality only seconds, the young men didn't respond, nor did they keep walking. And then the blonde, who afterward Felicity decided must have been their de facto leader, said, "Yeah, nice night. Have a good one!" He waved and continued walking away from their hotel, and the others followed.

It took a few moments for Felicity's heart to settle into its normal beat. Perhaps there'd been no reason to be frightened. Perhaps the men had always been harmless. Yet she couldn't help feeling that if Reed hadn't been so steady and strong—something she knew the young men had definitely sensed—the episode could have turned out differently.

"Ready to go back?" Reed said.

She nodded.

He bent for his shoes, then kept his arm firmly around her shoulders as they walked back to their hotel and onto its grounds. "You weren't frightened, were you?" he finally asked.

"Only for a moment," she admitted.

His hand tightened on her shoulder.

"But then I realized I'm safe when I'm with you."

He stopped. They were now close enough to the hotel that she could clearly hear the band still playing on the patio of the restaurant.

This time, when he closed her into his arms and kissed her, there was more than an awareness of the physical desire between them. There was also a feeling of inevitability. Somehow Felicity knew she was meant to be here, in this place, with this man, at this exact moment in time. Maybe they would never have more than this week together, but that was okay.

This week would be enough.

This week would give her something to think about on cold winter nights when she was once more alone.

This week would even be worth setting the Eastwick gossips' tongues wagging, should they somehow find out about her being here with Reed.

Now she *really* wished she hadn't made that silly bargain with him. Why waste the few precious days they had together?

"Let's go up to our suite," he murmured, ending the kiss.

"I'm ready," she said, knowing then that if he gave any indication at all that he wanted to put an end to their agreement to wait until Wednesday night before making love, she was ready for that, too.

Felicity Farnsworth was special.

Very special.

They could be very good together.

And tonight, if she didn't insist on abiding by the rules they'd agreed to earlier, he would get started on showing her just how good.

Yet Reed also knew he'd better be careful. He didn't want to make another mistake. Before he lost his heart to this woman—and that was a distinct possibility—he'd better think hard. No matter how good they might be together or how special he found her, he had to remember she'd been burned badly and how she now felt about permanent commitment.

Maybe I could change her mind.

It was too soon to know. Reluctantly he decided maybe he'd better cool it. Give them both a chance to get to know each other better, just as she'd suggested, before plunging into something they might not be able to stop before it burned *both* of them.

Even though Felicity had decided she would let Reed take the lead on whether they stuck to their agreement or not, she figured there was no harm in increasing the temptation. So once they were back in their suite, she said, "First dibs on the bathroom."

He smiled. "Fine with me. Want me to look at the guide and see if I can find a good old movie for us to watch on TV?"

"That sounds great."

"And how about if I order a bottle of champagne sent up?"

"Only if it's accompanied by chocolates."

His smile grew bigger. "I knew you were a girl after my own heart."

I'm definitely after your heart.... The moment the thought formed, it stunned Felicity. *Was* she after his heart? What of her vow never to marry again? Surely she didn't want him to fall in love with her unless she was ready to fully commit to him, did she?

The question unnerved her, even as she followed her plan to make it impossible for him to resist her tonight. Taking a black satin teddy and its companion robe from the drawer where she'd placed them earlier, she went into the bathroom to change. She didn't want Reed walking in on her in the bedroom. She wanted the element of surprise.

Before entering the bathroom, she looked with approval at the king-size bed, which the maid had already turned down. She'd also turned on one of the bedside lamps, and the softly lit room looked inviting. All it needed now was Reed in that bed, waiting for her.

Just the thought made Felicity's pulse speed up.

She took her time undressing, freshening up, spritzing herself lightly with her favorite fragrance and putting on the teddy and the robe. Sliding her feet into black satin mules—which she knew made her legs look fantastic—she took a deep breath and opened the bathroom door.

Earlier she'd heard Reed in the bedroom, but he was gone when she emerged. Now she heard the low hum of the television set in the sitting room and smiled. *Look out, Reed, here I come....*

He didn't see her at first, for she entered the sitting room quietly, stopping just inside the doorway. She purposely had not belted her robe, which would give him an unobstructed view of what she was wearing underneath. She knew the picture she made, and she had a pretty good idea of what its effect on him would be.

She wasn't disappointed.

When he turned and saw her, he went completely still, except for his eyes, which widened and then slowly traveled the length of her, and back up. When their gazes finally met, she saw everything he was thinking and feeling, and her heart hammered in her throat.

She wet her lips.

"Felicity," he said gruffly. "What the hell are you trying to do to me? I'm not made of iron."

She could see that. His erection strained against his gray silk pajama bottoms, which was the only garment *he* was wearing. Now Felicity swallowed. "Uncle," she said, forgetting that she'd wanted *him* to make the first move, forgetting everything but the hunger for him hollowing out her insides.

For a moment he didn't move, and she wondered wildly if she'd made a mistake.

And then, in one lightning-fast leap to his feet, he was by her side, crushing her to him.

They kissed greedily, as if they were trying to devour each other. He thrust his tongue deep and his hands—oh, those hands!—cupped her bottom and held her tight against him.

"Felicity," he groaned, burying his face in her neck, then moving down to her breasts. As he held her tight against his erection, his mouth found a nipple. Sucking it through the satin of her teddy, he quickly brought it to a hard nub that ached even as it wanted more…and still more.

Now she was moaning, her hands fisted in his hair

as he kissed and suckled and pulled at her nipples. "Let's go into the bedroom," she finally gasped. She was on fire, and she wanted him inside her. Deep and hard inside her.

He scooped her up into his arms, kicking the bedroom door wide. He put her on the bed none too gently. They were past the place where they might have enjoyed slow, teasing foreplay that built their anticipation. Right now there was only this primitive, wild need to satisfy their mutual hunger *now*.

When he joined her on the bed, she pulled at his pajama bottoms, then plunged her hands inside to grasp his penis. It was hard and hot, hers, all hers.

"I want you," she said, bending to take him into her mouth.

But he wouldn't let her. "Not that. Not now," he said raggedly. "You first."

When his tongue delved, finding that hidden pleasure point, she cried out. He slid his hands under her buttocks, holding her tightly as his tongue circled the throbbing nub at her center. In seconds her back arched and shudders racked her, as wave after wave of intense pleasure consumed her.

When her body finally stopped shuddering, he raised himself, put on a condom, parted her legs and entered her, driving deep. She wound her legs around him and they began to move together, finding their own rhythm. Soon Felicity was on fire again, and the need inside her built higher and higher until, with one great thrust, her body once more shattered around her. Seconds later Reed cried out with his own release.

Afterward, he collapsed on top of her, but a moment later he rolled over, bringing her with him, and held her close as their hearts slowed and their bodies cooled.

"My God," he said, "that was incredible."

Felicity felt stunned. Their lovemaking had been explosive, like nothing she'd ever experienced before.

His arms tightened around her. Gently he kissed the tip of her nose. "You okay?" he murmured.

"Yes." But she wasn't sure if she was okay or not. What she felt was part elation, part terror. For if he could bring out a wild side of her she hadn't even known she possessed, causing her to forget where she was and who she was and every single bit of her much-valued control, she knew she was in danger. Grave danger.

I can't love him. I can't. That path led to heartache, for more reasons than she cared to think about. *This is supposed to be a no-strings, fun-in-the-sun week. That's all. So get a damn grip on yourself!*

A sharp knock on the sitting-room door caused them both to stiffen.

"Who?" she said.

"It's probably room service. The champagne and chocolates…" Smiling down at her, Reed got up. "You stay there. I'll go." Unhurriedly he reached for his pajama bottoms, which had been discarded into a silky heap on the floor.

Felicity swallowed, getting a good look at him in all his magnificent male glory. No wonder she'd become putty in his hands. He was truly gorgeous.

But you know that's not the only reason. It's not even the most important reason.

Shut up, she told her inner voice. *Just shut up.*

Reed closed the connecting door when he walked out to the sitting room. While he was gone, Felicity reached for her teddy. One lacy strap had torn during its frantic removal, so Felicity donned her robe instead. Then she went into the bathroom to put herself back together again.

When she came out ten minutes later, Reed was sitting on the side of the bed waiting for her.

Their eyes met.

"Are you sure you're okay?" he said.

She nodded. Embarrassment had kicked in. Did he think less of her now? Did he think she had behaved wantonly? Somehow she couldn't imagine Emma ever acting like this.

Remembering Emma, guilt mixed with her feelings of embarrassment.

"Because," he said, "you're acting as if you're sorry about what we did."

Was she?

"*Are* you sorry?" he pressed. His blue eyes held concern.

Looking at him—his tousled hair, his kind face, his troubled expression, his beautiful body—Felicity felt ashamed. Of course he wouldn't think less of her. What was wrong with her? After all, they were both healthy, normal adults who desired one another. What was wrong with that?

"No," she said firmly. "No, I'm not sorry at all."

After a moment he grinned. "Let's do it again, then."

Now she laughed, the seriousness of the previous moment gone.

"That's better," he said. "Laughing is good for you." He patted the bed next to him. "Come sit by me."

"Where's that champagne you promised me?" she countered.

"Are you saying you'd rather have champagne than another bout in this bed?"

The incredulous look on his face—which he was striving hard to keep there instead of laughing—caused the last of any misgivings she might still have harbored to vanish. It was going to be okay. All she had to do was remember the terms under which she was here.

No strings.

Just fun.

For both of them.

So she'd gotten a little carried away in their lovemaking. So she'd attached a little more importance to it than was really there. No harm done. She hadn't said anything to Reed that she couldn't take back. And obviously he was just fine with what had happened between them. *So chill,* she told herself. *Match his tone and all will be well.*

"Champagne first, chocolate second and bed third," she said.

"You sure drive a hard bargain."

"I think you've said that before."

He stood and held out his hand. "Okay, you win. Let's go have some of that champagne."

Seven

Reed liked watching Felicity sleep.

She lay on her stomach, her legs sprawled out in abandon, almost as a child might sleep. Her breathing was slow and measured, with an occasional soft snore erupting from those luscious lips of hers.

She was no child, though.

No way. She was a gorgeous, sexy, wonderful woman, and she did things to him and made him feel things and want things that should be against the law.

Reaching out, he laid his palm against her tight, rounded bottom. She stirred slightly, murmuring, then settled back into sleep. He smiled, put a little more pressure into his touch. He sure did like her bottom. Bending, he kissed it.

"Hmm," she said, sighing. But her eyes didn't open.

He smiled again and drew back. He would let her sleep. Quietly, so he wouldn't disturb her, he got out of bed, and after getting some clean underwear he went into the bathroom to shower. For the first time in many weeks he could hardly wait for the day to begin.

Felicity awakened to the sun on her face and the most wonderful sense of well-being. Stretching like a cat, she let herself remember everything that had taken place yesterday.

She blushed when she thought about how she and Reed had made love twice more last night. Once in the sitting room on the sofa with the lights out and the moonlight streaming into the room from the open balcony doors, and then again in bed, slowly and sweetly and so wonderfully that Felicity had almost cried from the sheer joy of it.

Afterward he'd held her close, spoon fashion, one hand cupping a breast, the other caressing her hip, and they'd fallen asleep that way.

Where was he now? she wondered. Out on the balcony? Or in the sitting room? She didn't hear the TV. What was he doing?

Getting up, she reached for her robe and put it on. Then she padded over to the door that led into the sitting room and opened it. The smile on her face died. Reed wasn't there. She frowned. She could see out to the balcony, and he wasn't there, either.

And then she saw the note, propped in front of a vase of flowers on the round table next to the sofa.

She walked over and picked it up.

Felicity,
I woke up early and took my shower. I've gone for a walk. When I get back, I hope you're awake and ready to go down and have breakfast and talk about what we want to do today. See you soon.
Love, Reed.

Love.

He'd signed the note "Love, Reed."

Oh, so what? that nasty inner voice of hers said. *People are always saying love to one another, especially in notes and e-mails. You do it yourself, all the time. Doesn't mean you really* love *that person.*

Despite her little lecture to herself, she was smiling as she headed into the bathroom for her own shower. Suddenly the day—the entire week—seemed filled with possibility.

It was going to be a wonderful week, she thought happily. A wonderful, wonderful week.

But a tiny, niggling fear wormed its way through her haze of sexual satisfaction and excited anticipation.

What if, despite all Felicity's precautions, Emma should find out where Felicity had gone this week… and with whom?

But that wasn't going to happen, Felicity reassured herself. No one knew they were here together.

And no one ever would.

Reed took his time going back to the suite. So it was after ten-thirty when he returned. He was powerfully hungry by then—having awakened at eight—and hoped Felicity was up and ready for breakfast.

When he walked into the sitting room, he immediately saw her. She had been standing looking out over the balcony rail at the diamond-dusted water beyond, but at his entrance she turned, a hesitant smile on her face.

He felt a rush of tenderness toward her. He knew she was remembering, as he was, everything they'd experienced together last night.

As he walked toward her and she took her first, tentative steps toward him, he thought again what a beautiful woman she was. Today her bright platinum hair shone in the morning sunlight, its messy style looking for all the world as if she'd just gotten out of bed. The look was enormously sexy, he thought. As was her red-and-white cropped top and matching red shorts, worn with flat red thong sandals.

And yet her appeal wasn't just in the way she looked. She might be successful and coolly competent in her career, sophisticated and worldly because of her background, even jaded because of her life experiences, but she was also vulnerable—something she tried hard not to show, maybe because she viewed vulnerability as a weakness.

Reed could understand that. Hell, most men could and did, because most men tried to hide their own vulnerabilities.

And, as she'd shown last night, Felicity was also warm and passionate. In short, everything a man could want in a woman.

"Hey," he said softly.

"Hey, yourself," she said equally softly.

A moment later he closed the distance between them and took her into his arms. She sighed as their lips met in a lingering kiss.

When the kiss ended, he smiled. "Ready for breakfast?"

"I am."

The color of her eyes reminded him of the delicate new leaves that appear in the spring. And how was it he'd never noticed that faint dusting of freckles across her nose? They made her appear younger and even more sexy, if such a thing was possible.

"Do you want to order from room service or go downstairs?" he asked, trying not to be distracted by the expression in her eyes, or else they'd *never* get any breakfast. "The café has a buffet. I checked it out. It looks pretty good."

"That sounds perfect."

Ten minutes later they were in the buffet line. After they'd finished eating, they lingered with their second and third cups of coffee—second for her, third for him.

"Oh, that was good," she said, leaning back and sighing. "If I keep eating like this while I'm here, though, I'll be in danger of not fitting into my clothes when it's time to go home."

"We'll work it off," he said.

She raised her eyebrows.

He smiled. "So what do you want to do today?" He knew what he'd like to do, but he figured she wouldn't want to spend her *entire* week in bed.

"What are my choices?"

"Well, we could spend the afternoon at the pool or swimming on the beach. Or we could take a boat out to one of the coral reefs and try some snorkeling. There's also deep sea fishing available or, if you'd rather, we could do some scuba diving off San Francisco Reef.

"Or…" He paused. "We could rent a dune buggy and go off exploring on our own."

"Oh, that sounds like fun."

"What, exploring on our own?"

"Yes. We can wear our bathing suits and take one of those beach blankets—I saw where the hotel provides them to guests. They'll even pack us some sandwiches and a cooler of soft drinks if we want—and we can just do whatever we feel like doing."

Felicity decided later that it was one of the most perfect days she'd ever had. The sun, the sparkling sea, the wind blowing through her hair as they drove over the narrow coastal road until they found the perfect spot to stop, the delicious sense of freedom from responsibility and all of her everyday frustrations and stress, but most all, being with Reed—all added up to a day she knew would live in her memory for a long time.

They were lucky. They found a fairly secluded spot, one where there were no other swimmers and only the occasional passing vehicle on the road above the beach, so they could be uninhibited and frolic and play and kiss without anyone watching.

They even made love.

It was incredible, even better than Felicity's dream. They were in waist-high water, jumping the waves, when Felicity's bikini top came undone in the back and floated up in front of her. When she tried to grab it and retie it, she lost her balance and fell.

Reed, laughing, grabbed her and pulled her up, then lunged for the bikini top, which by now had come off entirely.

When he turned to give it back to her, their eyes met, then his moved slowly down. Felicity just stood there, letting each wave come and briefly cover her, then, as it receded, expose her naked breasts once more.

And Reed watched.

Felicity could feel her body change under his gaze. Something deep inside pulsed insistently, and her breathing became shallow and labored. A moment later he was there, taking her into his arms, covering her mouth with his.

Felicity could never have imagined how incredible it would be to make love in the warm water, with the hot sun beating down on them. When Reed lifted her up, sliding into her and letting the motion of the water set his pace with slow, hard thrusts, Felicity threw her head back and let herself go.

When her climax came, it was so powerful, she cried out, her nails digging into his back. His response was as guttural as hers.

Afterward she clung to him. She was shaking from the intensity of her physical response to him.

It was only after her heart stopped thudding that she thought about her bikini. She could feel its bottom part around her right ankle, but she had no idea where the top had gone. Reaching down, she pulled her bottom up. "I've lost my top," she said.

"There's no one to see," Reed said. "You can dry off and put your clothes on. I'll hold up the blanket in case a car comes along."

She wanted to say they'd forgotten something else, too. A condom. But she didn't. What good would it do to worry about it now? Anyway, she thought she was safe. Her period was due next week, so she didn't think she was ovulating. *I won't think about it. Time enough to worry about it if I have to….*

But it was a measure of how thoroughly Reed had captivated her that the moment he touched her, she forgot everything. Suddenly some of the pleasure of the day faded, for if there was one thing Felicity hated, it was losing control. And when she not only lost

control, but also lost sight of her objectives and goals—
even jeopardized them, not to mention her friendship
with Emma—she knew she needed to reevaluate.

Being with Reed may be fun, but it's dangerous,
she told herself. *You are playing with fire, and you're
going to get burned...and badly...if you're not very,
very careful.*

Felicity was very quiet on the drive back to the
hotel. Reed wondered what she was thinking. Her expression gave nothing away as she gazed out at their
surroundings. She'd gotten a bit sunburned on the
tops of her shoulders, even though they'd slathered
on sunscreen, and he wondered if maybe she felt uncomfortable...or maybe she was just tired. The sun
could do that—sap away all your energy.

He hoped she wasn't quiet because she regretted
their lovemaking. Reed sure didn't. Making love to
her in the water had been incredible. *She* was incredible. His only regret was that he hadn't used a condom,
but hell, he hadn't even thought to bring one, and he
sure wouldn't have had it with him in the water.

What had happened between them had been spon-
taneous—a mutual desire on their part—certainly
nothing planned.

He almost said something to her about it, then
changed his mind. Maybe he was making something
out of nothing. She probably *was* just tired.

Deciding to test the waters, he said, "I could use
a nap. How about you?"

Finally she looked at him. Her green eyes looked darker now, whatever she was feeling hidden in their depths. "I *am* a little tired."

There. He'd been right. "And I promise to let you sleep this time."

She smiled, but she didn't respond the way he'd hoped she would, with some teasing remark.

"Tonight I thought we could have an early dinner, since we skipped lunch, then see the show." The hotel had two alternating Vegas-style revues in their theater at nine each evening.

"That sounds like fun."

Then smile as if you mean it. Finally he could stand it no longer. "Felicity, what's wrong?"

She blinked. "Wrong? Nothing's wrong."

"We both know that's not true. You've been quiet ever since we left the beach."

"I told you, I'm just tired."

"It's more than that," Reed insisted. "Are you sorry we…made love?"

Her throat worked, and she looked away.

Reed pulled over to the side of the road, into the beach grasses that grew wild along this stretch. He cut the engine and turned to face her, putting his arm across the back of the seat. "Look at me," he said softly.

Slowly she turned her head.

He was shocked to see tears glistening in her eyes. "Hey," he said gently. He touched her neck. Her skin was hot, and he could feel a faint pulse beating. He wanted to kiss her, but for the first time, he was scared to. "Please tell me what's wrong."

With an angry motion she brushed away the tears. "It's just hormones. Don't pay any attention to me."

Reed didn't often feel helpless, but in the face of female stuff, he was totally out of his depth. "You're sure?"

She took a deep breath and made a stab at a real smile. "I'm positive."

"And I didn't do anything to upset you?"

"No." Finally a teasing light appeared in her eyes. "But next time, let's make sure we have a condom before we do anything, okay?"

He squeezed her neck. "Deal."

If anything could have shown Felicity that she might have bitten off more than she could comfortably chew in believing she could keep this week with Reed simply one of fun, sun and no-strings sex, her reaction to Reed's concerned questions certainly had exploded *that* misconception.

Reality check, Felicity. Your heart is becoming involved. Maybe you'd better rethink what you're doing.

And if she didn't watch herself, he'd soon know how she felt. And then what? Felicity knew that despite what he'd said about not using her to get back at Emma, that had to be part of the reason he'd asked her to come to Cozumel with him. Maybe he didn't realize it, but that would be a normal reaction after you'd been dumped, especially for a man as confident and attractive as Reed.

So of course he'd wanted to show Emma and everyone else that he wasn't suffering. Having Felicity come to Cozumel was an ego booster for him. Yes, she knew he liked her. And yes, she knew he enjoyed the sex. But that was it.

He'd told her up front what the rules of the week were. No strings. So if she was going to stay in Cozumel with him, she'd better make darned sure she followed those rules.

Disengage your emotions. Put on a happy face, enjoy the food, enjoy the sun and enjoy the sex. But stop attaching more importance to what Reed says and does than actually exists.

These thoughts and more swirled through her mind as she attempted to nap. Reed had teasingly said he'd let her have the bed to herself for a couple of hours, that he didn't trust himself when they were sharing a bed.

Now Felicity was kicking herself for not responding in kind. But when he'd said this, she'd simply nodded gratefully. Now she wondered where he was. Was he trying to nap on the sofa? That sofa wasn't long enough for his six-foot-two-inch frame.

Jumping up, she went into the bathroom, hurriedly splashed water on her face and ran a comb through her hair. Then she went out to the sitting room. It was empty.

This time she knew where to look. Sure enough, there was another note on the side table.

Dear Felicity,
I decided to try to catch the Red Sox game in the sports bar. I'll be back by six.

The note was signed simply "Reed."

No love this time. Good. That's the way she wanted it. Emotions in check. No strings. No involvement of anyone's heart.

She looked at her watch. It was five-thirty. She just had time for a shower before he came back. She was halfway to the bathroom when she realized she'd wanted to buy a disposable razor because she'd forgotten hers, and her legs really needed shaving.

Damn.

If she went down to the gift shop, she wouldn't be finished getting ready by the time he returned. Well, no help for it. She'd just have to hurry, and so would he if they were to eat dinner and still make that nine-o'clock show.

Sliding her feet back into the sandals she'd worn earlier, she grabbed her wallet from her purse and headed out to find a razor.

The lobby was crowded with people. Some were just coming in from an afternoon spent on the beach. Others were dressed for the evening. Still others were afternoon arrivals standing in the check-in line. Several luggage carriers were piled high nearby, and there were a half dozen or so people waiting to talk to the concierge.

Felicity wove her way through the crowd, smiling as she passed a cute little girl with dark pigtails who was standing with a teenage boy who was obviously her brother. The gift shop was at the far end of the lobby, but Felicity finally found it. She picked up a pink disposable razor and, while she was at it, a copy of *Vanity Fair* magazine, just in case she wanted something to read. At the last minute she grabbed some breath freshener, too.

After paying for her purchases, she walked out of the gift shop.

"Felicity! Hi!"

Felicity's heart skidded into her throat. She tried to keep the shock off her face as she turned to see Cindy and Josh Pruitt—whose wedding she had planned and coordinated last summer. Oh, my God, she thought.

"What are you doing here?" Cindy Pruitt said, her fresh, open face wreathed in smiles.

Felicity's mind raced. "I—I'm on vacation."

Josh Pruitt rolled his eyes. "What did you *think* she was doing here, Cin?"

Felicity swallowed and told herself to calm down. The Pruitts didn't know who she was with, and even if they should see her with Reed, she didn't think they'd know him. After all, they didn't live in Eastwick. They lived in Littlefield, which was a good twenty miles from Eastwick, and they didn't move in the same circles.

"Are you here by yourself?" Cindy asked.

"No, I'm with a friend," Felicity said. "It's beautiful here, isn't it?"

"Gorgeous," Cindy gushed. "We've had *such* a great time here. I hate to go home."

"Are you going home soon?" Felicity hoped she didn't sound as eager as she was.

"Tomorrow morning," Josh said. "We came on a four-day package."

"I wish we'd booked a whole week," Cindy said. "If I'd known how wonderful it was here, I would have." She sighed. "How long are you staying?"

"All week," Felicity said.

"Oh, you're so lucky. We even tried to extend our stay, but they're completely booked," Cindy said.

"That's too bad. Well, enjoy your last night here. Um, are you planning anything special?"

Cindy smiled, giving Josh one of those adoring glances that meant the honeymoon was still alive and well. "We're having a nice dinner and then we're going to see tonight's show."

"Well, have fun. I'd better go. My friend is expecting me."

They said their goodbyes, and Felicity, dodging people at every turn, hurried across the lobby to the bank of elevators. On the way back to the room she tried to think of what she could do to persuade Reed to change his plans, because there was no way she was going to eat in the restaurant and go to that show. Not if the Pruitts were going to be there. She could not take that chance. Even if they *didn't* live in Eastwick or run with her crowd, they did know some of them. And if they saw her with Reed, she'd have to introduce them. And then what? They might mention seeing her in Cozumel to the wrong person. She couldn't take that chance.

She had to lie low until they left tomorrow morning.

She entered the suite to see Reed pouring himself a glass of wine at the bar.

"There you are." He smiled. "Want a glass?"

"Sure. That sounds good." Setting her purchases on the coffee table, she walked over to join him.

"Here you go," he said, handing her a glass.

She tasted her wine, then said, "Reed, would you be too disappointed if we just had dinner sent up here tonight and skipped the show?"

For a moment he seemed taken aback. His questioning eyes met hers. "What's the matter? Aren't you feeling well?"

"It's not that. While I was downstairs at the gift shop I ran into someone I know."

"Really? Who was it? Anyone I know?"

"I don't think so. This is a couple whose wedding I planned. They live in Littlefield. Cindy and Josh Pruitt."

He shook his head. "Nope, doesn't ring a bell."

"Anyway, I told them I was here with a friend, and I don't want them to know who that friend is. I mean," she said hurriedly, seeing the frown on his face, "I can't take a chance on them saying something to someone and then having the information get back to Eastwick."

"I see."

"Don't look at me like that, Reed."

He shrugged. "I just think you're worrying for nothing. Hell, if Emma *should* find out about us, I don't think she'd care. It's not like *she* wants me and you've stolen me away."

"Maybe she wouldn't care, but I still wouldn't want her to find out about this week from someone else. If she needed to know, I'd want to be the one to tell her. But she doesn't need to know, does she? I mean, what purpose would it serve? It's not like you and I are going to be an item. After all, we *did* agree this was just going to be one week of fun and sun, with no strings, didn't we?"

He didn't answer for a moment. Finally he said, "Oh, all right, Felicity. You win. We'll lie low tonight. But what about the rest of the week?"

"The rest of the week we can do whatever we please. The Pruitts are leaving in the morning."

He finished off his wine and set his empty glass on the bar. "All right. Fine. I think I'll get my shower. While I'm doing that, why don't you look over the room-service menu and decide what you'd like to have?"

Setting her half-full glass down next to his, she said softly, "I've got a better idea." Hell, she might as well pack as much sex into the week as she possibly could, since she probably wouldn't be getting more for a very long time. "Why don't I join you in that shower?"

He smiled slowly. "You're right—that's a much better idea."

Eight

Reed decided this must be a dream.

He couldn't really be kneeling in front of Felicity, slowly moving a bar of soap down the insides of her legs while a jet of hot water streamed over both of them, could he?

Finishing with her legs, he buried his face in the nest of blond hair that was so temptingly there. He knew she liked it when he explored her with his tongue. He could feel the way she stiffened, hear the way her breath hitched, and her pleasure was a distinct turn-on for him, making him want her even more.

And yet he liked the anticipation of waiting. He liked bringing her to the point where she abandoned control and allowed her passions free rein, because if he'd learned anything about Felicity in the past week, he'd learned that keeping control was paramount in her life.

"Oh," she moaned as his tongue circled that little spot that throbbed against him.

"Do you like that?" he asked gruffly, drawing back so he could see her face.

"Yes, yes," she groaned. "Oh, yes."

"And this?"

"Yes, yes…oh, please don't stop."

And yet he did, for he knew the longer he could keep her on the brink, the more intense her orgasm would be. So he teased her, rubbing the tip of his penis against her, probing at that sweet spot until she was practically weeping.

Only then did he go back to her with his tongue, and this time he sucked hard. In seconds he felt the spasms begin and he held her trembling body fast. When the spasms finally stopped he rose to capture her mouth.

Winding her legs around him, she wrenched her mouth free, crying, "Take me now!"

He drove in deep and hard. She grasped handfuls of his hair, calling out as her body convulsed around him. When his release came, he shook from its intensity, gripping her buttocks and holding her close until he was spent, and his heart stopped its frantic beating.

Afterward, exhausted, they washed each other gently, then toweled off with two of the gigantic, fluffy towels warming on the towel rack.

They didn't talk, but several times their eyes met,

and they smiled. Reed wished he could say everything he was feeling, but he knew it could be a fatal mistake to rush Felicity.

Besides, he reminded himself, he'd already made one mistake. He didn't want to make another. *No strings. That's what you told her. So take it slowly. Enjoy the week. Then see what happens after you get back to Eastwick.*

"You ready for some of that room service now?" he asked, watching her as she combed her wet hair. Even with no makeup she looked beautiful.

"I could eat a horse," she said, meeting his gaze in the mirror and grinning.

"Me, too. Let's go look at that menu."

As they walked out into the sitting room, which was filled with the apricot glow from the setting sun, Reed found himself wishing he'd never made that dumb promise of no strings.

Because right now what he wanted most in the world was to tie up Felicity Farnsworth and never let her get away.

And to hell with going slowly.

The trouble with the heart was it didn't behave the way a person wanted it to, Felicity thought several days later. It had a mind of its own. And right now her heart didn't want to listen to her. She could tell it not to get involved with Reed all day long, but in the end, it was *already* involved, and no amount of denying it made a bit of difference.

Felicity sighed.

So much for no strings!

Well, at least Reed didn't know how she felt. And Felicity was determined he never would.

Even if it killed her.

"Penny for your thoughts," he said. The sun glinted off the blond streaks in his brown hair and made his eyes look darker than they were.

"They aren't worth a penny," she said, smiling. Slathered with sunscreen, they were lying on webbed chaises poolside. After eating an enormous breakfast, they'd come straight out to the pool and had been there most of the morning. Felicity felt an amazing awareness of all her senses as she sipped at a frosty rum drink and gave Reed covert admiring glances.

"There's something I've been meaning to ask you," he said lazily, turning to face her.

"What's that?"

"Why do you always wear some kind of butterfly in your hair?"

Felicity touched today's butterfly, this one a turquoise plastic barrette the same color as her bikini. "My grandmother loved butterflies. When I was little, she'd take me out to her garden and point out the different ones—she always planted the kinds of flowers and shrubs that would attract them—and she'd tell me their names." Felicity hesitated, then decided Reed would never make light of something this important to her. "Those were among my happiest childhood memories."

He seemed to sense there was more and said nothing.

"My granny Farnsworth was my idol." Felicity swallowed against a fresh feeling of loss, even though her beloved grandmother had been gone for many years. "She was knowledgeable about so many things, and she was kind and fair and…and she was the sort of person you could confide in. I always knew she'd never betray anything I told her."

Reed nodded. "Every kid needs someone like that in his life."

"Yes." Felicity had gained control of her emotions and she smiled in remembrance. "Anyway, I know it's probably silly, but the butterflies are my way of honoring her."

"It's not silly at all," he said softly.

"When she died, she left me a beautiful butterfly brooch made of diamonds. It was very old and worth a lot of money. The money wasn't important, though. What was important was that the brooch had belonged to her. Once she told me it was her most valuable possession." She looked at Reed. "Sam hocked it."

Reed stared at her. "He hocked it," he repeated flatly.

"Yes. He'd already run through my money— which, at the time, I still didn't know—and he was desperate. His gambling debts were piling up, and he was out of resources."

"So the brooch is gone?"

"No. I managed to get it back. I sold all my other

jewelry, everything he hadn't gotten his hands on. My wedding ring, my engagement ring, my mother's wedding rings and a few stock certificates Sam hadn't known I had."

"Jesus. What a bastard that guy was."

That statement said it all. Felicity couldn't help thinking how different her life might have been if she'd married someone like Reed. By now she would probably have had two point five children, one dog, one cat and of course, horses.

But she wouldn't have had Weddings By Felicity. And even though she sometimes wondered why she'd chosen to work in a business where people's emotions were so involved, she did love her career, and she was proud of the success she'd achieved.

No one ever gets everything....

"This week has gone fast," Reed said.

"Yes." It was Saturday. Felicity had now been in Cozumel five days. Tomorrow afternoon they were flying home. Monday she'd be back at work, and the days she'd spent here with Reed would just be a memory.

Sadness gripped her. It would be hard to give up what she'd found here. Yet give it up she must, because she knew she was not the kind of woman Reed wanted on a permanent basis. He wanted someone sweet and giving, someone with a kinder disposition than Felicity possessed or ever would possess, someone like Emma who loved working with children and would almost certainly put the man in her life first.

Felicity wasn't like that anymore.

Felicity had become more tiger than lamb.

And she would never again let any man take over her life.

Not even Reed.

Of course, he didn't want to, so her decision was a moot point.

The past few days had been glorious, though. They'd had a lot of fun together. They'd talked and laughed, gone scuba diving, snorkeling and deep sea fishing. They'd eaten tons of shrimp and crab and scallops and grouper, drunk elaborate concoctions made with rum, danced until Felicity's feet hurt, and made love in every conceivable place and way they could think of.

Remembering the sex—the most recent bout having come first thing this morning—she smiled in contentment. Her body hadn't felt this good and this sated since…actually, it had *never* felt this good or this sated.

"What are you thinking about now?" Reed asked, leaning over and brushing his lips against her ear.

She turned her head. Their eyes were only inches apart. Her breathing quickened. God, would she ever get enough of him?

Before she could censor herself, she said, "I was thinking about you."

"Let's go back to the room," he whispered.

"You're insatiable," she said, trying for a lightness she didn't feel. But her nether regions were already tightening against a pulsing need.

"I can't help it. You're too tempting."

"Well, okay," she said, pretending reluctance while knowing she didn't fool him one bit.

All the way back, as they walked through the hotel hand in hand, as they waited for the elevator, as they rode up to their suite, as Reed unlocked the door, all Felicity could think about was the way he unleashed her hidden desires, the way he made her practically beg him for more…and more.

No one seeing the cool and collected Felicity Farnsworth in action at work would ever imagine she could be so wanton and abandoned, so greedy to experience everything Reed had to offer.

They were barely inside the suite before they were tearing off each other's bathing suits. They never even made it to the bed. They made love on the floor of the sitting room, with Felicity on top, a position she found gave her the most intense orgasm of all—not just because Reed could go deeper, but because she could watch him watching her, and she could see as well as feel the reaction of her body when he rubbed her nipples or put his finger between their bodies to give her two pleasure points at once.

Afterward they shared a shower, then Felicity decided she would take a nap so that she wouldn't be tired tonight. She knew Reed had planned a special evening, since it would be their last one there.

"I'm not tired," he said when she told him what she planned, "but you go ahead. I may see if I can't get in a tennis game or two." He'd discovered there were always available partners, and had even made friends with a couple of the men.

"Okay. What time do you want to go down to dinner tonight?"

He looked at his watch. "It's two o'clock now. I've made reservations for eight. We should leave here no later than seven-thirty. So I'll make sure I'm back here by six-thirty, because I'll probably need another shower."

"Okay. I'll be ready by then." Felicity kissed him goodbye, then he left.

Wrapping herself in the thick terry robe the hotel provided, she lay down on the bed. The combined effects of the sun, the potent rum drink and the terrific sex lulled her almost immediately into sleep. She was in the middle of a wonderful dream featuring her and Reed stranded on a desert island when something jarred her awake. It took her a moment to realize it was the phone. Still a bit groggy, she picked up the bedside extension, fully expecting to hear Reed's voice.

"Hello?" she said, her voice rough with the remnants of sleep.

For a moment, there was only silence.

"Hello?" she said again, this time more firmly. "Is anyone there?"

"I'm sorry," said a male voice—a *familiar* male voice. "I must have gotten the wrong room. I was looking for Reed Kelly."

Felicity's heart slammed into her throat. Dear God. No wonder the voice sounded familiar. It belonged to Max Weldon. Shock, followed by panic, froze her voice so that she was utterly incapable of saying another word.

Finally she managed to stammer, "Th-that's okay." Her hand shook as she placed the phone back in its cradle.

Had Max recognized her voice?

Would he call back?

Sure enough, the phone rang again. Felicity stared at it, counting the rings.

Two. Three. Six.

Finally the ringing stopped. A few seconds later the message light began to blink red.

Still paralyzed with fear, Felicity sat on the bed and tried to calm her wildly careening thoughts.

What was she playing at?

She knew what she'd been playing *with*. Fire. She'd known how dangerous this game was, yet she'd gone ahead and played it anyway.

And for what?

For some truly incredible sex and some lovely memories, that's what. But no matter how incredible the sex, it was ending tomorrow, anyway. And the memories, well, were they worth losing Emma's friendship?

The truth was, if Reed loved her, and if Felicity thought they had a future together, she would risk everything. She realized that now. But he didn't love her. Because if he did, he'd had plenty of opportunities to say so, and he hadn't. He'd said she was incredible. He'd said the sex was fantastic. He'd said he enjoyed her company. But he'd never, not even in the throes of a climax, said he loved her.

And didn't men, if they were ever going to say it, say it then? Either that or they said it to *get* a woman into bed. Reed hadn't done that, either. He'd been honest with her from the beginning. He'd said this week was about having fun, getting some sun and having no-strings sex.

Period.

Suddenly her panic faded. Even if Max had thought her voice was familiar, he would never imagine she was here with Reed. Would he?

She swallowed, remembering how Max had seen her rushing out of the stables after Reed had kissed her that first time. She knew he'd wondered if something was wrong, because she was sure her face had betrayed her embarrassment. What if he remembered that day now? What if he put two and two together?

But even if he did, Max was not the kind of man to spread gossip. Besides, he liked her. Felicity knew he did. In fact, she thought he felt paternal toward her, partly because of his friendship with her father, and partly because he'd first met her when she was still a child.

I'm safe from Max. He wouldn't do anything to hurt me or Reed.

So as long as Reed kept his promise and didn't tell anyone about her being here with him—which she was sure he would, because he was an honorable man—then she had nothing to worry about.

But even as she told herself all this, an enormous ache of sadness squeezed her heart. Maybe Max or Reed would never deliberately hurt her, but she was hurting herself. And the longer she stayed here, the more intense that hurt would be.

I have to get away....

She knew Reed hadn't done it purposely, but the truth was, he was using her every bit as much as Sam had. The fact that she'd been using Reed, too, was beside the point. She had to face it. The longer she stayed here, the more it would hurt her when it was time to go home. And going home *with* Reed, having to spend all those hours on the plane with him, knowing when they got back to Eastwick they would be going their separate ways...she knew she wouldn't be able to stand it.

And then when they got back to Eastwick, what? Would they shake hands and say thanks, it's been fun, see you around?

No, she couldn't handle that. She might do something stupid, like cry. And then Reed would feel awkward. Oh, God. It didn't bear thinking about. The best thing she could do, for both of them, was make a quick, clean break and go home now.

Decision made, she jumped up. The digital clock read 4:00. Even though Reed had said he wouldn't be back until six-thirty, she knew she needed to hurry so she could be sure to get away in plenty of time.

Thank goodness she had her return ticket. She was sure if she was willing to add more money to it, she could get on a flight today, just as she had coming down to Cozumel.

By five, she'd packed up all her belongings, changed into khaki pants, a black knit top and comfortable black clogs. Ten minutes later she followed the bellman to the elevator. By five-twenty, she was climbing into a cab and on her way to the Cozumel airport.

Eyes blurred with tears, she didn't look back.

Reed had just finished three vigorous games of tennis and felt great. In fact, he couldn't remember when he'd felt better. He knew the sun and water and good food had something to do with his sense of well-being, but the main reason he felt so good was Felicity.

She continued to surprise him, revealing hidden facets of her personality piece by piece. When she'd talked about her grandmother and the butterfly brooch today, he'd realized once again how much she'd gone through in her short life, and how much courage she had. His life had been a piece of cake compared to hers.

"Hey, Reed, want to join Jenny and me for dinner tonight?"

"Thanks, Brad," Reed said to his tennis partner. "But I've already made reservations at Mesa 17." He'd been lucky to get them. The restaurant was one of the newer ones on the island and in a very short space of time had become one of the hottest.

Waving goodbye to Brad, Reed headed for the lobby and the elevators. The first thing he saw when he entered the suite was the blinking message light on the telephone.

"Hey, Felicity, I'm back," he called out, figuring she must be in the bathroom. Then he walked over to the phone and pressed the button to retrieve the message.

"Reed," he heard. "This is Max. I'm sorry to bother you while you're on vacation, but I've got one quick question. Call me back when you get a chance."

It took a few minutes for the hotel operator to put the call through, but once she did, Max answered almost immediately.

"Hey, Max, what's up?" Reed said.

"You remember Hugo Manchester?" Max asked.

"The Brit who visited Rosedale last fall?"

"That's the one."

"What about him?"

"He called today. He's going back home next month. Wanted to know if we were interested in buying out his stock."

Reed thought fast. Manchester had some fine horses, including a stud that Reed had coveted since first laying eyes on him. "How much does he want?"

Max named a figure and Reed whistled. "I don't know if I can raise that much. I don't suppose he'd consider splitting the stock."

"I asked him that. I figured you'd want Sir James, but Manchester said it's all or none."

"Damn," Reed muttered. "Well, call him back,

and tell him I'll need at least a week before I can make a decision."

"Okay."

"Anything else?"

"Uh, just one thing. The first time I tried to get you today, I thought the operator there put me through to the wrong room, 'cause a woman answered the phone."

Reed froze. Felicity. *Shit.* "And?" he said cautiously.

"I apologized, then tried again, and the second time I got put through to your message box."

"Well, good."

"Thing is, boss, before the operator put me through the second time, I told her she'd gotten the wrong room when I'd called before. And she said, no, she was sure she'd given me the right room. And I said, well, it couldn't have been, because some woman answered the phone."

Reed knew what was coming next.

"And then *she* said, well, it was probably Señora Kelly."

Reed hated liars, but in this case, he knew he had no choice. "Okay, you've found me out. I'm not alone here."

"Yeah, well, I figured as much. But here's what bothers me. That woman who answered the phone… she sure did sound like someone I know, and the more I thought about her voice, the more I thought it was Felicity."

"Felicity? You mean Felicity Farnsworth?"

"Yeah, that's who I mean."

Jesus, now what should he do?

"So here's the thing, boss," Max continued relentlessly. "I realize you could tell me it's none of my goddamn business, but let's just say it *was* Felicity who answered the phone. I don't know if you're aware of this or not, but her father was a real good friend of mine, and I've always had a soft spot in my heart for her. She's had some tough times, losing her parents like that, and then that son of a bitch ex-husband of hers screwing everything in skirts while he was married to her, not to mention stealing her blind. So I don't want to see her get hurt again. Not by *anyone*."

Nine

Reed stared at the phone. If anyone else had talked to him this way, he would have lashed back. But he respected Max. And he wanted Max to keep respecting him. "I don't want to see her get hurt again, either," he finally answered.

"Good. That's good. I'm glad we understand each other. Okay, boss, I'll let you go. See you Monday."

"Yes, see you Monday," Reed echoed.

After hanging up the phone, he didn't immediately go looking for Felicity. Instead, he stood there thoughtfully, going over everything Max had said to him. The Hugo Manchester proposition, something he would normally consider high priority, took a backseat to what Max had had to say about Felicity.

Damn. Reed wished he'd been in the suite when Max had called initially, because the last thing he wanted was for his call to have upset Felicity. But maybe she hadn't realized who had called. Reed hoped that was the case. He didn't want her worrying about Max, because Max obviously wasn't going to cause tongues to wag. From what he'd said, it was obvious he wanted to protect Felicity just as much as Reed did.

Well, he guessed he'd soon find out how she was feeling. Walking into the bedroom, he fully expected to see a closed bathroom door, but instead it stood open.

He frowned. "Felicity?"

Silence greeted him.

Where was she? He walked into the bathroom and looked around, then went back out to the bedroom. Had she gone down to the lobby for something? Maybe she'd needed something in the gift shop.

Well, wherever she'd gone, she knew he was coming back by six-thirty, and it was almost that now, so she'd probably be there soon.

He'd better get his shower. Taking clean underwear from a drawer, he entered the bathroom again. He showered quickly, and ten minutes later was reaching for the toothpaste to brush his teeth when he realized her toothbrush was gone. Frowning, he scanned the length of the vanity countertop. His heart thumped painfully when he saw that her toothbrush wasn't the only thing of hers missing. Her face cream, her perfume, her makeup kit…they were *all* gone.

A moment later he was staring into the closet. None of Felicity's clothes were there. Only his jackets, pants and shirts hung from the bar, and only his shoes were lined up on the floor.

Reed grabbed a pair of pants and a shirt, stuffed his sockless feet into loafers, then headed downstairs to the desk.

Fifteen minutes after that, frustrated, angry and feeling completely impotent, Reed apologized for yelling at the clerk who had just told him he had no idea when Señora Kelly had left the hotel.

It wasn't until Reed questioned the bellmen that he discovered Felicity had left at least an hour and a half earlier. By now she would be at the airport. In fact, for all he knew, she'd already managed to get on a plane.

He thought about calling the airline, then changed his mind. If she wanted to go home, it was best to just let her go. But this wasn't the end of it. Because when he got home himself tomorrow, the first thing he was going to do was go to see Felicity.

Whether she wanted to see him or not.

Felicity was exhausted by the time the limo dropped her at her town house. It was two o'clock in the morning, and except for the street lamps, her neighborhood was dark. Everyone was in bed. Which was exactly where she intended to be very soon.

On Sunday morning she didn't awaken until nearly eleven. Reed would just be leaving for the airport about now, she realized. She wondered what he'd thought when he'd come back to the suite last night and found her gone. Had he been mad...or hurt?

Now that she was over her first panic, she felt bad. She should have at least left him a note. That would have been the decent thing to do, especially when he'd treated her with so much consideration and kindness. Then again, maybe leaving the way she had was for the best. Now he'd think less of her. Which would make everything easier.

After all, Felicity and Reed, as a couple, were history.

From now on, their only relationship would have to do with business. And once the Newhouse wedding was also history, Felicity might be able to avoid Reed altogether.

She told herself she was fine.

None the worse for the experience.

And if she knew she was lying to herself, she didn't admit it.

Reed debated whether to call Felicity when he got home. He was still debating when he reached the outskirts of Eastwick. But when he came to the crossroad that would take him south toward Rosedale, he impulsively turned north toward town.

He knew the general area where Felicity lived. Once when they'd been driving to the club to watch a golf match, Emma had pointed out Felicity's townhouse complex. Whipping out his cell phone, he called information and, with a bit of cunning, managed to get her exact address.

He still wasn't sure what he'd do when he got there, but for some reason he felt it was important to confront her as soon as possible.

After parking his truck in front of the row of town houses that contained her unit, he walked up the pathway and around the corner until he reached her front door. All the wooden blinds were closed, so it was impossible to see if she was home.

Reed rang the doorbell. Nothing happened. He rang the doorbell again, then followed that by knocking hard at the door and calling out, "Felicity! It's Reed."

Still nothing.

He stared at the peephole in the door. Was she there? Maybe even now looking out at him? It was impossible to know. Deciding he would walk around back and see if her SUV was parked there, he set off. But when he reached the back of her row, he saw that each unit had its own garage, and the door of hers was closed. It had no windows.

Damn.

For all he knew, she *was* home, but avoiding him.

Well, she couldn't avoid him forever. He knew where she'd be tomorrow morning. And he would be there, too.

Thank God he'd gone.

Felicity knew it was ridiculous to be so shaken,

but Reed's appearance on her doorstep had totally unnerved her. She felt bad about pretending not to be there, but what else could she do? She knew if she'd let him in, she wouldn't have been able to keep to her resolve, because where he was concerned, she was weak, her much-vaunted control AWOL.

It was safer this way.

Much, much safer.

Yet she knew she couldn't hide from him forever. If he wanted to see her, he would eventually find her.

So she'd better be prepared.

"Oh, thank goodness you're back!"

"What's wrong?" It was eight o'clock Monday morning, and Felicity had just walked into the office.

Rita literally wrung her hands. "Portia Newhouse has broken her engagement!"

"You're kidding, right?"

Rita shook her head. "I wish I were."

Felicity's mind whirled. The Newhouse wedding was less than two weeks away. Every arrangement had already been made. She thought about the spectacular Vera Wang wedding dress designed for Portia, the bridesmaids' dresses made from imported Brussels lace, the three catering companies, the florist who had ordered exotic orchids that cost the earth, the tents and chairs and tables that had been rented, the special tablecloths, the china and silver and crystal, the hundreds and hundreds of gifts, the bartenders and waiters, all the musicians, Bo…

The people and vendors had been booked for months. Wedding or not, they would still have to be compensated. It would be a nightmare. "When did this happen?"

"Thursday. I—I didn't know how to reach you. I tried Serendipity, but they said you weren't there. I didn't know any other spa to try."

Felicity could feel a headache coming on. All she needed now was for the Pruitts to tell someone they had seen her in Cozumel. *Then my goose will well and truly be cooked.* "What have you done about cancellations?"

"I haven't done anything. I didn't know what to do. I didn't know if I *should* cancel. I mean, what if they patch things up?"

"So Portia and Corky had a fight?"

"Apparently. Madeline didn't give me details. The truth is, she was furious when she told me. She could barely hold it together. And when I told her you were away for the week, she hung up on me."

Felicity closed her eyes. Why? Why was this happening to her? Wasn't it bad enough that her heart ached and her life was a mess? Did she have to contend with chaos at work, too? Sighing heavily, she opened her eyes and looked at Rita. "Surely she gave you some idea of what she wanted us to do."

Rita grimaced. "No, she didn't. I'm sorry, Felicity. You would have handled things better, I know." She looked as if she were going to cry.

It wasn't like Rita to get so rattled, but then,

Madeline Newhouse was not an ordinary client. She detested being questioned, always looking as if she thought you were an imbecile because you couldn't read her mind. Felicity could almost understand Rita's reluctance to try to pin her down. Sighing again, Felicity sank into the chair behind her desk and put her head in her hands. "Welcome home," she muttered.

"So where *were* you?" Rita asked.

"I went to a place in New Mexico called The Silver Bell."

"Really? Why New Mexico?"

Felicity shrugged. "I read about the place and went to their Web site and on the spur of the moment, I made the reservation." Thank goodness she'd had the presence of mind to actually find that spa so that she'd have a place to tell people about.

"Well," Rita said, "I want to hear all about it later, but first, I'd better return some phone calls."

"All right. I'll call Madeline, I guess."

But when Felicity phoned the Newhouse home, she was curtly informed that Mrs. Newhouse wasn't taking any calls.

"I must speak with her," Felicity said. "Please tell her it's Felicity Farnsworth and I'm calling about the wedding."

"I'm sorry, Ms. Farnsworth," said the woman who'd answered the phone. "Mrs. Newhouse left explicit instructions. No calls. Instead, I'm to put you through to Alicia Delgado, her secretary."

Felicity impatiently tapped her foot—clad today in Jimmy Choo slingbacks—until Alicia came on the line.

"I'm sorry, Felicity, I don't know what to tell you," Alicia said.

"Well, surely she told you what she wants? I can't wait until the last minute to cancel everything. It's going to cost a fortune as it is."

"She refuses to discuss the wedding," Alicia said in a pained voice.

Felicity closed her eyes. Damn these prima donnas. Damn these movie star wives. And damn all these spoiled, rich, idiot brides. No wonder fifty percent of marriages ended in divorce. They were doomed before they had even begun. Yet for all her inner ranting, she didn't allow her frustration to cause her to lash out against Alicia. The secretary sounded miserable enough, poor thing. After all, she had to be around Madeline Newhouse every day.

"At least tell her I called," Felicity said. "And that I have to know her wishes."

Alicia's sigh was audible. "I'll try."

"What about Portia?

"She's gone."

"Gone? Gone where?"

"Paris, I think."

Felicity sat thinking after the call ended. She really had no choice. She couldn't sit around twiddling her thumbs and waiting for Madeline to deign to give her some direction. At the very least, she needed to warn her vendors. Thank God she hadn't been the one to order the wedding dress or the brides-maids' dresses. Madeline had done that directly, so Felicity was off the hook there.

She and Rita spent the next two hours calling everyone concerned and telling them there was a possibility the wedding would not take place and asking them to prepare an invoice for their expenses in that event.

Felicity sat back with a deep sigh when the last call had been made. "Well, we've done everything we can," she said to Rita.

"Um, not everything."

Felicity frowned. "What do you mean? Did I forget something?"

"You still have to call Reed Kelly. About the wedding photos."

Felicity hoped her face didn't betray the jolt she'd felt just from hearing the sound of his name. "Um, I'll wait on calling him. If, by some miracle, Portia changes her mind, I'm afraid he won't give his per-mission a second time to take pictures there."

Rita nodded. "You're probably right."

Just then the phone rang, and Felicity was glad, because she didn't want to talk about anything that even remotely had to do with Reed. She was afraid if she did, she would give herself away.

Even this brief mention of him had caused butter-flies in her stomach.

"Felicity?"

Felicity jumped.

"Sorry. Didn't mean to startle you. It's Emma on the phone."

Felicity waited until Rita had disappeared into her own office before picking up her extension. "Emma?" she said.

"Hi, Fee. Did you have a good trip?"

For one startled moment Felicity thought Emma knew about Cozumel. But just in time, she realized Emma, like everyone else who'd called here in the past week, thought she'd gone to a spa. "Yes, it was great. I really needed some time away from here."

"I know. You've worked so hard the past couple of years."

Emma's sympathetic response made Felicity feel even guiltier than she already had.

"So where'd you go? Serendipity?"

"Um, no. They were booked solid, since I waited till the last minute to try to get in. I, um, tried this new place in New Mexico called The Silver Bell."

"Is it in Santa Fe?"

"No, north of there." Oh, God. She hated lying to Emma. Hated it.

"Well, I hope you had a wonderful rest and feel like a new woman."

"I did, and I do. I even got a tan."

"Good for you. I can't wait to see you. Lunch next week?"

"Just you and me or all the Debs?"

"I thought just you and me. We can catch up on everything."

They fixed a time and day, then Emma said she had a customer and had to go. Her art gallery, Color, was a popular place, not just with locals, but with tourists as well, and stayed busy, especially in the summer.

After they hung up, Felicity sat staring into space.

Did Emma suspect something?

Felicity knew she was being paranoid, but she couldn't help it. *We can catch up on everything.* What did that mean?

She was still stewing over the phone call from Emma when the phone rang again. This time it was Alicia Delgado. "Felicity? Madeline said to cancel everything. The wedding's definitely off. She also said not to worry about the money. She realizes she'll still have to pay for everything."

"How'd you pull off that miracle, Alicia?"

Alicia laughed and lowered her voice. "I didn't. Alex did."

"Ah. Well, thank you."

Felicity wondered if something was in the air. Too many brides were having second thoughts. First Emma. Now Portia. Determinedly, she pushed Reed and all thoughts of their week together out of her mind. It was over and done with. Time to move on. And hope that Emma never found out that Felicity had lied to her about where she'd really gone last week.

It was after eleven before Reed could leave for Felicity's office. He'd wanted to be there earlier, but there were too many things hanging fire at Rosedale, and it wasn't fair for him to make Max handle them when he had been handling everything for the past week. Not that Max would have complained. He might have raised his eyebrows or wondered what in the heck was going on, but he would have quietly done whatever Reed had asked of him.

When he finally pulled into the parking lot in front of her office, he was relieved to see her silver SUV.

He still wasn't sure how he was going to play this. He'd been angry Saturday when he'd realized she left Cozumel without so much as a note of explanation, but his anger was gone now. He realized Felicity had been scared. That she had no reason to be frightened of gossip, from either him or Max, didn't matter.

When he opened the door to the office, she and Rita, her assistant, were standing at a display table discussing something. They both turned at the sound of the door opening. Rita smiled uncertainly—what was *that* about?—and Felicity's face froze.

"H-hello, Reed," she said.

"Hi. Do you have a few minutes? I need to talk to you about something." This was said for Rita's benefit.

"Um, sure." She looked at Rita.

"I'll just go into my office," Rita said. Her brown eyes were filled with curiosity.

When she'd gone and closed the door behind her, they both spoke at once.

"Reed, I'm—" Felicity said.

"Why'd you leave—" Reed said.

They both stopped. The silence hummed between them.

"What were you going to say?" Reed finally asked.

"I was just going to say that I'm sorry I left without saying goodbye," she said softly.

"What happened?"

"Look…" She cut a glance at Rita's closed door. Her voice fell to practically a whisper. "I can't talk here."

"Let's go get a cup of coffee somewhere."

"I can't. I have an appointment at eleven-thirty. They'll be here any minute."

"Later, then."

"All right," she said reluctantly. "Although…"

"Although, what?"

"There's really no point."

"Dammit, Felicity." Now he was getting mad all over again. "You owe me an explanation, and I'm not going to go away until I get it."

"Okay, okay. But it'll have to be tonight. I can't take any more time off right now. Things are a mess here, and Rita's had to handle everything by herself long enough."

"Fine. I'll come to your place tonight. What time?"

She looked as if she wanted to say no, not her place, but she obviously thought better of it, for after a brief hesitation she said, "Eight o'clock."

"I'll see you then." He started to leave, then stopped. "And Felicity?"

"Yes?"

"Don't pretend you're not there like you did last night, because I'm not going away."

Ten

Why had Felicity agreed to let Reed come to her place? Why had she agreed to see him at all? What earthly good would it do?

You had no choice, that's why. As he said, he wasn't going away. And with Rita in the next room, probably listening at the keyhole…

The thought had no sooner formed than Rita's office door opened and she came back out to Felicity's office. "Did he hear about the Newhouse wedding?" she said. "Is that why he came?"

"Yes," Felicity said, thankful not to have to make up something else.

"Is he angry?"

"No. He just said to let him know."

"Really? Gee, that was awfully nice of him. Do you think he'll charge Madeline Newhouse the money anyway?"

Felicity shrugged, because she honestly had no idea what Reed would do when he found out about the canceled wedding. "We'll see. Now…where were we?"

For the remainder of the day, no matter what she was doing, Felicity fought to keep her thoughts far away from Reed, but they kept going there no matter how hard she tried. Finally the day was over, and she could wearily head home. It was after seven when she finally pulled into her garage, and she was bone tired. The last thing she wanted to do was fence with Reed, yet she knew if she called and tried to cancel their appointment, he wouldn't agree.

Besides, it was probably better to just get the whole thing over with. Then she could start the miserable process of forgetting him and their glorious week together and try to move on with her life.

Figuring she'd feel better if she had a quick shower and could change into something comfortable before he arrived, she immediately headed upstairs to her bedroom. Twenty-five minutes later, dressed in a cool sundress and sandals, she came back downstairs and opened a bottle of her favorite Riesling. She also found a nice chunk of cheddar cheese and opened a packet of crackers. Maybe with something to eat and drink, they'd be more relaxed and could talk without Reed getting mad or her getting too nervous.

She'd just gotten a couple of wineglasses out of the cupboard when the doorbell rang. Her traitorous heart started beating too fast, and Felicity had to stand in the kitchen and take several deep breaths before she felt calm enough to go and answer the door.

As always, the sight of him was enough to undo any calm she might have attained. Why was it she couldn't seem to control her emotions where he was concerned? "Hi. Come on in," she said. Luckily, her voice didn't betray her inner turmoil.

He looked around briefly before following her into the living room, where she'd already placed the cheese and crackers on the coffee table, along with the open bottle of wine.

"Nice place you've got here," he said.

"Thank you. I like it."

"Have you lived here a long time?"

Felicity shook her head. "Only a year. Before that, I was renting a condo near the office." She was grateful for the small talk. "Want some wine?" she said, lifting the bottle.

"Sure." He sat on one of the love seats flanking the fireplace.

Felicity poured his wine and handed him the glass. For a moment their eyes met. Her heart knocked painfully. *Oh, Reed, why did I go to Cozumel? It was a mistake, and now I'm going to pay for it for a long time....*

Lifting her own glass, she said, "Cheers," and

took a swallow. Then she sat across from him on the other love seat.

He leaned back and looked at her. An uncomfortable silence enveloped them. Felicity was trying to think of a way to break it when he said, "Well? Are you going to tell me why you ran out on me?"

Felicity sighed. "Look, I'm sorry. I know I should have left you a note, but I was upset and I wasn't thinking."

"Why were you upset?"

"I'm sure you know by now that Max called you."

"Yes."

"When I heard his voice, I panicked. I was terrified he might have recognized my voice, and suddenly I knew I shouldn't be there. I should *never* have been there. It—it was a mistake."

"A mistake."

She knew by the way his eyes narrowed and his jaw hardened that she'd made him angry. "Yes." She was proud of herself for not allowing her voice to falter.

He set his wineglass on the table, then got up and walked to where she sat. Reaching down, he took her wineglass out of her suddenly nerveless fingers and put it down next to his. Then he clamped her hand in his, hauled her to her feet and yanked her against him.

A second later his mouth claimed hers, and she was powerless to resist. Didn't even want to resist. Where Reed was concerned, her body and her heart completely overruled anything her head might tell her. Soon they were kissing as if they'd never get enough of each other, and before Felicity's brain even registered the fact that he had lifted her into his arms, they were on their way upstairs, where he unerringly found Felicity's bedroom.

Setting her on her feet, he said, "Do you want me to stop?"

If he stopped, she would die.

His eyes bored into hers. "Tell me. I want you to say it."

"I—I don't want you to stop," she whispered.

"I didn't think so," he said right before his mouth claimed hers once more.

Five minutes later their clothes lay where they'd fallen, and the two of them were tangled together on top of her bed. There was no subtlety, no foreplay, just a furious intensity that built to a shattering crescendo and left them both gasping.

Afterward, Felicity wanted to cry. What was wrong with her? Why was she torturing herself like this?

"You can't tell me now that our being together is a mistake," he said.

Knowing she would not be able to do what must be done if she stayed on the bed, Felicity pulled away from him and gathered up her clothes. She turned her back and hurriedly dressed. Only then did she answer.

"It *is* a mistake," she said, turning to face him. She was relieved to see that he'd begun to dress, too. She wasn't sure she'd have been able to continue if she'd had to look at his body, the body that would no longer be beside her in the morning—or any other time.

"Look, Reed, whether you want to admit it or not, you're on the rebound. Once you get over being jilted by Emma, you'll be ready to move on. And that's for the best, because I know you want different things than I do. You want to get married, and I'm not wife material, am I? Because I'm not interested in marriage. I did that once, and I won't do it again."

His eyes were like blue chips of ice. "So I have no say in this."

She shrugged. Her heart was beating so hard, she was sure he could hear it. Why was this so hard? Wasn't it better for her to make this break now than to wait for him to do it? And he *would* do it. There was no doubt at all in Felicity's mind that he would eventually walk away from her. "What's there to say?"

He looked at her for a long moment. "Fine," he finally said. "If that's the way you feel, I guess you're right—there really *is* nothing else to say."

Seconds later he was gone.

Reed was thoroughly fed up with women.

They blew hot, then they blew cold. They couldn't make up their minds about anything. Take tonight. Why the hell had Felicity been so willing to climb into bed with him if she was just going to tell him to take a hike afterward? What was she playing at, anyway?

Frankly, he was sick of being accused of feeling things he wasn't feeling and thinking things he wasn't thinking. Why couldn't she believe him when he told her something? What made her think she knew him better than he knew himself?

He climbed into his truck and sat there fuming. Women could make a man crazy. Especially *that* woman! He glared at Felicity's closed door.

He was halfway home before he finally calmed down enough to consider that maybe Felicity's beliefs had some merit. Maybe, in his zeal to give her time and not rush her, he had instead made her feel all he cared about was her body.

Dammit, that wasn't *all he cared about.*

Was it?

Although it was nearly eleven, he turned around and impulsively headed for his sister Shannon's house. He desperately needed a sounding board, and he'd always been able to talk to Shannon. Besides, she was a woman. Maybe she'd be able to give him some perspective about this mess with Felicity.

When he arrived, he was relieved to see lights on in the living room. He should have known she'd be awake. His sister was a night owl.

He pulled into the driveway, cut the lights and ignition and got out of the truck. At the front door he didn't ring the bell. He knew John went to bed early. In fact, he and Shannon often laughed about their completely opposite sleep patterns, saying it was a miracle they'd ever managed to conceive a child.

Shannon opened the door only seconds after his knock. She didn't even ask why he was there, just took one look at his face and told him to come in.

"How about a drink?" she asked. "You look as if you could use one."

"How about some coffee instead?"

"Instant okay?"

"Sure."

He followed her into the kitchen, where she put a mug of water into the microwave.

"What happened?" she asked, leaning against the counter.

"That obvious, huh?"

"Reed, when you're glowering like that, it's clear something is going on."

"No lectures, okay?"

She grinned. "Aw, not even one little bitty lecture?"

"Shannon…" he said in a warning tone.

The grin got bigger. "Okay, no lectures."

The microwave dinged. Removing the mug, she added instant coffee, a teaspoonful of sugar, stirred, then handed the mug to him. "Want to go sit where it's comfortable?"

"Here's fine." He pulled out a kitchen chair.

"How about some German chocolate cake to go with the coffee?"

Reed eyed the glass-covered cake plate sitting on the countertop. "Homemade?"

"Compliments of Barrett's." Barrett's was a locally owned bakery whose cakes were renowned in the area.

"Talked me into it," he said.

She cut him a wedge and put it on the table in

front of him. "Just let me go get my glass of wine, and I'll be back."

A couple of minutes later, glass in hand, she settled herself across the table from him. "This is about a woman, right?"

"How'd you know?"

"I can't imagine you wanting advice about anything else. I mean, Mr. Perfection in person."

Reed grimaced. "Stop calling me that. I'm not perfect."

"Tell that to Mom."

"Are you through needling me? 'Cause if you're not, I'll just eat my cake and go home."

Shannon rolled her eyes. "My, you're touchy tonight. Okay, tell all."

She didn't interrupt, although she did give him an incredulous look when he told her how he'd decided to ask Felicity to go to Cozumel with him. When he finished—leaving out the personal details that were nobody else's business—he said, "Now I'm not sure what to do."

"Tell me something, Reed. Are you in love with her?"

This was the million dollar question. "I think I *could* be," he finally said.

She raised her eyebrows.

Reed heaved a sigh, finished off his cake and drank the last of his coffee. When he set his mug down, his eyes met Shannon's.

"What is it that's keeping you from making up

your mind about her?" Shannon asked quietly. "Is it that you're not sure about *her* feelings?"

"It's more than that," he admitted. "Hell, Shannon, what if she's right? What if, down deep, I *did* use her to get back at Emma?"

At some point after Reed had left, Felicity finally admitted to herself that she was in love with him. Deeply, completely, totally and hopelessly in love with him. And if he'd once said he loved her she would have happily said good riddance to all her supposed convictions about not marrying again.

Oh, Reed, why couldn't you love me? Why did it just have to be about sex?

Over and over she relived the days in Cozumel, all the things they'd said and done, all the times he'd been so sweet and attentive.

Face it, Felicity. It didn't cost him a thing to be nice to you. After all, he was getting what he wanted, wasn't he? He doesn't love you. It's over. Forget about him and forget about Cozumel and get on with your life.

At two o'clock, cried out and exhausted, she finally fell asleep.

"Bad night?"

Felicity grimaced at Rita. "You could say that."

"Well, the coffee's ready and I even brought in some fresh doughnuts from Barrett's."

Normally, Felicity would shun the doughnuts, but this wasn't a normal morning. Heading for their little kitchenette, she decided that in addition to the doughnuts, a couple of Advil might also be advisable.

Luckily, it wasn't a bad morning. Now that all the Newhouse wedding vendors and participants had been notified of the canceled wedding—except Reed, she thought guiltily—things at the office were back under control. There were just a few last-minute details to take care of for the Staunton wedding this weekend, but they were minor, nothing Felicity and Rita couldn't easily handle.

In fact, by ten o'clock Felicity wished she had more work facing her, because right now she had too much time to think. And thinking was the last thing she wanted to do.

She had just logged on to the Internet, deciding to use her free time productively and check out competing event-planning businesses in the area, when the outside door opened. A smiling Emma, accompanied by her fiancé, Garrett Keating, entered.

"Hi," Felicity said, thinking how beautiful and happy Emma looked today in her pretty blue flowered dress. "What brings you two here?"

"What else? We want to secure your services," Emma said.

Felicity grinned. "Really? You two have set a date?"

"We have," Garrett said, putting his arm around Emma and giving her a loving smile.

He really was a pretty decent guy, Felicity thought, and so much more suitable for Emma than Reed had been. But Felicity couldn't think about

Reed. Thinking about him, especially in Emma's presence, was a recipe for disaster.

For the next forty minutes the three of them discussed details of what Emma and Garrett might want. Since the wedding needed to take place before Emma's thirtieth birthday on August 31 so she could inherit her trust fund, there wasn't much time for anything elaborate.

"That doesn't matter," Emma said. "I don't like elaborate weddings, anyway. In fact, I just want one attendant and family and close friends." She looked at Garrett. "And Garrett agrees."

Although Felicity had told herself not to think about Reed, she couldn't help wondering how he'd feel about Emma getting married so soon after their breakup. "Will you have your reception at the club?"

"Yes, I'm afraid so."

"Why do you say that?" Felicity asked.

Emma sighed. "What I'd *really* like is to have it at the gallery."

"At Color?"

Emma nodded. "Yes. You know I've hosted openings there, and it can easily accommodate a hundred and fifty people, which is the most we'll want at the wedding, anyway."

"I think Color would be a wonderful place to hold the reception." Emma's gallery was located in the historic district of Eastwick, in a two-hundred-year-old house. It was a lovely place, with tall, skinny casement windows and beautiful grounds surrounded by a white picket fence. Felicity could just see the interior of the house festooned with flowers and draped with ribbons and lace. Maybe Emma could even find a Victorian wedding dress. "So why *can't* you have it there?"

"My mother had a fit when I suggested it," Emma said, "and the truth is, I just didn't feel like fighting her on this. That's all we've done recently is fight, and really, what difference does it make? Garrett and I will be married. That's what counts."

Garrett nodded. "We've decided to pick our battles. This one didn't seem that important."

Felicity knew their decision was probably a good one, but she couldn't help feeling bad for Emma. Why couldn't her parents be more understanding?

"I want you to be my maid of honor," Emma said. "Wearing blue, of course." Blue was Emma's favorite color, and Felicity wore it a lot herself.

"Oh, Emma." Guilt and remorse caused her heart to ache, and she could hardly meet Emma's eyes as she stammered her thanks and acceptance.

"Is something wrong?" Emma said anxiously. "Don't you want to be in my wedding?"

"Nothing's wrong. I'm just so touched, that's all." Felicity felt like a worm. Lower than a worm, even. Emma was such a wonderful friend, so loyal and true. *And you're pond scum. You shouldn't have lied to her. You should have trusted her and told her the truth.*

What would happen now if Emma should find out where Felicity *really* spent last week?

With a sinking heart, Felicity wondered if it would be possible for their friendship to survive.

Oh, God, if she lost Emma on top of losing Reed, she wasn't sure she could stand it.

Eleven

At four o'clock that afternoon Felicity had a meeting of the Eastwick Country Club's social committee—formerly chaired by Bunny Talbot and now taken over by her daughter, Abby. Felicity didn't really feel like going, but she knew she'd better. She'd missed the two previous meetings because of work commitments. If she didn't show up today, they might decide to replace her permanently.

When Felicity arrived at the club, Abby and Vanessa were already there waiting by the bar and talking with Harry. "Hey," Abby said, giving Felicity a hug. "Glad you could make it."

"Me, too." Now that she was there, Felicity found

she *was* glad. Maybe being with her friends would help take her mind off her problems. *Off Reed.*

Reed. Why couldn't she stop thinking about him?

"Mary's poolside," Vanessa said. She was referring to Mary Duvall, an old friend and new member of the committee, who had recently moved back to Eastwick. "We said we'd join her there."

"Want something to drink?" Harry asked.

"How about a tall iced tea?" Felicity said. Turning to her friends, she added, "Why don't you two go on out? I'll be there in a minute."

"So how you been?" Harry asked as he fixed her tea.

"Fine. Busy."

"Nice tan you've got there. You been away?"

Why was he asking? Felicity wondered. Did he suspect something? Oh, God. She really was paranoid. Harry was just making conversation, the way he always did.

"Yes, I had a week at a spa."

"Good for you. All work and no play…"

Felicity smiled, paid for her tea, left him a nice tip and waved goodbye. When she arrived at the pool she found the other three seated at one of the umbrella tables.

"Hi, Mary," she said, giving her a kiss on the cheek. Mary had gone to Europe after her college graduation.

Mary's brown eyes were warm as she returned Felicity's embrace. "It's so good to see you."

It was pleasant outside today, not as hot as it had been, and there was a nice breeze. Sitting under the umbrella, sipping at her iced tea and listening to her friends talk about upcoming events, Felicity felt almost happy. But a moment later a tall man with brown hair appeared on the other side of the pool, and her heart gave a sickening jolt. By the time she realized the man wasn't Reed, as she'd first thought, she had spilled her tea down the front of her taupe linen dress.

"What happened?" Vanessa said. "You jumped like a scalded cat."

"I don't know," Felicity said, totally shaken. "Haven't you ever had that happen to you? Something startles you and you're not even sure what it was?"

"No," Vanessa said.

"No," Abby said.

Felicity forced a laugh. "Okay, so I'm weird." She stood. "I'd better go put some water on this before my dress is ruined."

While in the ladies', Felicity told herself to calm down. Good grief, if she was going to go to pieces every time she saw someone who looked like Reed, what would she be like when she actually saw him in person? *I have to get myself under control. Have to.*

After scrubbing at her dress, she once more joined her friends poolside.

"You okay?" Mary asked.

"I'm fine," Felicity said. "Just mad at myself for being so jumpy. Must be all the caffeine I've had today."

They continued their discussion, and when they'd finished, they lingered around the table and watched the kids splashing in the shallow water. One, a particularly cute toddler with red curls, threw a ball that missed its mark—a boy who looked like her brother—and it rolled up and onto the decking, to end up at Mary's feet.

Mary picked it up and tossed it back to the little girl, who grinned at her. When Mary turned back to the table, Felicity was startled to see tears in her eyes, which she quickly brushed away.

Something about the poignancy of Mary's expression made Felicity want to cry, too. But she had done enough crying the night before. Besides, no man was worth crying over, she told herself angrily. They all let you down in the end.

"Guess what?" Abby said, breaking into Felicity's thoughts. "The police are finally taking me seriously and they've begun to reinvestigate my mother's death."

"Good," Vanessa said. "It's about time."

"What made them change their minds?" Felicity asked.

"The coroner's report," Abby said. "It said my mother had no digitalis in her system, but I *know* she faithfully took her heart medication up until the day she died. I *saw* her take it. And now her pill case has disappeared."

"That's odd," Vanessa said.

"Yes, I know. And there's something else. You know Edith Carter, my mother's housekeeper?"

They all nodded.

"Well, she overheard a woman yelling at my

mother the day she died, and now the police are trying to find the woman to question her."

"Do the police believe this woman, whoever she is, killed your mother?" Mary asked.

Felicity frowned, finding Mary's question odd. So, it appeared from her reaction, did Abby, who gave Mary a strange look. "I have no idea. They haven't told me anything except that they're reopening the investigation."

Mary nodded in a preoccupied way.

Felicity, forgetting her own troubles for a moment, wondered if Mary was unhappy. She certainly didn't seem like her old self at all. Emma had told Felicity that when she and the other Debs were all in school together, and then during their debut season, Mary had been the life of every party—a true wild child, ready for anything. But since she'd come back to Eastwick from Europe she'd been awfully quiet and subdued, even sad at times, the way she'd been a few minutes ago when she'd thrown that ball back to the little girl. Felicity wished Mary would talk about whatever it was that was bothering her, because obviously something was, but so far, she hadn't confided in any of them.

I guess we all have our secrets.

At five-thirty Vanessa said she had to run, and that was the impetus for the rest of them to start getting ready to leave. They all hugged and kissed goodbye with promises to get together soon.

"Don't forget our next Debs lunch," Abby said to

Mary, who shrugged, murmuring something about maybe she would come.

Yes, Felicity decided as she drove back to her office, there was definitely something bothering Mary. Maybe she'd had an unhappy love affair when she was in Europe. *Oh, you've got unhappy love affairs on the brain. Just because that's your problem doesn't mean it's hers.*

Trying to push reminders of Reed far away, Felicity turned her thoughts to how Mary had questioned Abby concerning the woman the police were looking for. Although Felicity didn't want to, she couldn't help wondering once more if Rita could possibly be involved. Bunny's housekeeper had said a woman was there, not a man.

Oh, God. Felicity could feel a headache coming on. Between her guilt over deceiving Emma, her unhappiness over Reed, her concern for Mary and her suspicions about Rita, she was a wreck.

And the next few days were no better. Emma, who was naturally excited about her upcoming wedding, called several times to reschedule their canceled lunch.

Felicity knew she'd soon run out of excuses, but she didn't feel up to being in Emma's company. She was just too miserable, and being with Emma only served to remind her of Reed and how she'd deceived her best friend and jeopardized their relationship.

And for what?

One week of fabulous sex and a lifetime of regrets.

Was it worth it?

Felicity didn't know.

She only knew it was too hard to keep up a happy, innocent front around Emma.

So she kept dodging Emma's company, and she knew Emma was probably beginning to wonder what was going on.

And then there was Rita, who was with Felicity every day. Every time Rita asked a question that had anything to do with any of Felicity's friends, Felicity would start worrying about Rita's possible involvement in the murder of Bunny Talbot and all the blackmailing taking place. If it should turn out that Rita was responsible for any of it, what would Felicity do?

Plus there was work. Although so far everything was running smoothly for the Staunton wedding at the club on Saturday, Felicity knew she couldn't let down her guard for a moment, because Jemima Staunton was the granddaughter of one of the club's founders, so the wedding had to be nothing less than perfection.

All these problems took their toll.

Felicity didn't sleep well, and she was grouchy and tired and felt as if she was coming down with the flu or something. By Friday she knew everyone she'd dealt with that week had been wondering what on earth was wrong with her.

And she still hadn't told Reed that the Newhouse wedding had been canceled. Knowing she was being a coward and not caring—it was better than making a fool of herself in front of him!—she finally sent him a carefully worded e-mail.

Hi, Reed,

Sorry to have to tell you that Portia Newhouse
has called off her wedding, so we won't need
to use Rosedale to take any pictures. If you
would like compensation, please send a bill
here to my office, and I'll send it on to
Madeline Newhouse.

Thanks,

Felicity.

Her finger hovered over the send button for a long
moment before she pressed it.

There, she thought. That was it. There was now
no more reason to ever talk to Reed again. Unexpectedly, tears filled her eyes. And at just that moment
Rita walked out of her office.

"Felicity! What's the matter? What happened?"

Although Felicity tried to pretend she was fine,
she couldn't seem to stop the tears. They rolled down
her face, and seconds later she found herself being
hugged and patted by Rita, who kept murmuring,
"There, there, dear. It'll be okay. Everything's going
to be fine."

When Felicity finally calmed down, Rita handed
her the box of tissues, and she wiped her eyes and
blew her nose.

"Want to tell me about it?" Rita asked gently.

Felicity looked at her—at the sweet face, the
warm and friendly eyes, the genuine concern in her
expression. She swallowed. Rita *couldn't* have

anything to do with that horrible blackmailing. She simply couldn't. "I do, but first I want to confess something."

Rita waited quietly.

"I'm embarrassed to tell you this, but for a while now, I've been thinking there was a possibility that you're the one who's been blackmailing my friends."

"Blackmailing your *friends?*"

"Yes."

"But…who's been getting blackmailed?"

"I really can't tell you that, Rita. The things I know were told to me in confidence. But it all started after Bunny Talbot died. Apparently her journals were stolen. At least, they went missing. And soon after that, certain people who had some things they preferred others not know about starting getting extortion letters."

"Oh, that's terrible!"

"Yes, it is."

"And you honestly thought *I* had something to do with this?"

"I didn't really think so, but there *was* a possibility." She grimaced. "I'm so sorry, Rita. Down deep I knew you couldn't be involved."

"Well, I'm not. I would never do anything like that. Never. It's a crime."

"Yes," Felicity said, "it is. But that sure hasn't stopped whoever's doing it."

"Did you get a letter?"

"Me? No. I don't have anything to hide."

But the moment the words were out of her mouth she knew she did. The knowledge settled in her breast like a stone. In that moment she knew what she needed to do.

"Rita," she said, "we'll talk later, okay? Right now I have something important I have to do."

Twenty minutes later Felicity parked her SUV in the parking lot behind Emma's gallery.

"Fee!" Emma said when Felicity walked in the door. "What a nice surprise."

The two friends hugged, then Emma offered her a soft drink and invited her back to her office, where they could talk privately. "I'll hear the bell if someone comes in," she said.

Once they were settled in the office, Felicity took a deep mental breath and said, "Em, there's something I have to tell you. It's been bothering me a lot to keep this from you, and today I knew I couldn't do it any longer."

Emma's violet eyes widened only a fraction—the only indication Felicity's statement had surprised her. As Felicity talked, telling her about going out to Rosedale that first time and what happened, then how Reed had invited her to Cozumel, and how she'd gone, Emma listened quietly.

As Felicity talked, she could feel that stone being lifted, and she knew she'd done the right thing. "Please say you forgive me," she said when she'd finished.

"Oh, Fee, there's nothing to forgive," Emma said

with a tremulous smile. "I'm glad Reed has found someone else, and I'm so happy that someone is you."

Once again, Felicity felt like crying. What was wrong with her today that she couldn't hold it together? "You're such a good person," she said. "Such a generous friend. I've always wished I could be more like you."

"And *I've* always wished I could be more like you," Emma said, grinning. "You're so strong, so self-sufficient. We all admire you."

As they hugged again, Felicity told herself she was very fortunate to have so many wonderful people in her life. Emma, Rita, the other Debs. So what if Reed didn't love her? She had gotten along just fine without him before.

And she would get along just fine without him again.

Reed looked at the e-mail from Felicity. He thought about whether or not he should answer it.

He decided not to.

He didn't want to write to her. He wanted to see her. He wanted to touch her. He wanted her to admit that she felt the same way.

Dammit. They *weren't* a mistake.

But how was he going to get her to believe that?

Suddenly something struck him. When he'd wanted her to go to Cozumel, and he'd tried to talk her into it, she'd said no.

But when he'd sent the flowers and the condoms, she'd changed her mind.

Jesus, it was so *obvious*. Why hadn't he seen that before? Felicity wasn't the kind of woman you talked into anything. She was the kind of woman who required action.

He smiled.

He knew exactly what he needed do.

Twelve

The fragrance of hundreds of roses floated in the air as Felicity went through her mental checklist. She was standing in the foyer of the church, watching as Rita arranged the folds of Jemima Staunton's creamy satin train. From inside the church she could hear the anticipatory murmur of the wedding guests as they waited impatiently for the appearance of the bridal party.

The very air seemed to tremble in the moments after the prelude ended and the organist began the first stately notes of Bach's "Air in D Major," the piece Jemima and her mother had chosen for the processional. It was a perfect choice, Felicity thought, well suited to the regal bride and this elegant, subdued church.

Walking over to the lead bridesmaid, Felicity quietly reminded her to walk slowly down the aisle.

"I know," the pretty blonde said, dimpling as she smiled. "There's no rush. Hesitate between steps."

"Exactly."

Felicity slipped into the back of the church and watched as the wedding party processed without a hitch. Once the bride and her father were on their way, Rita joined her.

Earlier, Felicity had scanned the guests to see if Reed might be among them. But she didn't see him, and she breathed a sigh of relief. She had a reprieve. She knew she'd run into him sooner or later, but she'd rather it was later, when she was more in control of her emotions.

She hadn't gotten an answer to her e-mail. Not that she'd expected one. She was sure he had washed his hands of her.

"Dearly beloved," the minister intoned. "We are gathered here today in the sight of God and in the face of this company to join together this man and this woman in holy matrimony, which is commended to be honorable among all men, and therefore is not by any to be entered into unadvisedly or lightly, but reverently, discreetly, advisedly and solemnly."

He continued with the traditional introduction to the vows, then said, "Who gives this woman in marriage?"

"Her mother and I do," said Wallace Staunton, his long, angular face beaming proudly as he placed his daughter's hand into the hand of her bridegroom. Still beaming, he took his seat next to his wife, Aurora.

After that, a friend of Jemima's sang the song "Always," which Jemima had told Felicity was playing when her father asked her mother to marry him.

Then it was time for the vows.

Looking down benignly on the couple before him, the minister began to talk. Normally this was the point in a wedding ceremony where Felicity's mind wandered. Usually she was thinking about what she needed to do once the ceremony was over or what might go wrong at the reception.

Today, though, for some reason, the minister's words caused a lump in her throat. "Marriage is the union of husband and wife in heart, body and mind," he was saying. "It is intended for their mutual joy and for the help and comfort that is given to one another in prosperity and adversity."

In prosperity and adversity, Felicity thought sadly. Would she ever have that? Someone to share all of life's joys and sorrows? Someone to lean on? Someone who really cared about her?

Oh, Reed...

Tears pooled in her eyes, and she reached for a tissue in her purse. She knew she had to get a grip on herself, but lately she'd had an almost impossible time doing so.

"This relationship stands for love," the minister continued. "For loyalty, honesty and trust, but most of all for friendship. Before Jemima and Phillip knew love, they were friends, and it was from this seed of friendship that they found their destiny. Do not think that you can direct the course of love, for love, if it finds you worthy, shall direct you."

The words, the sentiment were so beautiful, they made Felicity's heart ache. And she finally faced the truth that she'd been lying to herself for a long time. Of course she believed in marriage. She'd just been afraid of being hurt again, of giving her heart and soul to someone who didn't value them, the way Sam hadn't valued them.

Oh, Reed, why couldn't you love me? Why did I just have to be someone to make you forget Emma?

Knowing she couldn't listen to any more, she leaned over and whispered to Rita, "I need to get some air. I'll be back."

Rita gave her a curious look, but she didn't say anything as Felicity hurriedly left the church. Outside, she took deep, calming breaths and told herself that the rest of the day would be easier. Once they were at the club, she would have lots to do and lots to think about. And hopefully, none of it would remind her of Reed.

Reed watched Felicity from behind a tall plant near one of the open terrace doors. She didn't know he was there, and that's the way he wanted it. Time enough to announce his presence later. Right now he just enjoyed watching her work.

She was a dynamo, no question about that. Here,

there and everywhere, overseeing everything. And all in a tight black lace dress and four-inch heels. He was reminded of what had been said about Ginger Rogers and Fred Astaire—how she did everything he did, only backward and in high heels.

The club looked beautiful tonight, decorated with hundreds of baby orchids and white roses. The fountains outside sparkled in a rainbow of colored lights, lending a magical feel to the ballroom, where the reception was being held. He wondered if Felicity had had a hand in the decorations. Probably. He imagined she'd had a hand in everything.

Everyone in the ballroom was dressed to the nines—the men in suits or dinner jackets, the women in cocktail dresses and dripping with jewels. Reed knew many of them, including the groom's parents, although not well enough to have gotten an invitation. Still, he didn't think anyone would call him on the fact he'd crashed this shindig. They were all too busy having a good time.

"Well, if it isn't Reed Kelly!"

Reed whipped around to see a smiling Lucia Peretti, the wife of one of his clients, standing there. She looked striking, as always, in a bright red sequined dress that hugged her voluptuous figure.

"Hello, Lucia," he said, hoping no one had heard her calling out his name in her distinctive, accented voice. He sneaked a glance in Felicity's direction, but she was turned away from him, busy talking to one of the wait staff.

"What are you doing hiding out behind that plant?" Lucia demanded, dark eyes flashing in amusement.

"I'm not hiding."

"Certainly looks like it to me."

Reed didn't want to keep denying what he was so obviously doing, so instead he said, "Where's Antonio? I don't see him."

"He hates weddings," Lucia said. "He figures if he sends an expensive gift, that's all that's required of him. But he doesn't care if I come. He knows how much I like parties. And he likes to keep me happy."

Reed bit back a smile. That was an understatement. Lucia Peretti had her husband twined around her little finger.

Just then the band, which had been on a break, started playing a lively salsa number and a dozen or more couples began to move out onto the dance floor.

"Come and dance with me," Lucia said, reaching for Reed's hand. She was already swaying with the rhythm.

"Uh, thanks, Lucia, but I—" He never finished his sentence, because Lucia paid no attention to his reluctance and insistently pulled at him to come out from behind the plant.

"Don't worry, this kind of dancing is easy," she said.

"It's not that. It's—" He stopped. Now that his cover was blown, he figured he might as well do the gentlemanly thing and dance with her.

Once among the dancers, Reed steered her to the middle of the floor where they'd have more room.

He knew the exact moment Felicity saw them. For a brief second her eyes met his, then she quickly looked away. But not before he'd seen the shock in her eyes, or the way her face paled. Seeing him had upset her. He hoped that was a good sign.

"You're a wonderful dancer, Reed," Lucia gushed. "I may have to commandeer you for the night. You didn't bring a date, did you?"

"No, but—"

"Good."

"Look, Lucia," Reed said, tired of her presumptuous behavior. "I may not have brought a date, but I do have other plans."

"Oh, pooh." Her full lips with their bright red lipstick pouted. "I thought you liked me."

"I do like you. So does Antonio," he reminded her.

"So I'm married. That doesn't mean I'm dead." Her smile turned coquettish. "Who's the gal?"

In answer, he only smiled. "You'll see soon enough."

"Why so secretive?"

"Because I have something planned, and I don't want it ruined."

"Well, I hope she knows how lucky she is."

"I'm the lucky one," Reed said. *That is, if things go as I hope they will.*

What was he *doing* there?

Felicity had felt she might faint when she'd first spied Reed on the dance floor. She knew his name was not on the invitation list. She'd checked it when she'd first arrived. So was he a last-minute invitee? Or had he crashed the wedding? And if he'd crashed it, why?

Her hands were trembling as she shifted the flowers on the main food table a couple of inches to the left.

Oh, God. Was he going to stay the entire evening? Was he deliberately trying to torture her?

She'd recognized the woman he was dancing with. Lucia Peretti. Wife of electronics tycoon Antonio Peretti. Lucia was a notorious flirt, and gossip had it that she slept around. A lot. And that her husband had no idea.

Was she Reed's newest acquisition?

Would she be the next woman to go to Cozumel with him?

Nausea roiled in Felicity's stomach. *You are such a fool,* she told herself. *Why did you ever allow yourself to get emotionally involved with him? Why did you allow yourself to get involved, period?*

But there were no answers to her questions.

She had and she did.

Now what she needed to do was somehow hold herself together until this blasted reception was over and done with. But she knew it wasn't just this reception she needed to survive. It was the rest of her life. For this wouldn't be the only time she'd see Reed with another woman.

She swallowed.

One of these days he'd find someone he wanted to marry. Even the thought made Felicity feel sick.

How could she bear it? Eastwick was a small town. Their social circle was even smaller.

I can't bear it. I'll have to leave.

"Felicity, you look worn out."

Pulling herself together by sheer force of will, Felicity turned to see a concerned-looking Rita standing beside her.

"Why don't you get yourself something to drink and go sit down?" Rita said. "Everything's fine. You can relax now and enjoy yourself. I know some of your friends are here. I saw Abby Talbot dancing just a minute ago."

"Rita, I'm okay."

"Why are you so stubborn? You're *not* okay. Anyone can see that."

Because arguing with Rita would take more energy than Felicity had, she finally said, "Fine, you win. I'll go sit down somewhere."

"Good."

Snagging a flute of champagne from a passing waiter, Felicity looked around for Abby. Of all the Debs, she was the only one on the guest list, for Jemima Staunton was much younger than Felicity's friends, but Felicity knew Abby's and Jemima's mothers had served on one of the big charity boards together.

She had just spied Abby near one of the open terrace doors when a hand touched her shoulder. Turning, expecting to see Rita again, she instead found herself gazing into Reed's blue eyes. Her mouth went dry.

"May I have this dance?" he said.

"I—I'm working."

He looked at her glass of champagne. "Really."

Deciding bluster was her best defense, she lifted her chin. "I'm allowed to have something to drink."

"Of course you are. Just as you're allowed to have a dance."

She shook her head. "I can't." But even as she was saying no, she put the flute of champagne on a nearby table.

"Good girl," he said, smiling. Then, taking her hand, he led her onto the dance floor.

Short of making a scene, Felicity told herself she really had no choice. But when he put his arm around her and drew her close, she knew she should have made a scene. Done anything to stay away from him. Because right now, if he threw her down on the floor and wanted to make love to her, she knew she'd let him. This man could ask anything of her, and she would have no will to resist.

It was heaven dancing with him and remembering everything they'd shared.

It was hell dancing with him and knowing this was all she'd ever have.

"You look beautiful tonight," Reed said against her hair. "But then, you always look beautiful."

Her heart beat a crazy tattoo. Why was he doing this to her? Didn't he know how unfair this was?

"I've been watching you for a while," he continued, "admiring the way you handle your work so efficiently."

"Th-thank you."

"You're a remarkable woman."

What did he *want?*

His arm tightened around her. "Look at me, Felicity," he whispered.

Slowly she raised her eyes.

"There's something I need to know," he said.

"What?"

The song ended and the band leader announced that the band would be taking a fifteen-minute break. People started to walk off the dance floor.

But Reed didn't move or loosen his hold. Instead, looking down into her eyes, he said, "I need to know if you love me. Because I love you. I love you more than I ever thought I could love anyone, and I want us to spend the rest of our lives together."

Felicity's heart stopped. Had she really heard those words? Or had she wanted so badly to hear them that she'd imagined them?

But then, in a moment that would live forever in her memory and that she would one day describe to her children and grandchildren, Reed dropped onto one knee. Ignoring all the people around them—people who had stopped talking and were now standing there watching—he said in a voice meant to be heard by everyone, "Felicity Farnsworth, will you do me the honor of becoming my wife?"

Once again, Felicity's eyes filled with tears. "Oh, Reed," was all she could manage to say.

He smiled, one of those crooked smiles she so loved. "Is that a yes?"

"Yes," she said. "Yes, yes, yes!"

And then he was standing and kissing her, and the hundreds of wedding guests were clapping.

When the kiss ended, he reached into his right pocket and pulled out a small blue velvet box.

Felicity gasped when he snapped it open. Inside was the most beautiful pink diamond she'd ever seen. The guests closest to them oohed and aahed.

Taking the ring from its niche, he slipped it onto her ring finger. Felicity looked at the ring, then at Reed, her heart filled with wonder.

"You still haven't said if you love me," he teased.

She knew she was grinning like a fool, but she couldn't help it. "I adore you, you nut," she said. And then she threw her arms around him and let her kiss say everything else that was in her heart.

* * * * *

THE BOUGHT-AND-
PAID-FOR WIFE

by
Bronwyn Jameson

Dear Reader,

When I was asked if I would like to participate in SECRET LIVES OF SOCIETY WIVES, I jumped in with an enthusiastic "Yes, please." Just hearing the series name conjured up all kinds of juicy, scandalous premises…not to mention the "it" TV show at the time. The invitation came, you see, midway through the first season of *Desperate Housewives*, and I'm a big fan.

Now, I live a long way – ten thousand miles, give or take – from Connecticut and a similar distance from the glamorous, high-society lifestyle this series embodies. But it was no hardship researching and inventing my little piece of Eastwick, Connecticut. From Vanessa's home to the polo charity benefit to the country club wedding, it was a Bentley-load of fun!

As for my hero…I have a New York friend to thank for Tristan. Jen's offhand comment about sexy Australian footballers in their short shorts and great legs inspired me to create this background for my rugged, difficult, take-no-prisoners alpha. I hope you enjoy him as much as Vanessa does!

Cheers,

Bronwyn Jameson

BRONWYN JAMESON

spent much of her childhood with her head buried in a book. As a teenager, she discovered romances, and it was only a matter of time before she turned her love of reading them into a love of writing them. Bronwyn shares an idyllic piece of the Australian farming heartland with her husband and three sons, a thousand sheep, a dozen horses, assorted wildlife and one kelpie dog. She still chooses to spend her limited downtime with a good book. Bronwyn loves to hear from readers. Write to her at bronwyn@bronwynjameson.com.

For all my readers, with a special mention to those who've written to me. I treasure every note and letter and card.

And to Mrs White, the number one advocate for my own little "Lew."

Thank you, K.

One

He'd seen pictures. He'd expected beautiful. After all, when a man chooses a trophy wife, he wants one other men will covet. But Tristan Thorpe hadn't appreciated the extent of that beauty—or its powerful clout—until the front door of the Connecticut colonial opened in a rush and she was there, five-and-a-bit feet of breathtaking impact.

Vanessa Thorpe. His father's widow. The enemy.

In every one of those society diary pictures she looked as glossy and polished as a trophy prize should… which had left Tristan speculating over how much was real—the platinum hair? the full lips? the petite but perfectly curved body?—and how much came courtesy of his father's wealth.

He hadn't wondered about the sparklers at her throat

and in her ears. Those, he knew, were real. Unlike her other multi-faceted assets, the diamonds appeared on the listed valuations of Stuart Thorpe's estate.

But here, now, seeing her in the flesh for the first time, Tristan didn't notice anything fake. All he saw was the very real sparkle in her silvery-green eyes and the smile. Warmer than the August sun at his back now that the rain had cleared, it lit her whole face with pleasure and licked his body with instant male appreciation.

That hot shot of hormones lasted all of a second, which was as long as it took for shock to freeze the smile on her perfect pink lips.

"It's...*you*."

Her whispered gasp came coated with dismay and, although she didn't move, Tristan saw the recoil in her expression. She wanted to back away. Hell, she probably wanted to slam the door in his face, and a perverse part of him wished she would give it a go. The long flight from Australia and the snarled afternoon traffic following a heavy rainstorm had him edgy enough to enjoy that kind of confrontation.

Logic, however, was Tristan Thorpe's master and it cautioned him to remain cool. "Sorry to disappoint you, duchess." And because he wasn't the least bit sorry, he smiled, as slow and mocking as his drawled greeting. "Obviously, you were expecting someone else."

"Obviously."

Tristan arched an eyebrow. "Didn't you say I was welcome here any time?"

"I don't recall—"

"Two years ago," he reminded her. After her husband's death. Seeing as she had to call his estranged family on the other side of the world to inform them of his passing, why not extend her largesse? An ex-waitress with expectations of a cool hundred million in inheritance could afford to appear generous.

Right now she didn't look so generous. In fact she looked downright inhospitable. "Why are you here, Tristan? The court date isn't until next month."

"If it's even necessary."

Surprise and suspicion narrowed her eyes. "Have you changed your mind? Are you dropping your contest of the will?"

"Not a chance."

"Then what do you want?"

"There's been a new development." Tristan paused, savoring the moment. He'd flown nearly ten thousand miles for this. He wanted to drag it out, to see her flail, before he brought her down. "I think you'll change your mind about keeping that court date."

For a second she stared at him, her expression revealing nothing but annoyance. Behind her, somewhere within the mansion's vast interior, a phone started to ring. He saw her momentary distraction, a glance, a tightening of her lips, before she spoke.

"If this is another of your attempts to obstruct execution of Stuart's will—" the hostility in her eyes and her voice confirmed that's exactly what she thought "—please take it to my lawyer, the same as you've done with every other *new development* the past two years. Nothing has changed in that regard. Now, if you'll excuse me…"

Oh, no. No way would he be dismissed. Not with that snooty voice, not with that imperious lift of her perfect little chin.

Tristan didn't stop to consider propriety or good manners. To prevent her closing the door on him, he stepped forward. To halt her leaving, he reached out and caught her by the arm.

The *bare* arm, he realized as the shock of her warm and female softness shot through his system.

Vaguely, beneath that purr of awareness, he felt her stillness and heard the hitch of her breath. Shock, no doubt, that he'd dare lay a hand on her.

"You don't want to close that door on me." His voice sounded rough, a deep growl in the tense silence. And he realized that the shrill ringing of the telephone had stopped, whether because someone had picked up or the caller had quit, he didn't know and couldn't care. "You don't want me taking this public."

"No?"

"If you're smart—" And she was. They might have dealt with each other largely through lawyers, but he'd never underestimated the smarts behind her platinum blond looks "—you'll keep this between you and me."

Their eyes clashed with raw antagonism and something else. The same something that still buzzed through his system and tightened his gut. The same something that made him release his grip on her arm without breaking eye contact, even when he heard the rubbery squelch of rapidly approaching sneakers on the foyer's marble floor.

"Take the call if you need," he said. "I can wait."

The owner of the sneakers stopped and cleared her throat and Tristan's attention switched to a trim middle-aged woman, even shorter than Vanessa. Despite her casual jeans and T-shirt attire, he pegged her as the housekeeper. Perhaps because of the old-fashioned feather duster poking out from under one arm.

"Sorry to interrupt." Even though she addressed her boss, the woman's gaze flicked over Tristan, not curious, not nervous, but sizing him up. The dislike in her expression suggested she recognized him. "Andy needs to speak to you."

"Thank you, Gloria. I'll take it in the library."

"And your…guest?"

The pause was deliberate. He got the distinct impression that, like her employer, she would relish tossing *the guest* out on his backside. And then turning the dogs on him.

"Show him to the sitting room."

"No need." Tristan's gaze shifted to Vanessa. "I lived here for twelve years. I can find my own way."

That registered like a slap of shock in her rain-on-water eyes but she didn't comment. Instead she inclined her head and played the gracious hostess. "Can Gloria bring you tea? Or a cold drink?"

"Would that be safe?"

The housekeeper made a sound that fell midway between a snort and a laugh. Her boss, however, didn't appear to appreciate his gibe. Her lips compressed into a tight line. "I won't keep you long."

"Don't hurry on my account."

She paused, just long enough to cast him a long,

frosty look over one shoulder. "Believe me. I never do anything on your account, Tristan."

Uttered with the perfect mix of scorn and indifference, it was a killer closing line—one he would have paid with a salute of laughter at another time, in another place. With another adversary. But this was Vanessa Thorpe and she was already halfway across the foyer, her head bent in earnest conversation with her employee.

He couldn't distinguish words, but the low lilt of her voice packed the same impact as her million-watt smile.

It created the same sting of heat as when he'd gripped her arm…and that heat still prickled in the palm of his hand. Flexing his fingers helped. Allowing his gaze to drop below her shoulders didn't.

She wore a little dress—a sundress, he supposed, although the milk-pale skin it revealed hadn't seen much sun. Very little skin lay bare; this was not a provocative dress. The silky material didn't cling as much as flow with the subtle curves of her body. It was classy, expensive and feminine. The kind of dress that whispered *woman* to every red-blooded male cell he owned.

At the door to the library, she gave final instructions to the housekeeper who hurried off. To fix his tea, with a side of lemon, milk and arsenic, he presumed.

For a long moment the only sound was the retreating squeak of rubber soles and then, as if she felt the touch of his gaze or the cynical whisper of his thoughts, Vanessa pivoted on the heel of one of her delicate sandals. The skirt flared out from her legs, revealing a hint of bare thigh.

Making his skin prickle with renewed heat.

Their eyes met, clashed, held, and he saw a flash of something in her face, quicksilver fast. Then it and she were gone, from the room but not from his blood.

Damn it to blazes, he could not be attracted to her. He would not allow it.

With a growl of aggravation, he shut his eyes and rubbed the back of his neck. Twenty-six hours he'd been traveling. Longer from when he left his Northern Beaches' home for the airport in Sydney's south end.

He was tired and he was wired, running on adrenaline and fixation on his goal.

How could he believe anything he felt right now? How could he trust anything in the turmoil of emotions elicited by his return to Eastwick, Connecticut? To this, the home where he'd grown up, where he'd felt cherished and secure, only to have that comfort blanket yanked from under his adolescent feet without any warning.

Guess what, darling? We're going to live in Australia. You and your sisters and your mother. Won't that be exciting?

Twenty years later he was back and his heightened responses—the heat, the bitterness—weren't all about Vanessa Thorpe.

He expelled a long breath and forced himself to move farther inside.

She'd changed things, of course. The colors, the furnishings, the mood. His footsteps echoed in the cavernous foyer, soaring to the two-story ceiling and bouncing off walls painted in a medley of pale blues. Where he remembered the warmth of a childhood home, now he felt nothing but an outsider's detachment.

Ignoring the tight sensation in his gut, he executed a slow three-sixty and took in the matched mahogany hall stand and side table, the pair of watercolor seascapes, the vase of long-stemmed blooms. The place was as perfectly put together as Vanessa Thorpe, as carefully executed as had been her plan to snare a multimillionaire three times her age.

For two years Tristan had fought the will that gave her everything bar a token bequest to him, Stuart Thorpe's only child, a deliberate act to show he'd chosen wife over son as his beneficiary. Tristan had filed motion after motion while he searched for a loophole, an angle, a reason.

He'd never doubted that he would win. He always did.

Finally, from out of the blue, he'd caught his lucky break. An anonymous allegation contradicting what his legal team had learned about the young widow. Initially, all they'd heard was good—Saint Vanessa with all her charity committees and voluntary work and her unstinting devotion to an ailing husband.

But a second round of discreet inquiries had revealed another slant on Vanessa Thorpe. No solid evidence, but enough rumors from enough different sources to point toward the smoke of a secretly guarded fire. Evidence would not be easily attained two years after the fact but it might not prove necessary.

He was banking on an admission of guilt to close this thing off, granting his mother all that was rightfully hers. Winning would not make up for her life's disappointments and unhappiness, but it would serve to reverse the gross injustice of her divorce settlement.

Twenty years late but it would redress the balance. It was just and fair. And at long last, it would set things right in Tristan's mind.

Vanessa put down the receiver and slumped over the library desk, weak with relief. Plans had changed. Andy would not be arriving at the door any minute, making her meeting with Tristan Thorpe even more difficult than it promised to be.

And she knew, from experience, that anything involving Tristan would prove more difficult than it needed to be.

Time after time he'd proven that, obstructing the execution of probate at every turn, refusing each effort to compromise, threatening to never give up until he had his due. All because he'd cast one look at her age, another at her background and thought *Hello, gold digger*.

Vanessa knew plenty about narrow-minded bigots, but still she'd given this one time to reassess. She'd called, she'd extended that invitation to visit, she'd given him every opportunity to take a fair settlement from the estate. She'd thought he deserved it, even though Stuart had decided otherwise.

But Tristan remained inflexible. A greedy, heartless brute and bully. Too bad she refused to be intimidated.

Reflexively she lifted a hand to rub at her arm. She hated that his touch had left a remnant warmth, that she'd felt the same heat from eyes the changeable blue of summer on the Sound. From the depth of his dark drawl and the scent of rain on his clothes and the contrast between civilized suit and uncivilized—

An abrupt knock at the library door brought her head up with a guilty start. But it was only Gloria, her brow puckered with concern. "Is everything all right, hon? Do you need to go out? Because if you do, I can deal with *himself*."

The last was issued with a sniff of disdain that made Vanessa smile. For a brief second she considered taking that option, mostly because it would tick him off. But she needed to find out what he wanted and why he'd felt a need to deliver his latest pain-in-the-butt objection in person.

Not that she believed he'd discovered anything new. At least, nothing that could influence the estate distribution.

"Everything's fine, thanks. Andy's had to cancel our trip to the city but that's turned out to be a blessing. As for *himself*—" she said it with a mocking smile as she rose to her feet "—I can handle him."

"I know you're plenty tough, but he's a big one."

"The bigger they are…"

Gloria harrumphed. "You better make sure he doesn't break anything valuable when he falls. And if he does fix on making trouble, I'm here."

"No," Vanessa said, getting serious. "You will not be here because your working day finished thirty minutes ago. Now, go home and fuss over your Bennie. As soon as I'm done with our guest, I'm heading up to Lexford anyway."

"Is everything all right up there? Is L—"

"Everything's fine," she repeated. And because she didn't want to extend the conversation by fielding further queries, she put a firm hand on Gloria's shoulder and propelled her toward the door. "I'll see you tomor-row. Now, shoo."

Wanting a glass of water before facing the dreaded enemy, Vanessa headed to the kitchen…and stumbled upon him en route—not in the formal sitting room as instructed, but in the keeping room.

No, no, no. Her heart beat fast with agitation. This was *her* place. The only room decorated with *her* things. The only room small enough and cozy enough and informal enough to relax in with a good book or to visit with friends.

Tristan Thorpe did not fit anywhere in that picture. Not the friends bit, and definitely not the small and cozy part. He'd made his mark as a pro football player in Australia, and she could see why he'd been such a forceful presence on the field. It wasn't only his height, broad-shouldered build and wide male stance. He also exuded an aura of purpose and determination, a hard edge that his tailored suit and expensive grooming could not disguise.

Even standing with his back to the door, without the full-on impact of his intense blue gaze and the decisive set of his strong-boned face, he created an uneasy awareness in Vanessa's flesh. She wasn't used to seeing a man in her house, especially one this blatantly male.

But he's here, she told herself. *He is what he is. Deal with it.*

That pragmatic mantra had pulled her through a lot in twenty-nine years—more difficulties of more impor-tance than Tristan. Most of them had been solved by her godsend marriage to Stuart and she could not afford to lose that resolution. Not now; not ever.

She started into the room and at the sound of her first footfall, his head came up. A thousand nerves jumped to life as he swung around to face her. She lifted her chin an inch higher. Straightened her shoulders and fixed her face with the cool, polite expression that had gotten her through the most terrifying of social events.

Let him call her *duchess*. She didn't care.

And then she noticed what had held his attention—what he now held delicately balanced in his big hands—and her heart lurched with *I-do-care* anxiety. It was the *Girl with Flowers*, the most treasured in her collection of Lladro figurines.

That fretfulness must have registered in her expression because he regarded her narrowly. "Bad news?"

Vanessa knew he referred to the phone call, but she nodded toward the figurine. "Only if you drop that."

Heart in mouth she watched him turn it over in his hands, first one way and then the other. As a football player he'd been magic with his hands, according to Stuart. But magic or not, she didn't want Tristan's hands on her things. She didn't want to look at them a week or a month or a year from now, and remember this man in her home.

As much as she wanted to keep her distance, she couldn't help herself. She had to cross the room and take the statuette from his hands.

"When I mentioned bad news, I meant the phone call."

The brush of their fingers unsettled Vanessa more than she'd anticipated. She felt the fine tremor in her hand and prayed he didn't hear the telltale rattle as she put the figurine down.

"There's no bad news," she said, recovering her poise. She indicated a wingback chair with one hand. "Would you like to sit?"

"I'm comfortable standing."

Leaning against a cabinet with the heels of his hands resting on its edge, he looked at ease. Except the tightness around the corners of his mouth and the tick of a muscle in his jaw gave him away. Not to mention the intentness of the sharp blue gaze fixed on her face.

Like a lion, she decided, lolling in the grass of the veldt, but with every muscle coiled as he waited for the chance to pounce. Paint her pelt black and white and call her zebra, because she was the prey.

The vividness of that mental image created a shiver up her spine, but she snapped straight in automatic reflex. *Do not let the enemy see your fear.* It was a lesson she'd learned as a child, one she'd tried to instill into her younger brother, Lew.

One she'd used often in her new life, adapting to the scrutiny of Eastwick society.

As much as she wanted to put distance between herself and the enemy, she stood her ground and met his unsettling gaze. "Would you care to tell me about this new development? Because I can't think of a thing that would make any difference to your claim on Stuart's estate."

"You're aware of every letter in that will, Vanessa. Surely you've worked this out."

"You've tried to obstruct every letter of that will. I can't believe there's one you missed!"

"We didn't miss this one, duchess. You were just clever enough to beat us…then."

Vanessa huffed out a breath. "I have no idea what you're talking about. Stop playing games, Tristan. I don't have the time or the patience."

For a long moment he didn't respond, although she realized—belatedly—that he no longer lounged against the cabinet. He'd straightened, closing down the gap between them. But she refused to ask for space. She refused to acknowledge that his proximity bothered her.

"Is he the same one?"

She blinked, baffled by his question. "Who?"

"The man you were expecting this afternoon. The one who put that smile on your face when you answered the door. The one who called."

Was he crazy? "The same what? What are you talking about?"

"I'm asking if this man—Andy, isn't it?—is the one who's going to cost you a hundred million dollars."

Vanessa's heart seized with shock and a terrible realization.

"Well?" he asked, not giving her a chance to recover, to respond. "Is he the man you were sleeping with while you were married to my father?"

Two

Oh. My. Lord. He was talking about the adultery clause. The one left over from Stuart's first marriage, to Tristan's mother.

When Tristan had signaled his intention to challenge the will, her lawyer, Jack Cartwright, had gone over every clause with painstaking care, making sure Vanessa understood and that he wouldn't receive any nasty surprises from the opposing attorney.

She'd given that clause no more thought. She had no reason to. But now Tristan thought she'd had a lover…that she *still* had a lover.

That comprehension took a moment to sink in, and then she couldn't prevent her shock from bubbling into laughter.

"You think this is funny?"

"I think," she said, recovering, "this is ludicrous. Where would you get such an idea?"

"My lawyer's asked around. There are rumors."

She stared at him in disbelief. "After almost two years of this dispute, you've decided to invent rumors?"

"I didn't invent anything."

"No? Then where did these rumors suddenly sprout from?"

He took a second to answer, just long enough for Vanessa to note that the muscle still ticked in his jaw. "I received a letter."

"From?"

"Does it matter?"

"Yes, it does," she fired back at him, her earlier disbelief growing indignant. "It matters that someone is slandering me."

He regarded her in silence, a long taut moment that fanned Vanessa's gathering fury.

"I'm giving you the chance to deal with me privately, here and now," he said finally, his voice low and even. "Or would you prefer to take this to court? Would you like to answer all the questions about who and where and how often under oath? Would you like all your society friends to hear—"

"You bastard. Don't you dare even think about spreading your lies."

"Not lies." Something glinted, brief and dangerous in his eyes. "I intend to dig deep, Vanessa, if that's what it takes to discover all your dirty little secrets. I will find every truth about you. Every last detail."

Vanessa's head whirled with the implications of his

threat. She had to get away from him, to cool down, to think, but when she tried to escape he blocked her exit. And when she attempted to stare him down, he shifted closer, hemming her into the corner where she couldn't move without touching him.

Her resentment rose in a thick, choking wave. She wanted to sound icy, imperious, but instead her voice quivered with rage. "You start by turning up at my home uninvited. You manhandle me. You threaten me with your nasty lies. And now you're resorting to physical intimidation. I can hardly wait to see what you try next."

Their eyes clashed in a lightning bolt that was eight parts antagonism, two parts challenge. She knew, a split second before he moved, before his hands came up to trap her against the wall, that the two parts challenge was two parts too much. And still she couldn't back down, even when his gaze dropped to her lips and caused a slow sweet ripple in her blood. Even when he muttered something low and unintelligible—perhaps an oath, perhaps a warning—beneath his breath.

Then his mouth descended to hers, catching her gasp of indignation.

For a second she was too stunned by the sensation of his lips pressed against hers to react. Everything was new, untried, unfamiliar. The bold presence of his mouth, the rough texture of his skin, the elemental taste of rain and sun and man.

Everything was unexpected except the electric charge that flushed through her skin and tightened her breasts. That was the same as when he'd touched her, the same as when he'd watched her walk away, the same as when she'd turned at the library door and caught him staring.

She heard the accelerated thud of her heartbeat and scrambled to compose herself, to reject that unwanted response. But then he shifted his weight slightly and she felt the brush of his jacket against her bare arm. For some reason that slide of body-warmed fabric seemed more intimate than the kiss itself, and the effect shimmered through her skin like liquid silk.

The hands she'd raised to shove him away flattened against his chest and the slow beat of his heart resonated into her palms. With a shock she realized that she wasn't only touching him but kissing him back, just now, for one split second. *Oh, no. A thousand times no.* Her eyes jolted open, wide and appalled, as she pushed with renewed purpose.

His mouth stilled for one measured second before he let her go. The message was clear. He'd instigated this. He was ending it. Damn him. And damn her traitorous body for reacting to whatever weird male-female chemistry was going on between them.

Red-hot anger hazed her vision and she lashed out without conscious thought. He dodged her easily, catching her arm before she came close to landing a blow. And that only infuriated her more. She wrenched at her captured arm and the jerky action caught the Lladro *Girl with Flowers* she'd set down on the cabinet.

In slow motion she saw the delicate figurine start to topple but she couldn't move fast enough. The sound of its shattering impact on the marble floor filled the silence for several long brittle seconds. Vanessa pressed the back of one trembling hand to her mouth, as if that might silence the anguished cry deep inside her.

But when she started to duck down, he intercepted her, his hand on her arm holding her steady. "Leave it. It's only an ornament."

An ornament, yes, but this one was a gift from her childhood—a symbol of where she'd come from and all she'd dreamed of leaving behind.

But only a symbol, her pragmatic side reminded her. She'd had to grow up too practical for dreams and symbolism. This incident signified only one thing: she'd allowed Tristan Thorpe to cut through her cool, to upset her enough that she'd lashed out in temper.

And she would eat dirt before she gave him the satisfaction of knowing how deeply he'd affected her.

"Are you all right?"

The softened edge to his voice caught her off guard, but she shrugged that aside along with his touch. He was probably worried that she'd start weeping and wailing. Or that she'd turn and throw some more of her *ornaments* at his infuriating head.

No doubt it was as hard and as cold as the marble tiles underfoot.

Gathering the shards of her poise, she turned and met his eyes. "I will be fine once you get out of my house."

The concern she'd detected in his voice turned steel-hard. The muscle she'd noted earlier jumped in his jaw again. "You enjoy your house while you can, duchess."

"Meaning?"

"It won't be yours once I prove your adultery. Not the house, not any of these pretty things you're so concerned about breaking. All bought and paid for with Thorpe money."

"Good luck with that," she said coldly, while the anger resurged with new fervor. She had to get out of here before she did start hurling things at him, if only to show how little they mattered. "If you'll excuse me, I have another appointment. If you have anything else to say, please say it through my lawyer."

"That's it?"

"Except for one last thing… Please close the door on your way out."

Tristan hadn't planned on following her. After closing the front door, he'd been intent on getting to one place only—his attorney's office in Stamford. He had a letter to deliver. He had instructions to employ the best investigator—a team of them, if necessary—to follow up every rumor about her secret assignations, to find this mystery man whatever the cost.

Even though he'd prodded her about seeing *the same man* today, he didn't believe she would be foolish enough to flaunt her lover so openly. Not when she stood to lose everything she'd set her cap at when she had married the old man.

With all his focus trained on what she'd said and not said, on what he'd done and wished he hadn't, Tristan drove straight through the intersection of White Birch Lane and Beauford when he should have turned right. Half a mile farther on he realized his error and pulled over. Waiting for a gap in the traffic, he beat himself up about missing the turn. And while he was at it, he beat himself up some more for making such a hash of his first meeting with Vanessa Thorpe.

Sure she provoked him. Everything about her had needled him long before he came face-to-face with her kick-gut beauty. But did he have to react to every goading statement, every challenging eye-meet, every disdainful lift of her chin?

Did he have to kiss her?

The hell of it was he didn't remember making a choice. One second they were going at it, biting verbal chunks out of each other's hides, the next he had her backed against the wall tasting the provocation of her lush lips. And the hell of *that* was how swiftly her taste had aroused his hunger.

He'd wanted so much more than one quick bite. His hands had itched to touch that distracting dip in her chin, to feel the creamy softness of her skin, to pull her tight against his body.

He could blame the long day, his lack of sleep, the edgy turmoil of returning to Eastwick, but in the end he could only hold himself responsible. He'd let her get to him.

He wouldn't make that mistake again.

The flow of traffic eased and he checked his mirror just as a champagne colored convertible whizzed by. He didn't have to see the vanity plates to know it was her. Everything on the list of possessions they'd sparred over this past year was indelibly printed on his brain.

He hadn't planned on following her any more than he'd planned on kissing her, but as he steered into a gap in traffic Tristan had a hunch that this would turn out a whole lot more fulfilling and less frustrating than that ill-conceived meeting of mouths.

"I'm so glad you suggested this," Vanessa said.

This was to meet by the water at Old Poynton, where the breeze drifting off Long Island Sound tempered the warmth of the late afternoon sun; where breathing the fresh marine air cooled the edgy heat of Vanessa's temper…a little.

And *you* was Andy Silverman, who'd suggested the outdoor walk-and-talk when he'd called earlier to change plans.

Andy had grown up in the same Yonkers neighborhood as Vanessa's family, and she'd recognized him as soon as he commenced working at Twelve Oaks, the special-needs facility that had been home to her younger brother for the past seven years. They met regularly to discuss Lew's program and his progress, and Andy had become more than her brother's counselor.

Now she counted him as a friend…the only friend who knew and understood Lew and the difficulties posed by his autism.

"Tough day at the country club?" Despite the light-hearted comment, she felt a serious edge to Andy's sidelong look. "You want to talk about it?"

"Haven't we just done that?"

They'd talked about Lew, as they always did, and about why Andy had cancelled their trip to the city. Storms, like today's, were one of several triggers that upset Lew's need for calm and routine order.

"Your brother has bad days all the time," Andy said now. "You're used to that."

No. She didn't think she would ever call herself *used to* Andy's autism or his most difficult, sometimes violently damaging, days. But she conceded Andy's perceptive point. He knew there was more worrying her today than Lew.

"I'm not sure you want to hear this," she said.

"Hey, I'm a professional listener."

That made her smile. "Do you charge extra for out-of-hours consultations, Dr. Silverman?"

They'd reached the end of the promenade. Andy paused and leaned against the stone wall that separated the walkway from the beach. He folded his arms across his chest. His open face and calm expression were part of what made him so good at his job. "Go ahead and spit it out. You know you want to."

Not so much *want to* as *need to*, Vanessa silently amended. Her gaze shifted beyond her companion, tracking two windsurfers as they rode a gust of air across the clean blue surface of the Sound. Then one of the surfers slowed, faltered, and toppled into the water, his charmed ride on the wind over.

"Wouldn't it be nice if we all had such soft landings," she mused out loud.

"You've lost me."

With a small sigh, she turned her attention back to Andy and his invitation to *spit it out*. "It's Tristan Thorpe."

Andy tsked in sympathy. "Isn't it always?"

"He's here. In Eastwick."

"For the trial? I thought that wasn't till next month."

"He's here because he thinks he's found a way to beat me without going to court." All semblance of relaxation destroyed, Vanessa paced away a couple of steps, then swung back. "Which he hasn't, but that won't stop him making trouble."

"Only if you let him."

She laughed, a short, sharp, humorless sound. "How can I stop him? He has it in his head that I'm a nasty sly adulterer and he's here to prove it!"

To his credit, Andy barely blinked at that disclosure. She supposed, in his line of work, he heard all manner of shockers. "That's not a problem if there's nothing to substantiate."

"Of course there's nothing to substantiate!"

"But you're upset because people might believe that of you, despite your innocence?"

"I'm upset because…because…"

Because he believes it. Because he kissed me. Because I can't stop thinking about that.

"My point exactly," Andy said, misinterpreting her stumble into silence. "Your friends know you well enough to not believe whatever he might put about."

"My friends know. You know. I know," she countered hotly, "but he's always thought the worst of me. Now he believes I'm not only an Anna Nicole Smith clone who took advantage of a susceptible older man, but I kept a lover on the side to share my ill-gotten spoils." She exhaled on a note of disgust. "I don't even know why I'm surprised."

Andy regarded her closely for a long moment. "He's really got you stewing, hasn't he?"

Oh, yes. In ways she didn't want to think about, let alone talk about. She'd let him kiss her, she'd breathed the scent of him into her lungs, and then she'd raised her hand, for pity's sake, when she despised violence born of temper and heated words and uncontrolled emotions.

"He got me so riled," she said with quiet intensity, her stomach twisting with the pain of those long-ago memories. "I wanted to hit him, Andy."

"But you didn't."

Only because he stopped me.

She could still feel the steely grip of his hand, the pressure of his fingers wrapped around her wrist, and the need to lash out raging in her blood. And the worst of it? Not the loss of her treasured gift but the acknowledgment, on the hour-plus drive up here, that she hadn't been lashing out at him but at her fickle body's unexpected and unwanted response.

"I told myself not to let him get under my skin. I invited him into my home when I wanted to slam the door in his face. I tried to be polite and calm. But the man is just so…so…" Unable to find a suitable descriptor, she spread her hands in a silent gesture of appeal. Except she doubted the dictionary contained a single word strong enough, hot enough, complex enough to cover all that Tristan had evoked in her that afternoon. "And it's not only him that has me stewing."

Suddenly she couldn't stand still any longer. Hooking an arm through one of Andy's folded ones, she forced him into motion, walking back toward the strip of tourist boutiques and sidewalk eateries opposite the small beach and marina.

"Someone sent him a letter. An accusation. That's how this latest crusade of his started." She tugged at his arm in agitation. "Who would do such a thing?"

"Did he show you this letter?"

Vanessa shook her head and in Andy's raised brows she read another question. "Are you thinking that this letter might not exist?"

"If I were you," he said carefully, "I'd want to see it."

At the time she'd been too astounded and too het up by his allegations. She hadn't thought of asking to see the evidence. Frowning, she walked and she chewed the whole exchange and its implications over in her mind. "Why would he invent this letter and come all the way over here to prove its claims? That only makes sense if he believes he *can* prove it. And that only makes sense if someone—such as his correspondent—has convinced him they have something on me."

And that made no sense because she had never slept around.

Not once. Not ever.

"It's not as if I have a pool boy," she continued, "or a tennis pro or a personal trainer. The only male staff I employ regularly is Gloria's Bennie, and that's only for odd jobs to keep her happy. I see Jack, my attorney, regularly but everyone knows he's a besotted new husband and soon-to-be father."

"And you see me."

Andy's evenly spoken comment hung in the air a second before she grasped its significance. Then she stopped in her tracks, shaking her head with a slowly dawning realization. Usually they met behind the walls

of Twelve Oaks' sprawling estate, in one of the formal
meeting rooms or the less formal library, or they walked
around the estate's spacious grounds.

But on occasions they did meet in the nearby town
of Lexford, for lunch or a coffee. And they'd also met
once or twice here at the shore where Andy lived.

"Do you think some busybody could have seen—"
she waggled her hand between them, unable to voice the
us that might link their friendship in a nonplatonic way
"—and misconstrued?"

"It's possible."

Vanessa stared at him wide-eyed. Then, pity help
her, she couldn't suppress an involuntary giggle.

"Pretty funny, huh?"

"I'm sorry." Sobering instantly, she reached out and
put her hand on his arm. And that was the thing with
Andy—she could touch him and feel no spark, no jolt,
no prickling of heat. Nothing but a comfortable warmth
similar to what she'd established with her husband and
still missed so very much. "I didn't mean to offend you.
You know I love you like a brother."

"*I* know that, but what about someone watching us?"

Shock immobilized her for a split second. Then she
drew back her hand and her body, suddenly aware of
how close they stood. As they'd done on countless other
innocent occasions.

With an audience?

They continued walking, but Vanessa couldn't stop
herself from glancing at each car and passing pedestrian.
Scores of people were out enjoying the gorgeous
summer twilight, yet she felt exposed.

Despite the warmth of the air she felt a chill run over her skin. "I hate the thought that someone might have been following me."

"That's something I've never quite understood."

She cut him a narrow look. "The fact that I don't like being spied on?"

"The fact you've kept Lew and your visits to Twelve Oaks secret."

"That has nothing to do with being spied on."

"Maybe not," he said in his usual mild manner. "But if the good folk of Eastwick knew about your brother, then they'd also understand why you need to drive up here so often and why you meet with me. That would take care of one possible misinterpretation."

As usual, Andy was right. Except up until now she hadn't seen any need to share this most personal part of her life. Only Stuart—plus a handful of trusted professionals and some old friends from her pre-Eastwick days—knew about Lew. Together they had decided to keep his long-term tenancy at Twelve Oaks private.

"Are you ashamed of—"

"Of course not!" Vanessa swung around to face Andy, all thoughts of being spied upon lost in the fierceness of her answer. "Don't you dare suggest that Lew is some sort of embarrassment. I would take out a paid page in the *New York Times* if I thought it would help, but what would be the point? All that would accomplish is a whole lot of talk and finger-pointing from small-minded people who don't understand."

"And this is the society you want to live in?"

"No. This is the society I *chose* to live in when I married Stuart."

Because that choice included Twelve Oaks, the exclusive facility that provided Lew with the best environment, the right therapy, everything he needed to grow and flourish as an individual. She hadn't even dreamed of accessing such an expensive option before she met her future husband. In fact she'd been at the end of her tether, out of options for caring for Lew and dealing with his increasingly violent tendencies as he grew from a boy into a man.

"Besides," she continued, "not everyone in Eastwick is narrow-minded. If they knew, my friends would want to visit, to help, and you know how Lew is with new people and changes to his routine. He is happy and I'm happy visiting and doing my voluntary work without it being talked about all over town. I've had enough *poor Vanessa*s to last a lifetime, thank you very much!"

They resumed walking, Andy silent in a way that suggested he didn't agree. Was she being selfish, making it easier on herself, protecting her cushy life? After Stuart's death she had wanted to confide in her friends, because Lord knows she'd felt so incredibly alone and lonely. But then she had Gloria, who'd come from the same background, who knew Lew. Plus Andy. Two of the best friends she could have because, unlike her Eastwick friends, they'd known her when she was plain Vanessa Kotzur.

It had been easier to keep the status quo, for so many reasons.

What about now? her pragmatic side wanted to know.

"I need to see the letter," she said with quiet resolve.

Before she made any decision on what else to do, she had to see the evidence.

Andy nodded grimly. "And you need to set him straight about me."

Vanessa's whole system bucked in protest. She could actually feel her feet dragging on the pavement as they neared the street where she'd parked her car.

"Perhaps I can do this without even mentioning Lew. I'll say I do voluntary work at Twelve Oaks." Which she did. "And we're working together on a program…a new music therapy program which I'm looking at funding. And that I'm interested in extending the equestrian therapy facility."

This wasn't even bending the truth. She intended making a very significant donation from Stuart's estate, once it was finalized, to help with both of those programs as well as funding positions for adolescents from low-income families.

Andy's frown looked unconvinced. "He's looking for proof of adultery, Vanessa. He'll have you investigated."

"And find out what? That I drive up to Lexford two or three times a week, to a special-needs home where I'm listed as a volunteer?"

"A home with a resident who shares your surname. Any investigator worth his salt is going to make the connection."

Didn't he ever tire of being so calm and logical and right? Blast him. Because he *was* right, and already her mind had leaped ahead to the next correlation a professional investigator—or his eagle-eyed employer—may make.

Lew Kotzur had moved into Twelve Oaks the same month that his sister Vanessa quit her two waitressing jobs to marry Stuart Thorpe. The man who pulled strings to get young Lew into the place. The man behind the trust fund that paid all his bills.

A sick feeling of fatalism settled over her as they stopped beside her car. Even before Andy spoke. "The way I see it, you have two options, Vanessa."

"I get to choose my poison?"

He didn't smile at her attempt at levity. His calm, level gaze held hers as he laid those choices on the line. "Either you let Thorpe investigate and risk him spreading nasty stuff about why you keep your brother hidden away from your new society friends. Or you tell him yourself and explain your motivation. There're your choices, Vanessa. It's up to you."

Three

There wasn't any choice. Sitting in her car, watching Andy's loping stride carry him off toward the marina, Vanessa knew exactly what she had to do. Swallow her poison quickly, before she had time to think about how bitter it would taste going down.

She dug her cell phone from her purse. Stared at the keypad so long that the numbers swam before her eyes. Closed her eyes until the crashing wave of dread passed.

This isn't about you, Ms. Pragmatist lectured. *Think about Lew. Think about how disruptive and upsetting this could end up for everyone at Twelve Oaks if an investigator started hanging around, grilling staff and residents.*

She didn't have Tristan's cell number, but she did have several Eastwick hotels in her phone's directory. How hard could he be to find?

Not very, as it turned out.

On her second attempt, the receptionist at the Hotel Marabella put her straight through to his suite. She didn't have a chance to second think, or to do any more than draw a deep breath and silently wail, *why the Marabella?* She preferred to think he'd have chosen one of the big chains instead of the tasteful Mediterranean-style boutique hotel whose restaurant was among her favorites.

Perhaps his secretary chose it. Or a travel agent. Business executives did not make their own—

"Hello."

Vanessa started so violently she almost dropped her phone.

By the time she'd recovered and compelled her heart to stop racing and pressed the tiny handset to her ear, he was repeating his greeting and asking if anyone was there. His voice was unmistakable, a deep, thick drawl colored by his years down under. That color matched the sun-tinged ends of his rich brown hair, the deep tan of his skin, but not the alert intensity of his eyes.

She felt a ripple of hot-cold response, as if those eyes were on her again. Those eyes and his mouth—

"It's Vanessa," she said quickly, staunching that memory. "Vanessa Thorpe."

Silence.

"I wasn't expecting to find you in."

"You weren't expecting…" he murmured, slightly puzzled, slightly mocking. "And yet you called?"

"I thought you might be out for dinner. I intended leaving a message."

"A different message to the one you left me with earlier?"

Vanessa counted to five slowly. He knew she'd been spitting mad when she ordered him out of her house. And he knew why, blast him. She was not going to let that cynical taunt get to her. She had to do this. For Lew. For Andy. For her own guilty conscience. "I need to talk to you."

"I'm listening."

"I meant, in person."

In the next beat of silence she could almost feel his stillness, that hard-edged intensity fixed on her from fifty-odd miles away. Ridiculous, she knew, but that didn't stop a tight feeling of apprehension from gripping her stomach.

"Tomorrow?" he asked.

With a full schedule of committee meetings plus a trip to Lexford to see how Lew was doing after today's dramas, her only free hour was first thing in the morning. And the idea of inviting him to her home, or arranging to meet for breakfast somewhere else, caused every cell in her body to scream in protest. Breakfast meant straight out of bed. Breakfast also meant a long night of worry and endless opportunity to change her mind.

"Tonight would suit me better." Vanessa closed her eyes and tried to block out how bad an idea this might turn out to be. "Do you have plans?"

"I have a dinner reservation downstairs."

"I'm sure they will hold your table."

"I'm sure they would," he countered. "If I asked them to."

She sucked in a breath, but she couldn't suck back her sharp retort. "Are you deliberately trying to antagonize me?"

"I don't think either one of us has to try. Do you?"

Okay. So he wasn't going to make this easy, but that didn't mean she would give up. "Are you dining alone?"

"Why do you ask? Would you like to break bread with me?"

"I would like," she enunciated, after ungritting her teeth, "to speak to you. If you're dining alone, I thought that may provide an opportunity without intruding on your plans."

Another pause in which she could almost hear him sizing up the implications of her request. Then, he said, "I'll have the restaurant add another setting."

"Just a chair," she said quickly. "I won't be eating so please don't wait for me. I'll be there in an hour."

"I look forward to it, duchess."

Tristan had drawled that closing line with a liberal dose of mockery, but he *did* look forward to Vanessa's arrival. Very much. He couldn't wait to see how she explained her rapid turnaround from *get out of my house* to *I need to talk*. He could have made it easy on her by changing his dinner booking and meeting her downstairs in the lounge bar or the more private library. He could have offered to drive out to her house, to save her the trip into town.

But after witnessing her rendezvous at Old Poynton, knowing she'd rushed helter-skelter to her lover right after scoffing at the letter's allegations, he was in no mood for making anything easy for Vanessa.

So. She wanted to talk. Most likely to spin a story concocted during that intense seaside heart-to-heart. He couldn't imagine her confessing but she might attempt to explain away her secret meetings with lover boy. Whichever way she played it, he was ready.

This time she wouldn't catch him unawares.

This time he would keep his hormones on ice.

Resisting the urge to check his watch, he poured a second glass of wine and pushed his dinner plate aside. He'd requested a table at the end of the terrace, where, in secluded peace, he could pretend to enjoy the food and the shimmer of reflected moonlight off the darkened waters of the Sound. Where he wouldn't be scanning the door for the distinctive shimmer of moonlight-blond hair.

Still, he sensed her arrival several minutes later. Without turning he knew her footsteps and felt the quickening of anticipation in his blood. When he started to rise from his chair, she waved him back down. Her warm smile was all for the waiter who fussed over seating her—not opposite but catercorner to him.

"So madam, too, can enjoy the view."

She thanked Josef and while he took her order for some ridiculous froufrou coffee, Tristan kicked back in his chair and tried not to notice that she still wore the same pink sundress.

Because she hadn't yet gone home? Because she'd spent all this time at Old Poynton...doing what?

Only walking? Only talking?

The questions—and the possibility in the answers—snarled through him, sharp and mean. For a long moment he continued to stare at her, waiting for Josef to leave. Waiting for her to acknowledge his presence. Waiting for the impulse to ask those questions to pass so he could speak with some civility.

He took a sip from his very civilized *sauvignon blanc*. "Traffic bad?"

She'd been fussing with her purse, setting it just so on the table, but she looked up sharply.

"You said an hour."

"Have I held you up?" Her expression was polite, her voice as cool and dry as his wine. "If you have another appointment, you should have said when I called. I didn't mean—"

"My only appointment is upstairs, with my bed. It's been a long day."

Across the table, their gazes met and held. Comprehension flickered in her eyes, like an unspoken wince of sympathy. "I'm sorry. You must have started the day yesterday, on the other side of the world."

And didn't that seem a long time ago? He should have been wiped out but instead he felt energized. By her presence, by her proximity, by the subtle drift of her perfume in the still night air. But mostly by the promise of another skirmish in their ongoing battle.

"I'm sure you didn't come here to talk about my long day." And there was something in her eyes or in his primed-for-combat blood, that pushed him to add, "Or my current need to get horizontal."

"No." She answered without pause, without dropping

eye contact, without responding to his deliberate provocation. "I didn't."

"So. What do you want?"

"I want to see the letter."

Tristan arched an eyebrow. "You don't believe it exists?"

"Is there any reason I should?"

"I've flown ten thousand miles today on the strength of it."

"So you say."

Rocking back in his chair, he met the steady challenge of her gaze. "If the lover doesn't exist and the letter doesn't exist, why are you worried?"

"Do I look worried?"

"You're here."

Irritation flared in her eyes but before she could respond, Josef arrived with her coffee. She smiled up at the young waiter, her annoyance instantly concealed by an expression as warm and friendly as when she'd opened the door that afternoon. Then Tristan cleared his throat and the subtle reminder of his presence wiped all the warmth from her face. Exactly the same as when she'd found him on her doorstep.

"I am here," she said tightly, "to see this letter. If it exists."

"Oh, it exists, duchess. Same as your lover." Turning the wineglass with his fingers, he waited a second before continuing. "A little young, isn't he?"

A frown marred the smooth perfection of her face. "Josef?"

"Lover boy. At Old Poynton."

"How do you…" Her voice trailed off and her eyes widened as the inference took hold. "You followed me this afternoon?"

"Inadvertently."

"You *accidentally* followed me? *For fifty miles?*"

One shoulder lifted in a negligent shrug. "I took a wrong turn. You sped by. I thought it might be interesting to find out who you needed to see in such a godfire hurry."

Vanessa stared across at him with a growing sense of horror and violation. Not the chill shivers of earlier, when she'd thought about being spied on, but a hot wave of outrage. Because *he'd* done this. Not some anonymous stranger, but this man. Sitting beside her and passing this off as if it were a big fat nothing.

For a long second she had to fight the urge to hurl something at him. The closest something was her cinnamon mocha macchiato, untouched and still hot enough to do serious damage. The need steamed through her, curling her fingers so tightly around the coffee cup's handle, she was afraid it might crack under the pressure.

Not good, Vanessa. Not cool. Not restrained. Not gracious.

Not any of the things she loved about this lifestyle she'd adopted.

Through sheer force of willpower she loosened her grip, but she couldn't risk speaking for fear of the words she might hurl in lieu of the physical. She couldn't even look at him, in case that fired her rage anew. To remind herself of the very public venue and her very elegant surroundings and the very real need to gather some restraint, she looked past his shoulder at the restaurant and the other diners.

Even on a Tuesday night the Marabella's celebrated restaurant was close to capacity, the crowd an even mix of well-heeled tourists and business suits and elegantly dressed locals. Many she recognized; several she knew well enough to call friends. Frank Forrester, one of Stuart's old golfing buddies, tipped his silver head and winked broadly when he caught her eye.

Smiling back, she breathed a silent sigh of relief that Frank's company didn't include his wife. The last thing she needed was Delia Forrester sauntering over to flutter eyelashes and flaunt her latest chest augmentation at the new man in town. And if Delia were present, she *would* notice Tristan. She *would* saunter and flutter and flaunt because that's what Delia did in the presence of men, despite the husband she gave every appearance of doting on.

"What's the matter, duchess? Afraid you'll be seen with me?"

Tristan's soft drawl cut through her reflection, drawing her attention back to him. When her gaze collided with his—sharp, steady, the rich ocean blue darkened like night on the water—she experienced a brief pulse of disorientation, almost like vertigo.

"Not at all," she replied crisply, shaking off that weird sensation. What was the matter with her? Why did she let him get to her so easily, in so many ways? "We are here to discuss business, the same as these gentlemen—" she spread her hands, indicating the sprinkling of suits around them "—and the real estate reps over by the door."

When his gaze followed hers, taking in the company, Vanessa's heart gave a tiny bump of discovery.

She'd hit upon the ideal segue back to Andy and this afternoon's meeting and the ridiculous misconception about an affair. "I don't mind being seen with you, Tristan," she said in a smooth, even voice, while her insides tightened and twisted over where this conversation might lead. "It's no different from two people meeting, say, at the shore, to talk business."

"Your meeting this afternoon was business?"

Lifting her chin, she met his sardonic gaze. "I do voluntary work at a facility for the developmentally disabled up near Lexford. Andy works there as a counselor."

"And you meet him, about your volunteering, at the shore? After hours?"

"Not usually." She moistened her lips. Chose the next words with careful precision. "Andy isn't only a work associate, you see. We grew up in the same neighborhood, went to the same school. He's a good friend and we do meet after hours, sometimes, and not always to talk about my volunteering. Given his profession, Andy is a good listener."

"And today—this afternoon—you needed to talk."

"To vent," she corrected.

"About me."

"Who else?"

He didn't counter for a tick, and there was something in his expression that started a drumbeat of tension in her blood, a beat that slowed and thickened when his gaze dropped to her lips. "Did you tell him about our kiss?"

The intimacy of his words washed through her, at first warm and strong with remembered sensations and then all wrong. *Our kiss* denoted sharing. A lovers' kiss, hushed with reverence and sweet with romance, not imbued with bitter disdain and the bite of angry words.

She shook her head. "That wasn't a kiss."

"No?"

"It was a power play, and you know it."

A note of surprise flickered in the darkened depths of his eyes. "Was it really so bad?"

"As far as kisses go, it fell a long way short of good."

He rocked back in his chair, his expression trickily hard to gauge. Then he shocked the devil out of her by laughing—a low, lazy chuckle that stayed on his lips and tingled through her body like the sparks of a slow-burning fuse.

"Here's where I should say, I can do better."

"To which I would reply, you won't ever get that second chance."

Treacherous territory, Ms. Pragmatist warned her. She'd challenged him before. In the keeping room today, for example, and even before today's first face-to-face confrontation they'd employed words to cut and thrust, in terse e-mails and messages delivered via their respective attorneys.

But this verbal sparring held a different edge.

This came in the shadow of laughter, with a lazy smile and a dangerous shot of pleasure because Vanessa sensed that, finally, she had managed to surprise him in a positive way. That shouldn't have pleased her quite so much. She should have felt repelled by the prospect of another kiss, a real kiss, with no agenda other than exploring—

No. She jolted upright, appalled that she'd been staring at his lips. That she'd allowed the marine-scented air and the witchery of a full moon to lure her from her evening's task.

No more, Ms. Pragmatist admonished. *Get to the point and get out of here.*

"Andy is not my lover. He never was. He never will be." She laid it on the line in a resolute rush. "If he is named in that letter, I think it's only fair that he should know."

"There are no names."

"Can I see?"

"Now?" He showed his hands, palms up, empty. "Not possible. It's in my lawyer's hands."

"You didn't waste any time."

"You had your chance this afternoon, when I came to your house. It was you who suggested we deal through our lawyers."

Yes, she remembered. She also remembered what had made her so spitting mad that she'd kicked him out without seeing the letter. Blast him and her own sorry self for not asking over the phone. She could have saved herself the drive and the aggravation and the gossip she'd no doubt started by meeting him in this public place.

Tight frustration prickled at the back of her throat, but she lifted her chin and ruthlessly shoved that emotion aside. "Could you please arrange for a copy to be sent to my lawyer's office tomorrow?"

"First thing," he replied with surprising compliance.

Prepared for their usual slanging match, Vanessa stared at him through narrowed eyes. What was the hitch? What angle was he playing? He held her gaze for a long moment, steady, blue, guileless, and there was nothing left to say.

Nothing left to do, except get out of there before she started trusting his word.

"Fine." With a brief, decisive nod, she reached for her purse. A shadow fell across their table. And Frank Forrester's distinctive longtime smoker's voice rasped through the silence.

"Sorry for the intrusion, but I couldn't leave without saying hello to my second favorite blonde. Given my rusty old ticker—" he tapped a thin hand against his chest and winked "—I don't put off till tomorrow."

Although Frank often quipped about his age and his heart condition, Vanessa couldn't voice her usual light-hearted reproach. Not only because he'd interrupted her getaway, either. Up close he looked a decade older than his years, frail and slight and stooped.

Smiling up at him, she only hoped her shock at his appearance didn't show on her face.

"Your company is never an intrusion," she assured him. And because it was the gracious thing to do, she added, "Would you care to join us? For coffee or a nightcap?"

"No, no. I'm on my way home. Can't dally." But he made no move to leave and his gaze glinted with genuine interest—or curiosity—as it edged toward her companion and back.

As much as she'd have liked to, Vanessa couldn't ignore the hint. "Tristan, meet Frank Forrester. Frank, this is Stuart's son. From Australia."

"You don't say?" Frank shook his head slowly, his gaze beetling in on the younger man's face. "You've grown some since I last saw you, lad. You were a weedy young beanpole then. It must be at least fifteen years."

"Twenty," Tristan said. And he was on his feet, shaking hands. Being clapped on the back in the male version of an embrace.

"Welcome back to Eastwick, lad. Welcome home!"

Vanessa blinked with surprise. She hadn't considered they might know one another, despite the former bank president's longtime friendship with Stuart. And as for the *welcome home*—the concept of Tristan belonging here in Eastwick was almost as unsettling as seeing him in her home that afternoon.

"Suppose you're here on business," Frank mused. "You started up a telecom, didn't you? Heard you'd turned it into one of the Pacific's major players."

"I'm surprised you've heard of us."

Frank made a gruff sound. "Your father was a proud man. He wasn't above crowing your successes."

If this came as a surprise to Tristan, he didn't show it. No shift in his expression, no acknowledgment, no mention of his father. Just a smoothly offered, "I recently sold out of the company, as it happens."

"You don't say."

"It was an attractive offer."

"Made a killing, eh?"

Tristan's smile came quick and unexpected, its impact a devil of awareness that settled low in her belly. She had to force herself to concentrate on his words. Not the sharp line of his jaw or the curve of his lips. Not the sudden recall of those lips against hers, but his words.

He's sold his business. Does that mean this trip is open-ended? That nothing will prevent him staying in Eastwick for as long as it took?

"Are you asking as a friend or a banker?" he asked.

Frank chuckled. "I'm an old man. Retired, didn't you know?"

"Once a banker, always a banker."

Suppressing a smile, Vanessa looked away. Apparently she needed her own mantra: *once a brute, always a brute*. Just to remind herself what lurked behind that slow, charismatic grin.

"You'll have to come for dinner one night," Frank suggested. "If you're in town for more than a day or two."

"That depends—" she felt the glancing touch of a sharp blue gaze "—on my business."

"Are you staying with Vanessa? Even better. Why don't you both come?"

Staying with her? In her home? Her heart did a little stumbling hitch as their eyes met. *No way.*

They both spoke at once.

"He's not staying with me, actually."

"I'm staying here. At the Marabella."

Oblivious to the sudden tension in the air, Frank dug around in his jacket until he unearthed a card. He pressed it into Tristan's hand. "Even more reason to join us for a meal, lad. Call me when you know your plans."

They said their goodbyes and Frank started to leave. Then he stopped, one hand raised, as if struck by a sudden notion. He turned back. "Is that polo do this weekend, Vanessa?"

"It's on Sunday, yes. But I don't—"

"Perfect!" Frank spoke over the top of her objection. "Why don't you join us?"

"Polo?"

Tristan sounded dubious and Frank nodded sympathetically. "Damn sissy sport if you ask me, but my wife seems to like it."

Champagne, celebrities, studly Argentinean players. Of course Delia liked the polo.

Vanessa did not, particularly, but Sunday's match was a fund-raiser for *Eastwick Cares,* one of her favored charities since it dealt with at-risk youth. The kind of place she and Lew might have needed, had their lives taken a slightly different turn. So, no, she couldn't *not* go to the polo match, although the idea of sharing the same luncheon tent as Tristan and Delia made her stomach pitch.

"Everybody will be there," Frank continued. "Great chance to catch up. Ain't that right, Vanessa?"

Something sharpened in Tristan's gaze as it fastened on her face. A sense of purpose that she instantly recognized for what it was: he would go to the polo match, all right. And he would use the opportunity to quiz people about her.

"That's right, Frank. Anybody who's anybody will be there." She smiled, but the effort felt as forced as her jovial tone. "Unfortunately that means all the invitations were snapped up months ago."

Frank waved that away with a tremulous hand. "Delia will rake up a ticket if need be. Let me know, lad."

With a sinking heart, Vanessa watched his unsteady meandering departure. Delia could wangle an extra invitation if she set her mind and her saccharine-sweet charm and Frank's checkbook to it. There was nothing Vanessa could do without appearing petty or vindictive, and right now all she wanted was escape.

But as she gathered up her purse she felt Tristan's focus switch to her.

The instant she turned into the sharp cast of those blue, blue eyes, she knew what was coming next. Like a freight train barreling through the night, she saw the oncoming light and couldn't do a thing to divert the wreck.

"Who is Delia?" he asked, right on cue.

Twenty years ago, when Tristan left Eastwick, Frank had been married to his first wife. Now Vanessa would have to explain the new, younger, recently acquired model and he would draw the inevitable comparison. Vanessa had heard it all before. She and Delia were not kindred spirits—as Delia had wanted to believe when she first sailed into the choppy waters of Eastwick society—but they had both improved their financial and social status immeasurably when they married significantly older men.

She could not speak for Delia's motives, but she had married Stuart for his money. It was the one fact Tristan had got absolutely right.

Four

"Delia is Frank's current wife."

"His current wife?" Tristan asked. "How many Mrs. Forresters have there been, exactly?"

"Delia is the third."

Not unusual in a place as affluent as Fairfield County, with men as wealthy as Frank Forrester. Or Stuart Thorpe. "Has she been the current Mrs. Forrester for long?"

"Delia and Frank met at this same charity polo event last summer. She was working as a freelance journalist, I believe, and she chose to feature Frank in an article on business leaders who'd retired here on the gold coast. They married soon after."

Alerted by the measured choice to her words and the defensive tilt of her chin, Tristan narrowed his eyes. "Love at first sight?"

"Is that so hard to believe?"

"I haven't met Delia. You tell me."

"You know, that's never come up in conversation," she countered coolly. "I'm not that close to Delia and, frankly, I'm not comfortable discussing her."

Tristan studied her for a moment, his interest piqued by the words and the attitude. Obviously she got along fine with Frank…but not his wife? He had to wonder about that.

And since she was tucking her dinky little purse under her arm with a note of I'm-about-to-leave finality, he might as well wonder out loud.

"Is there something I should know about her before I start making social engagements?" He gestured toward the door, indicating she should precede him. Wariness clouded her green eyes and her mouth tightened slightly because, naturally, she'd have liked to walk away. Alone.

Too bad because he intended seeing her to her car.

And getting a response to his question about Delia.

"Is there a reason you're not close?" he persisted after they'd cleared the tables and were crossing the restaurant foyer. She wasn't exactly dawdling but he kept up easily, a hand low on her back steering her toward the elevators. "Because I'd have thought you would have plenty in common."

Halting abruptly, she turned to him. Green sparks flared in her eyes. "Don't presume too much, Tristan. You've never met Delia. And you only think you know me."

For a moment the inherent challenge in her words was secondary to the impact of her nearness. She'd turned into his ushering arm, so swiftly that the swing of her hair brushed his arm and shoulder. Several strands had caught against his dark jacket, and when he inhaled—a quick flare of his nostrils, a sharp suck of air—he breathed her delicate floral scent and the combination rocked his brain and libido with dizzying temptation.

He knew better than to touch but he did it anyway.

With his free hand he lifted those rogue strands from his jacket and coiled them around his fingers. Her hair was as fine and silky soft as he'd imagined but surprisingly cool, unlike the flush of heat in her throat and the softening of her full lips.

Completely unlike the bolt of energy that crackled in the air as their eyes met and held.

"Is that a challenge?" he asked.

She blinked slowly, as if lost in the moment and the dangerous vibration pulsing between them. "What do you mean?"

"To get to know you better."

Behind them the elevator announced its arrival. The subtle electronic distraction brought her head up and back, breaking eye contact and forcing him to release her hair. A couple exited the elevator, hand in hand and so absorbed in each other they'd have walked right through him and Vanessa—or a herd of stampeding buffalo—if he hadn't backed out of the way.

"Not at all," she responded once they were alone again. "It was a statement of fact. You haven't met Delia Forrester and yet you presumed a similarity between us."

"You're unlike?"

"We are different." She held his gaze. "Very different."

He thought she would say more—it was there in

her eyes, a darkening of purpose, a fleeting moment of gravity—but then she made a little gesture he interpreted as forget-about-it and started walking.

He caught up with her in two strides.

"I'm going to take the stairs," she said crisply. Then, when he continued at her side, she cut him a sharp look. "There's no need for you to accompany me."

"I'll see you to your car."

"I am valet parked. There's no need."

He didn't argue, he just kept walking, not to be difficult or perverse but to see her safely to her car. It was the right thing to do. So was letting go the subject of Delia Forrester—he would find out the differences soon enough.

He would make up his own mind.

While waiting for her car, they made stilted small talk about the hotel and its first-rate service and, when her Mercedes Cabriolet appeared, about the car itself. Then, before she slid into the driver's seat, came a moment of awkwardness, as she said goodbye in a stiffly formal way.

"Not goodbye." Tristan dismissed the valet with a look and met her eyes over the sports car's low door. "I will see you at the polo match. Frank said everyone will be there—I assume that includes you?"

"Please don't do this," she said in a rush of entreaty. "Please don't use this as a venue to ask questions about me."

"This afternoon you didn't have any qualms. I recall you wishing me luck."

"This afternoon you caught me by surprise."

The surprise of that kiss, of each touch, of their unwanted attraction, arced between them in the tense stillness of the night. Nothing needed to be said; it was all there, in the unspoken moment. As was the root of their conflict, the part that was no surprise. "And now you're suggesting I shouldn't ask questions about you?"

"I'm asking that you respect the privacy of others." She moistened her lips, and the sweet warmth of her kiss licked through his veins again. "You said this was between you and me, but it's not. You will hurt others, if you go around asking questions and starting rumors and drawing attention to our feud. Think about it, please. Think about doing the right thing."

Standing so close, Tristan felt the candor of her appeal reach out and take a grip. She'd never asked anything of him before, not so directly, not with a *please* that chased the memory of her taste and the scent of her hair on a wild scrambling scurry beyond his blood and his male hormones to a closely guarded place beyond.

"I am doing the right thing," he assured her…and reminded himself. "I've never doubted that."

For a brief instant he thought there was more, a response or another appeal, and deep in his gut he hoped for the latter. A *please, Tristan* that was only about them and had nothing to do with their conflict. But then she pressed her lips together and just before she slid into the driver's seat, he glimpsed something else deep in her eyes, something that shifted like a darkening shadow.

Whatever was going on with her, he would find out.

Steel coated his resolve and his voice as he watched the glossy vehicle glide from beneath the hotel portico onto the street. "If you have nothing to hide, duchess, then why that appeal? What do you have to fear? And who the hell are you protecting?"

A block away from the Marabella, Vanessa expelled a soft gust of held back breath. Finally she was able to breathe and think again—two basics she had difficulty with in Tristan's company. And now she was functioning at something like normality, the tight, sick feeling she'd experienced earlier returned with a vengeance.

Tonight had been a complete waste of time. Had she really thought she could sit at the same table and pretend he hadn't turned her world on its head with his arrival and his condemnation and his hot-blooded kiss?

"Not a kiss," she reminded herself vehemently, and a fat lot of good that did! Rolling her shoulders and gripping the steering wheel tightly did not halt the rush of heat, either. Even now, all these hours later, she could still feel the sizzle.

What was that about?

The sad part was, Vanessa didn't know. She'd never experienced anything like this before. Ever. No boyfriends, no stolen kisses, no illicit make out sessions. Nothing but work and caring for Lew and then a whole new world of opportunity through her friendship with Stuart Thorpe.

"Why him?" She thumped the steering wheel with one fisted hand. "Why did it have to be him?"

Tonight, unfortunately, she'd witnessed an unexpected side to her nemesis. Smiling in the moonlight, challenging her over his kissing technique, charming and at ease with Frank Forrester, showing her to her car like a gentleman.

She growled low in her throat and thumped the wheel again.

And what are you going to do about it, duchess?

Hearing the silent question in *his* dark chocolate drawl did not help her mood of frustrated disquiet.

"Nothing," she muttered, but that response hung over her like a dark-shadowed indictment of her failure tonight. She shifted in her seat and reconsidered. Okay. About this unwanted attraction, she would do nothing.

But that wasn't her real problem...

She still had no proof of the letter's validity, and he believed he had grounds to steal her security and Lew's future away from her.

Paused at an intersection, she checked for traffic. Down the street to her left stood the offices of Cartwright and Associates, a place she'd come to know oh so well in the past two years. The place where she should have taken the news of Tristan's arrival and allegations this afternoon.

As Stuart's lawyer and now hers, Jack Cartwright was one of the handful of people who knew about Lew, and right now she could do with his clear head and logical approach. She checked the dashboard clock and winced. Although Jack and his wife Lily were close friends, they were expecting their first baby in a month's time and calling this late felt like an imposition.

Not that she wasn't tempted...but, no. First thing in the morning she would call and arrange a meeting. The earlier the better.

* * *

After sleeping poorly Vanessa was up and dressed before dawn, but she managed to hold off calling the Cartwright home until seven o'clock. Then she kicked herself because Jack had gone into the office already. She exchanged small talk with Lily for all of six seconds before the other woman picked up on the strain in her voice. "Is everything all right, Vanessa?"

"No, not really. Tristan Thorpe's in town." Which, really, was the sum total of her problems. "I need to talk to Jack. I'll call him at the office."

"I have a better idea. Why don't you come over here and have breakfast with us?" Lily suggested. "Jack will be home in an hour or so. He went in early to brief an associate on a court appearance because he's taking the morning off. Doctor's appointment."

"Is everything all right?"

Lily chuckled. "As far as I know, but Mr. Protective insists on taking me, every time."

Vanessa didn't want to intrude on their morning plans but Lily insisted. And right on eight o'clock she was following her heavily pregnant friend into the kitchen of the Cartwrights' two-story colonial home. And it was a home, as bright and cheerful and welcoming as the glowing Lily.

Lily was a recent addition to the circle of friends known as the Debs Club and Vanessa had felt an immediate kinship. Possibly because she, too, had grown up in a tough environment unlike the rest of the group who truly were debs. Lily, too, had struggled to fit into this privileged society in the early months of her marriage, but she and Jack had worked things out and now the happiness she deserved showed on her face.

"Jack's not home yet." Lily rolled her eyes but with a cheerfulness that said she didn't mind. Her man would be home soon and that suited her fine. "I called to let him know you were coming over so he shouldn't be long. Can I get you coffee? Tea? Juice?"

"Oh, please, you don't have to wait on me. Sit down."

"And take a weight off?"

"Yes. Exactly." For the first time she let her eyes rest on the other woman's belly and she felt an unfamiliar twinge of longing, a reaction she hid behind a smile. "Are you sure that's not twins in there?"

"Sometimes I swear there are three." Lily paused in the middle of making a pot of tea. Her expressive blue eyes grew dreamy. "Not that I would mind."

Of course she wouldn't. Her down-to-earth honesty combined with her caring nature and a street-smart wisdom had made her a wonderful social worker and would make her an equally wonderful mother.

Lucky kids, Vanessa thought, and the pang in her middle intensified.

"So." Teapot in hand, Lily waddled across to the table and lowered herself carefully into a chair. "Tell me about Tristan Thorpe."

For once Vanessa was relieved to bring him into the conversation—anything to stifle this bizarre attack of motherhood envy. She had no idea where that had sprung from, all of a sudden. "He arrived yesterday. He's staying at the Marabella. He's even more aggra-vating face-to-face."

"You've seen him already?" Lily propped her chin in a hand, all eager-eyed curiosity. "Do tell."

Where should she start? What could she say without giving away the depth of her confusion and conflict? Just saying *face-to-face* had brought a guilty warmth to her cheeks, mostly because it put her in mind of mouth-to-mouth.

And hadn't *that* wild sensual memory kept her company all through the night!

"There's probably no need for me to tell you anything," she said, recalling one of the other things that had kept her awake. "You will hear it all on the grapevine soon enough."

"All?"

"I met with him at the Marabella restaurant last night."

"You went to dinner with him?" Surprise rounded Lily's eyes. "Did anyone survive?"

Vanessa pulled a face. "Barely. As luck would have it, Frank Forrester happened along."

"With Delia?"

"No, but he'll tell her that he ran into us. You know Delia. She needs to know everything that's going on."

"Unfortunately, yes."

Delia had really stuck her claws into Lily, for no apparent reason other than her friendship with the Debs. That ugliness had exposed a whole new side of Delia Forrester—a side that turned Vanessa ice-cold with anxiety when she thought about—

"Hey, what's the matter?"

Vanessa blinked, and realized that her worried frown had drawn Lily's question. She started to wave her friend's concern aside, then changed her mind. Of all the Debs, Lily would most likely understand.

"I was thinking about how these people—the Delias of this world—can tear a person apart for no reason. A whisper here, a catty comment there, and before you know it everyone is talking and wondering." She took a breath. "Have you heard any rumors about me?"

"What kind of rumors?"

"Oh, that I'm meeting a man in secret. That I have been for years."

"Where on earth did this come from?" Lily's eyes narrowed. "Tristan?"

"He says he got a letter, from someone over here—" she spread her hands to indicate Eastwick, their home "—claiming there is proof."

Something flickered in Lily's eyes and she sat up straighter. She opened her mouth, about to speak, but then her focus shifted, distracted by the sound of footsteps. As her husband came into view her expression transformed, growing bright and soft and incandescent with love.

Although Jack greeted Vanessa with an apology for his tardiness, it was a fleeting acknowledgment of her presence. Because then he was smiling at his wife as he leaned over and pressed a chaste kiss to her forehead and touched a gently protective hand to her stomach.

It was nothing and it was everything, a symbol of the intimacy of their small family circle and a reminder of what she, Vanessa, had never experienced and could never contemplate for herself.

Suddenly her throat felt thick with a desperate sense

of yearning. It was ridiculous, hopeless, frustrating. She didn't even want this love, this coupledom, this family deal. She had everything she wanted, everything necessary and important, and there was no room or time or emotional energy left for anything else.

"So, I hear that Tristan Thorpe is in town." Jack straightened, his expression smoothing into business professional. It seemed that the news had traveled even faster than she'd anticipated. "Is he here to make trouble?"

"He got a letter," Lily supplied, and her husband went very still. His eyes narrowed on Vanessa. "The same as the others?"

"The…others?" Vanessa repeated stupidly, and in the same instant it struck her what they meant.

Two anonymous extortion letters had been sent several months back, one to Jack and one to Caroline Keating-Spence. She shook her head slowly, kicking herself for not considering this connection.

"I don't know. I haven't seen the letter yet." Her heart beat hard in her chest, a thick pulse of dismay, as she looked from Jack's still countenance to Lily's worried frown and back again. As the full ramifications took hold. "Do you really think this could be the same person? That it might be the same man…the one Abby thinks killed Bunny?"

Five

Tristan had a breakfast meeting, too. Not with his lawyer but with the private investigator engaged by his lawyer to look into Vanessa's alleged adultery. The P.I. turned out to be a retired cop who was punctual, professional and personable.

Tristan dismissed him anyway.

His decision was split-second, gut instinct. Sitting in a Stamford coffee house watching the guy demolish a towering stack of pancakes while he delivered the lowdown on his snooping techniques, he pictured Vanessa's face when she'd appealed to his sense of fair play. Same as last night, he felt the grip of her emotion as she looked him in the eye and hit him with the reminder that this was between the two of them.

That didn't mean he'd changed his mind, only his tactics.

Instead of employing a third party to dig into her affairs, he'd take up the shovel himself.

Instead of arranging for the letter to be sent to her lawyer, he collected it and brought it back to Eastwick. His aim: to deliver it personally.

Turning into White Birch Lane, he pulled over to make way for a horse float and the need to brake and control his deceleration alerted him that he'd been driving too fast. Worse, he realized that his haste was geared by a different anticipation from his first visit to her home. Edgy, yes, but colored by memories of her smile and her taste and the spark of a fiery inner passion when she faced up to his hard-line tactics.

Vanessa might look the picture of Nordic cool but he'd seen her gather that poise around herself like a protective cloak. Measured, learned, practiced—whatever, he knew it was fake and he couldn't help wondering why she felt the need to adopt a facade. He couldn't help wondering what she was hiding, and a frown pulled hard at his brow.

He'd spent a good portion of the night wondering about her, uncomfortable with how much he wanted to know. It was an alarm and a warning.

Get to know her, yes, but don't forget why.

After the lumbering trailer disappeared, Tristan continued at a more sedate pace. He allowed himself to glance around, to take in the big homes set back from the road on finely manicured acreages. His frown deepened as he contemplated Frank Forrester's reference to coming home.

He didn't feel any more sense of homecoming today

than yesterday, not even when he turned into the drive where he'd learned to ride a bicycle, not passing the first tree he'd climbed, not even looking out over the grass where he'd first kicked a football.

All he felt was the same gut-kick of bitterness and the keener edge of anticipation. He had to remind himself, again, of his purpose.

He wasn't here to see her, to visit with her, to spar with her—he was here to deliver the letter.

That didn't prevent the crunch of disappointment when the housekeeper—Gloria—opened the door and informed him, with great glee, that Mrs. Thorpe was out and not expected home until late in the afternoon.

Okay. This could still work. In fact, if Gloria didn't mind talking, this could work out even better.

"I didn't ever get that tea yesterday." He smiled and was rewarded with the suspicious narrowing of the woman's eyes. "Is the invitation still open?"

"I guess I could manage a pot of tea."

She stepped back and let him precede her into the foyer.

"So," he said, picking up his shovel and turning the first sod. "Have you worked for Mrs. Thorpe a long time?"

After visiting with Gloria, Tristan returned to his hotel to catch up on some business. He'd sold his share in Telfour very recently and was still fielding calls and e-mails daily. Then there was his position on two company boards plus an enticing offer to join a business start-up, which had influenced his decision to sell.

He was still considering that direction and monitoring a couple of other options.

The busyness suited him fine. He didn't know how to do nothing and immersing himself in his normal business world served as the perfect touchstone with reality. He'd needed that after the last twenty-four hours.

Thus immersed, he picked up the buzzing phone expecting to hear his assistant's voice, only to be disappointed.

Delia Forrester hadn't waited for him to call. He didn't much care for the woman's overly familiar manner but he accepted her invitation to join their party at Sunday's polo match, regardless.

After the call, his concentration was shot so he headed to the hotel's pool. His natural inclination was to swim hard, to burn off the excess energy in his limbs and his blood and his hormones. But after a couple of hard laps he forced himself to ease off to a lazy crawl. He refused to cede control to a situation and a woman and an untenable attraction.

Up and down the pool he loped, distracting himself by thinking about last night's encounter with Frank Forrester, conjuring up vague memories of him and his first wife—Lyn? Linda? Lydia?—spending weekends out of the city at the Thorpe home.

And now, for all the brightness of his conversation, Frank looked worn out. Had his father aged as badly? Had he grown frail and stooped?

Worn out from keeping up with a young, fast, social-climbing wife when he should have been taking it easy with his life's companion, enjoying the rewards he'd earned through decades of hard work?

Without realizing it, Tristan had upped his tempo to a solid churning pace, driven by those thoughts and by the effort of *not* thinking about his father with Vanessa.

Too young, too alive, too passionate.

All wrong.

He forced himself to stop churning—physically and mentally—at the end of the lap. Rolling onto his back, he kicked away from the edge and there she was, standing at the end of the pool, as if conjured straight out of his reflections.

Or possibly not, he decided on a longer second glance.

Dressed in a pale blue suit, with her hair pulled back and pinned up out of view, her eyes and half her face hidden behind a pair of large sunglasses, she looked older, stiffer, all polish and composure and money.

She didn't look happy, either, but then he'd expected as much when he decided not to leave the letter with Gloria.

He knew he'd hear about it—and that she'd possibly come gunning for him—but he hadn't expected her this early in the day. Not when he'd been told she had a full day of important charity committee meetings.

Despite all that, he felt the same adrenaline spike as last night in the restaurant and this morning walking up to her door. The same, only with an added rush of heat, which didn't thrill him. To compose himself, he swam another lap and back, forcing himself to turn his arms over—slow and unconcerned.

Then he climbed from the pool in a long, lazy motion and collected his towel from a nearby lounger. All the while, he felt her watching him and his body's unwelcome response undid all the good work of those relaxing last laps.

Thank God for jumbo-size hotel towels.

Walking back to where she stood, Tristan subjected her to the same thorough once-over. Payback, he justified. She didn't move a muscle, even when he came to a halt much too close, and he wondered if her shoes—very proper, with heels and all to match the suit—had melted into the poolside tile.

"A little overdressed for a dip, aren't you?"

A small furrow between her brows deepened. She moistened her lips, as if perhaps her mouth had all dried out. "I didn't come here to swim."

"Pity. It's the weather for it."

"Yes, it's hot but—"

"You want to get out of the sun?" Tristan inclined his head toward the nearest setting with a big shady umbrella. What a difference a day makes. Twenty-four hours ago he'd been in the business suit, knocking at her door. Now she was on his turf and he aimed to milk the reversal in power for all it was worth.

"No." She shook her head. "I only came for the letter. Gloria rang to tell me you'd called around but you wouldn't leave it."

"I didn't know if I should."

She made an annoyed sound with her tongue and teeth.

"Last night you specifically asked that we keep this between you and me," he reasoned.

"Which is why you insinuated yourself into my house and interrogated my housekeeper?"

Ah. He'd thought she mightn't approve of that. "Gloria kindly made me tea."

"Did she kindly tell you what you needed to know?"

"She told me you were tied up with meetings all day." He allowed his gaze to drift over her charity-meeting outfit. "Yet here you are."

He sensed her gathering frustration, but she took a minute to glance around the surroundings and the little clusters of tourists and the discreetly hovering staff. If she'd been about to stomp on his bare foot with one of her weapon-shaped heels or to launch herself fully clothed into the pool, she resisted. Her elegantly dimpled chin came up a fraction. "I am here to fetch the letter. Do you have it or don't you?"

"I have it, although—" he patted his hips and chest where he might have found pockets, had he been wearing clothes "—not on me."

Despite the dark Jackie O.-size shades, he tracked the shift of her gaze as she followed his hands down his torso. Then, as if suddenly aware of what she was doing and where she was looking, her head snapped up. "I didn't mean *on you*. Is it in your room?"

"It is. You want to come up and get it?"

"No," she replied primly. "I would like you to go up and get it. I will wait in the lounge."

Vanessa didn't give him a chance to bait her further. She turned smartly on her heel and walked away. Yes, he tracked her departure all the way across the long terrace. Yes, that filled her sensory memory with images of his bare tanned length wet and glistening from the pool. Of those muscles flexing and shifting as he toweled himself off. Of the blatant male beauty of a strong toned abdomen, of dark hair sprinkled across his chest and trailing down his midline and disappearing into his brief swimming trunks.

Heat flared in her skin then shivered through her flesh as she crossed from the wicked midafternoon sunshine into the cool shade of the hotel interior. She chose a secluded seat away from the terrace windows and surreptitiously fanned her face while she waited.

And waited.

She ordered an iced water and checked her watch. And realized the waiting and waiting had actually been for little more than five minutes. Time, it seemed, had taken on a strange elongated dimension since she opened the door exactly twenty-four hours ago.

In that time so little had happened and yet so much had changed. None of it made sense…except, possibly, the buff body. He'd been an elite athlete, after all, and any woman with functional eyesight would have found herself admiring those tight muscles.

It wasn't personal.

Vanessa exhaled through her nose, exasperated with herself. She didn't check her watch again.

Assuming he showered and dressed, he could be five or ten minutes or more. And although she hoped he did shower and dress, she didn't want to think about him showering and dressing.

To pass the time she scoped the room, wincing when she noticed Vern and Liz Kramer at a table not too far away. Vern and Stuart went way back. While she liked

the Kramers, she didn't want to deal with another introduction and everything-is-fine conversation like last
night's episode with Frank. She just wanted to get the
letter and get out of here.

The letter.

Another shiver feathered over her skin with the realization of a purpose and an anxiety forgotten from the
second she saw Tristan's strong, tan body slicing effort-
lessly through the azure water. Finally she would get to
see this piece of evidence. She could make her decision
on how to proceed: whether to take Andy's advice and
tell all, or follow Jack's counsel in revealing as little as
necessary.

Since this morning's breakfast discussion, she'd had
little time to weigh the options. Jack's version tempted
her because doing nothing, saying nothing, was always
easier. But was it best for Lew? She just didn't know.
But seeing the letter—her heart raced as a tall, familiar,
fully-dressed figure entered the room—she hoped,
would make up her mind.

Although she'd watched him arrive, Vanessa looked
away to take a long sip from her water. Then he was
there, standing beside her chair, an envelope in his hand.
Her whole stomach went into free fall and she had to
close her eyes against a dizzying attack of anxiety.

"Are you all right?" he asked.

She nodded. From the corner of her eye she saw Liz
Kramer peering their way and she sucked in a quick
breath. "Can we go somewhere more private? I'm afraid
some more old friends are about to come over here."

To his credit, he didn't turn and look. "There's the

guest library downstairs. Or I could arrange a private meeting room—"

"The library will do fine. Thank you."

Tristan stood back, hands in pockets, while she turned the envelope over in her hands. He tried not to notice the pale trepidation on her face. Or the tremor of her fingers as she drew the single sheet of folded paper from inside.

But he couldn't ignore the tightening in his chest and gut, the desire to reach out and…hell…do what? Take the bloody letter back? Ignore his reason for holding onto it this morning, so he could hand it to her and judge her reaction?

Logic said she wouldn't look so uncharacteristically nervous—she of the cool poise and composure—unless she were guilty.

Damn it all to blazes, he needed that guilt. He should be turning up the heat, pushing and prodding her into a hot-tempered admission. Except she looked too fearful and vulnerable and he couldn't. Not yet.

"It's white," she murmured, so low he wouldn't have made out the words if he weren't so intensely focused on her face. Her lips. The wide bemused eyes she suddenly raised up to his. "This is the original? Not a copy?"

"That's the original." Then, when she continued to sit there studying the paper and the envelope, he asked, "Aren't you going to read it?"

Perhaps she'd been building up her nerve or delaying the inevitable, because now she unfolded the letter and scanned it quickly. When she got to the end, she stared at the page for a full minute. He couldn't tell *what* she was thinking only that she *was* thinking. In the silence of the large library room, deserted but for them, he could almost hear the wheels turning and the gears engaging.

But when she finally spoke it wasn't to point out the lack of concrete proof in the letter's content, as he'd expected. It was to ask, "Why would somebody do this?"

Hands deep in his pockets, Tristan shrugged. "To create trouble for you."

"Well, they've succeeded there," she said dryly, surprising him again…and reminding him of her first baffling reaction.

He nodded toward the letter. "You commented on the white paper." She'd also asked if it was a copy. "What's going on, Vanessa? What aren't you telling me?"

"I…"

Vanessa paused, her chest tight with indecision. Despite Jack's instructions to divulge as little as possible, she wanted to share. Yesterday, no. Out by the poolside, no way. But this man had shown a new consideration, in fetching the letter so promptly, in whisking her away to a private room without question, in standing aside and letting her read in peace.

Besides, telling him about the letters would take the focus off her and the secret she didn't want to share. This one he would probably hear anyway, if he hadn't already, on the town grapevine.

"A couple of months back," she commenced slowly, decision made, "two people I know here in Eastwick each received an anonymous letter. I thought…I had thought…this one might be connected."

"Now you think not, because the paper's different?"

"And there's no demand of any kind."

He went still. "Are you saying these other letters contained extortion demands?"

"Yes."

"Demanding what? What's the link?"

"Did you know Bunny Baldwin?" she asked. "Lucinda was her real name but everybody called her Bunny. She was married to Nathan Baldwin, a friend of Stuart's. I thought you might have known them when you lived here."

"It's been twenty years."

"You remembered Frank Forrester."

"He and his first wife spent a lot of time at our house."

Oh. She looked away, unaccountably stung by the sudden hard cast to his eyes. *Our house*. Did he still feel that attachment? Was that why he was so bound and determined to win the estate back?

She wanted to ask, to know his true motivation, but he cut through her thoughts and reminded her of the subject at hand.

"I take it this Bunny Baldwin is the link between the letters?"

"Yes." A sick, tight feeling twisted her stomach as she thought about poor Bunny. Although the woman had been fearsomely intimidating—and had cast some speculation about Vanessa marrying so spectacularly well—she'd also been mother to one of Vanessa's closest friends. "She passed away a few months ago. They thought it was a heart attack but Abby, her daughter, discovered her journals missing. Long story short, the police are now reinvestigating her death."

"Because of some missing journals?"

"Have you heard of the *Eastwick Social Diary*?"

His answer was a noncommittal, "Refresh my memory."

"It's a gossipy newsletter and Web site column about who's who and doing what—" or *whom* "—in Eastwick. Bunny was the writer and editor, and the journals contain her notes and sources plus all the material she chose not to print."

"Chose not to?"

Too agitated to sit, Vanessa rose to her feet and slowly circled the seating arrangement. This connection to his letter and its allegations had to be broached, as much as she dreaded how the conversation would go down. "I gather she thought some stories were too scandalous or damaging or potentially libelous to print."

That's all she had to say. The sharp speculation in his eyes indicated he'd joined the dots without needing further clues. "These journals were stolen and the thief has attempted to blackmail persons named in the journal?"

"That seems the likely explanation."

"And you think it's possible the same person sent the letter to me?"

"I thought so." She lifted her hands and let them drop. "But then it's not the same stationery."

"You think a blackmailer uses the same paper every time?"

"I don't know. I don't know what to think. Do you?"

"There's no hint of extortion," he said after a moment's pause. "And if this person did have blackmail in mind, he'd have sent the letter to you. To entice *you* to pay hush money."

She exhaled on a long note of resignation. Yes, he was right. Although… "Do you believe there's no connection to Bunny and the journals? Because this is rather a big coincidence, a third anonymous letter whose source could have been the same as the first two."

He regarded her silently for a long second. "What are you trying to sell me here? What's your angle?"

"I don't have an angle. I'm just trying to work out the motivation behind this letter."

"And?"

Surprised he'd detected the nebulous hint of more in her words, she looked back at him warily. Then, she decided to tell him. "What if the thief read something in the journals and misinterpreted? What if the person referred to as having an affair wasn't me at all? A lot of the diary pieces are *guess who, don't sue*. Names are not named. What if he has the wrong person?"

"That doesn't explain why he sent the letter to me."

Vanessa narrowed her eyes. "You aren't prepared to listen to my side at all, are you?"

"I listened."

"And now what? You'll have me investigated?"

"Yes," he said, that blue gaze unflinchingly direct. "I will continue to investigate. I also think we should speak to the police."

"The police?"

"You said they were investigating Bunny's death and, I imagine, the extortion demands. Whether it's connected or not, they should see this letter."

Six

"I heard a whisper that Tristan Thorpe's in town."

Felicity Farnsworth's casual comment dropped like a brick into the calm pool of after-lunch conversation, bringing all eyes straight to Vanessa.

Blast.

She'd rather hoped the drama surrounding Emma's upcoming wedding—she wanted small, while her parents had invited half of Eastwick—would keep the focus off her. That's the way she preferred things anyway, including at the regular Debs Club luncheons. These women—Felicity, Lily, Abby Talbot, Emma Dearborn and Mary Duvall—were her friends. Smart, warm, kind, inclusive, they'd invited her into their group, onto their charity committees and into their confidence.

Now, more than ever, she felt the weight of guilt

because she hadn't been so forthcoming. In six years of regular get-togethers she'd tiptoed around her past and her reason for marrying Stuart and becoming part of Eastwick society.

Although she had shared much of her angst in battling Tristan over the will, hence the girlfriends' questions now.

"Is he here about the will contest?" Abby asked.

"Where is he staying?" Caroline wanted to know. "Have you met him, Vanessa?"

"Yes, have you seen the beast?" Felicity continued.

Carefully Vanessa put down her coffee. "Yes, I've met with him." *I've also fought with him, kissed him, ogled him in swimmers, and accompanied him to the police station.* "He's staying at the Marabella and, yes, he is here about the will. In a way."

"You sound remarkably calm," Emma decided. "Is that a good sign? Or are you sedated?"

"Is he dropping the contest?" Felicity asked. "He must know he's beating a dead horse."

"Tristan doesn't think so," Vanessa replied. "In fact, he's here because he believes he's found a way to beat me."

They all responded pretty much at once, a mixture of scoffing remarks and how-so questions. And so she filled them in on the letter's allegations, the no-adultery clause in Stuart's will, and finally this morning's meeting with the detectives handling Bunny's case.

Silence followed, an unusual happenstance when this group met. Abby recovered first, although she looked pale and strained. Not only had she lost her mother in sudden and suspicious circumstances, but she'd had to fight tooth and nail to have her suspicions recognized. "What did the police say?"

A lot, Vanessa answered silently, most of it uncomfortable questions about her relationship with Tristan and the—nonexistent—man referred to in the letter. To her friends she said, "They took us seriously enough when we showed them the letter. They asked a lot of questions, but in the end I'm not sure they think it's the same person."

"Why not?" Abby leaned forward, intent and focused. "It sounds exactly like the others."

Felicity nodded. "The lowlife who took the journals is selecting blackmail opportunities straight from the pages. It's only a matter of time before he hits pay dirt."

They all fell silent a moment, considering, before Emma asked, "Wouldn't he have tried to blackmail Vanessa though?"

"Would you have paid?" Felicity turned to Vanessa. "If the letter had come to you?"

"Why would I pay when the allegation is false?"

A couple of them exchanged looks, no one met her eye, and in the ensuing silence the bottom fell out of Vanessa's stomach. "You think I had a lover? While I was married to Stuart?"

"No, sweetie." Emma put a hand on hers. "Not us."

"Then…who?"

"There's been some talk," Caroline said.

And they hadn't told her? Hadn't mentioned these suspicions once? In all this time?

"You have to admit, you do keep parts of your life off-limits."

Felicity had spoken no less than the truth. Vanessa

had been secretive and this was the perfect opportunity to confide in her friends and garner their advice. That's what friends were for, after all. Not that she had much experience, especially with her peers, and that made this hard task even tougher.

Her intentions were good, but the words lodged in her throat. Before she could coax them free, Lily returned from the bathroom and there was much fussing over how long she'd been gone.

"I ran into Delia Forrester," she explained. "I couldn't get away."

"Poor you," Caroline murmured.

"Whatever did she want?" Emma asked.

"A favor." Lily pulled a wry face. "She needs an extra invitation to the polo benefit. Vanessa, it seems she's invited your good friend Tristan Thorpe."

Polo turned out to be a hard, fast and physical game—not for sissies as Frank Forrester had maintained. After several chukkers and with the help of some sideline experts, Tristan was catching on to the skilful intricacies of play and enjoying the breakneck end-to-end pace. As Frank's binoculars rarely strayed from the field, he wondered if the old bloke had been referring to the off-field action rather than the polo itself.

Tristan had a healthy cynicism for the games played by the beautiful people, and this charity benefit had brought out the best—and worst—players. Which brought his thoughts winging straight to Delia.

Frank had introduced his wife as "My favorite blonde," instantly tying her to the woman he'd referred to as his second-favorite at the Marabella restaurant. In those first few seconds Tristan rejected the connection out of hand. The two women were as different as Vanessa had claimed.

With her glossy facade and saccharine-sweet affectations, Delia was the kind of woman he'd expected—and wanted—to find living in his father's house. Vanessa Thorpe was not. The truth didn't slam into him. It had been creeping up on him for days, with every meeting, every new discovery, every disarming touch of warmth or vulnerability.

Acknowledging his error of judgment did unsettle him, however.

If he'd misjudged her character by the width of the Nullabor, could he also be wrong about other things?

Since seeing her response to the letter he'd been thinking a lot about the sender's motivation. He'd assumed someone had a vendetta against her. Back in Australia he'd believed it—a pushy young social climber could make plenty of enemies without even trying. But since arriving in Eastwick, the worst he'd heard about her was, "She holds her cards close to her chest."

A loud cheer rolled through the spectators' gallery, rousing Tristan from his introspection. The local team's number three had goaled, leveling the score. He'd learned early on that the Argentinean import was a great favorite with the partisan polo crowd.

Vanessa, too, had her fans. This Tristan measured from the locals' responses to him.

Too polite for blatant rudeness, many met him with a cool look or shook his hand with stiff formality. Others were more direct. Vern Kramer, for example, stated outright that he sympathized with his plight—"You're his son, after all"—but didn't approve his tactics. Vern was another of his father's oldest friends and one of the more vocal sideline polo experts.

Right now he was protesting an umpiring decision with much gusto. His wife took a large step back, disowning him with a wry shake of her head. "He's not mine. I don't know him."

Tristan waited a moment, watching the umpire award a penalty against the local team and smiling at the roasting that ensued. Then he acknowledged Liz Kramer whose large backward step had brought her—unwittingly—to his side. "How are you, Mrs. Kramer?"

"Well, thank you." Her greeting was polite, her tone frosty. Par for the course, although from Liz it stung. She'd been a close friend of his mother's, a frequent visitor at their home, and he remembered her fondly. "And you, Tristan? Are you enjoying being back home?"

Not the first time he'd been asked a variation of that question and he didn't understand the assumption any better with each repetition. "My home is in Sydney," he said, sick of making the polite answer. "This is a business trip."

"And are you enjoying that?"

There was a bite to her voice that suggested she knew his business. "Not particularly."

"Which makes me wonder why you're persisting."

"I have my reasons."

Eyes front, watching a melee of horses and mallets, he felt rather than saw Liz's gaze fix on his face. "How is your mother?"

"Recovering."

"She's been ill?"

He cut her a look and saw genuine concern in her eyes. It suddenly struck him that of all the conversations he'd had since arriving in Eastwick, Liz was the first to ask after his mother. He decided to tell her straight. "Breast cancer. She's had a tough few years."

"I'm sorry to hear that."

They watched the game in silence for several minutes. Then Liz said, "I hope she found the happiness she was chasing."

Tristan frowned. "Chasing?"

"When she left your father."

"I'd hardly define being tossed out with nothing as leaving."

He tried to keep the bitterness from his voice but wasn't sure he succeeded. Not when Liz made a soft clucking noise with her tongue, part sympathy, part reprimand. "She took *you*, Tristan, the most valuable thing from her marriage. Stuart was a long time getting over that."

But he *had* got over it. With the help of a beautiful new wife, and that stuck in Tristan's craw in a dozen disturbing ways now that he'd met Vanessa.

His gaze shifted beyond Liz, and—as he'd had done countless times in the past hours—he unerringly found Vanessa in the crowd. Despite the number and size of the hats blocking his view, despite the subtlety of her dress, despite the way she'd pinned her distinctive hair beneath a pretty little lace and net construction.

The awareness was there, like a visual magnetism. He didn't seek her out. He looked up and like sunshine, she was there. Since acknowledging how much his attitude to her had changed, since recognizing the dangerous pull of this attraction, he'd kept his distance. Not exactly avoiding her, just proving to himself that he could resist the urge.

"He was so lucky to find Vanessa. She is a treasure."

He looked back at Liz, found she'd followed the direction of his gaze. "I've heard that more than once today," he said dryly. "A treasure. A good gal. An angel."

"Feeling like you've been cast with horns and a trident?"

"Somewhat."

With a soft chuckle, Liz lifted her empty champagne flute and looked him in the eye. For the first time he saw the familiar sparkle of her humor. "If you'd like to take the first step toward redemption, you can fetch me a refill."

Vanessa thought she felt him watching her. Again. But when she turned in that direction—and all day she'd known exactly where he stood, sat, lounged—she found her imagination was playing tricks. Again.

This time he was intent in conversation with Liz Kramer. With his head dipped toward the shorter woman so a lock of sun-tinged hair fell across his forehead, he looked younger and warmer and more at ease than Vanessa had seen him. Then someone moved and blocked her view and she turned away, heart racing and her mouth gone dry.

Anxiety, she decided. And trepidation because of what he might be discussing with Liz and with countless others before her.

And who are you kidding?

Not her pragmatic self, obviously. She knew these responses had nothing to do with their conflict and everything to do with the man.

Was he ignoring her on purpose?

No, Ms. Pragmatist answered. *He is doing what he set out to do.* Mixing, meeting, talking. And learning absolutely nothing because there was nothing for him to discover—at least nothing that wasn't rumor and whispers about her secretive side.

Thinking of the *talk* her friends had told her about took her mind off Tristan, at least. Not that being talked about was a biggie for Vanessa—she'd grown up with fingers pointed her way. *That's the girl with the freakoid brother. Did you hear her daddy got arrested again last night? They're such a loser family.* She didn't care what others said about her; she did mind that her friends might have believed her capable of infidelity.

And she hated that she'd frozen when she should have told them the reason for her mysterious behavior.

The sea of summer frocks and lightweight suits, of hats and champagne flutes and imported longneck beers shifted again, parting as if by a divine hand to reveal him again. Walking toward her, a bottle of vintage Veuve Clicquot in one hand, a pair of flutes in the other. Dressed simply in a pale gray suit and open-necked white shirt— no more, no less than a hundred other men in the crowd— he commanded attention with his size, his presence, the way he moved with an athlete's grace and purpose.

She felt a burst of sensation, as though the pop of a

champagne cork had sent all the bubbles fizzing through her veins.

Not good, Vanessa. Not good at all.

In a bid to appear involved, she turned back to Felicity and Reed, Emma and Garrett, Jack and Lily…and discovered that while she'd been lost in introspection they'd moved on. Vaguely she recalled Lily wanting to sit down. Or Jack insisting she sit. Possibly she'd waved them on.

Now she was alone. And feigning surprise when she heard the rich drawl of Tristan's voice at her back. His actual words were swallowed by the thumping of her heart as she swung around.

He stood close enough for her to feel the impact of his electric blue gaze. A thousand watts all plugged in to her. He probably bought the whole wow-where-did-you-spring-from act because her mouth had gone slack and her throat tight and breathless while she just stood there staring up at him.

Help, her pragmatic self whimpered weakly. She feared that side of her was about to go down for the count.

"I noticed your lack of champagne." The corner of his mouth quirked in a kind of crooked half smile. "I gather that's a transgression here."

The only transgression she could think of was her weak-kneed, weak-willed desire for a man she'd declared her enemy five days ago. How could this be happening?

That deadly attractive half smile had turned quizzical and Vanessa gave herself a mental shake. "Thank you," she said, a trifle huskily. "But no."

"This bottle is straight from Liz Kramer's stash, just opened, unspiked. Scout's honor."

"So you say, but you don't look like a Boy Scout. Can I trust your word?"

Something flickered in his eyes and in her blood. Perhaps that was the last gurgle of Ms. Pragmatist going under, because she appeared to be flirting with him. She, Vanessa Kotzur Thorpe, who had never flirted in her life.

He filled one of the slender glasses, then handed her the bottle. She regarded it suspiciously. "Take it," he said. "So I can defend my Boy Scout honor."

Their fingers brushed as she took the bottle, a thrilling little contact of skin on skin. She had barely recovered when he lifted the glass to his mouth. Their eyes met over the rim as he took a long, slow sip and the connection somehow seemed steeped in intimacy.

Without breaking eye contact, without saying a word, he held out the glass and temptation whispered through her blood. She wanted to take it from his hand, to place her lips on the same spot, to taste his heat on the icy cool glass.

More, she wanted to stretch on her toes and lick the golden chill from his lips. To kiss him the way she'd wanted to the first time.

"You still don't trust me?"

Vanessa wet her lips. "It's not that. I'm not drinking."

"Driving?"

"I don't drink." She volunteered the information without thought…and then kicked herself sharply. *Pay attention.* She didn't want to explain why she never touched alcohol, nor did she want to see in his eyes that he'd worked out the reason by snooping into her background.

She switched her gaze to the game, pretending to watch without seeing anything but a blur of activity. A team of monkeys mounted on camels could have taken to the field and she wouldn't have noticed...although she supposed they'd have needed extra-long-handled mallets.

After a moment the thick ache in her chest reminded her to relax and breathe. Today Tristan appeared relaxed, as if he were enjoying this as a social occasion rather than as an investigative opportunity. Perhaps he'd taken her appeal outside the Marabella to heart.

Perhaps he was biding his time.

Play thundered by close to the sideline and the air thickened with the scent of sweat and earth and the clash of contact between players. Vanessa blinked and focused. The umpire blew a foul eliciting a heated debate on who'd crossed whose line on the ball.

"How are you enjoying the polo?" she asked, genuinely curious.

"I like the game."

"But not the rest?"

He considered that a long moment, appearing to give it more weight than the casual inquiry commanded. "I'm enjoying today more than I'd thought. I hadn't realized so many people would remember me or want to know me. Given your popularity, I thought I might be the pariah."

"You're not?"

His small smile caused a large clamor in her system. "Can't say I haven't felt some coolness."

"Which hasn't dulled the curiosity."

"No."

Vanessa cast a glance over the crowd and found a degree of that curiousity trained on them. Many of the locals—her friends included—would be conjecturing over her chumminess with the enemy. A frown pulled at her brow so she considered the changed dynamic between them. She couldn't work out what had changed. The heat, the awareness, the attraction, she'd felt before, but today there was another element she couldn't pin down.

They weren't exactly comfortable and relaxed together but the tension had altered.

It reminded her of the one time she'd sat on a horse. The riding lessons were a birthday present from Stuart, but when the instructor hoisted her into the saddle she hadn't enjoyed the sensation one little bit. She'd hated losing touch with earth, of not knowing if the exhilaration would last or bring her crashing onto her backside.

She cast a cautious sideways glance at Tristan and caught him watching her. A weird sense of yearning fluttered to life in her chest, and her frown deepened as she quickly looked away. *Oh yes,* Ms. Pragmatist nodded. *You are so going to land on your backside.*

"Worried about what they're thinking?" he asked.

"Well, I am fraternizing with the enemy."

"I'm not the enemy, Vanessa." He eyes on hers were darkly serious. "Your real enemy is the person who wrote that letter."

Vanessa lost Tristan to Delia during the halftime divot-stomp and didn't see him again—no, that wasn't true, she couldn't help *seeing* him, but she didn't *talk to* him again—until she was walking toward her car at the end of the day. This time her wow-where-did-you-spring-from reaction wasn't contrived. One second she was picking her way carefully across a soggy patch of ground, trying not to identify the heavy weight pressing down on her chest as going-home-alone gloom, the next he was there at her side.

The weight lifted leaving her feeling ridiculously pleased…until she felt his gaze fix on her smile for an unnervingly long moment. Then she thought, *must stop grinning like a loon. Must think of something to say that doesn't sound like I'm ridiculously, pleased.*

"Did you enjoy the second half?" she asked, getting the smile under control. "I lost you during the break."

"I didn't know they really did that."

"Walk the divots? It's a time-honored tradition and the perfect chance to mix. Don't they do that at your Aussie football games?"

"Our mixer tradition is aimed at the kids. They all flock onto the ground for a kick at halftime."

Picturing the mayhem of hundreds of kids let lose on a football field, Vanessa allowed herself a half smile. "Slightly wilder and noisier than a divot-stomp, I imagine."

"Slightly."

"You looked as if you were enjoying yourself." Straight away she wished she'd kept that observation to herself. She also wished that the sight of Delia hanging off his arm, laughing, reaching up to brush something— or nothing—from his collar wasn't stuck in her visual memory. She had no hold on him and no right to the sharp stab of possessiveness.

"I enjoyed today," he said noncommittally.

"You seemed to fit right in."

He cut her a sideways look, as though trying to work out if she was having him on. Then something shifted in his expression, his gaze grew keen with perception. "And you, Vanessa. You fit in as if you were born to this life."

The warm glow of enjoyment brought on by his seeking her out and fanned by their banter, faded and died. But she might as well confirm what he'd probably already gleaned from Gloria or who knows where else. "My parents both worked for people like these, in the city. I spent some time observing the life."

"And you dreamed of living it?"

She shrugged. "What girl doesn't dream? It's the Cinderella fantasy."

They stopped beside her car, the last left in this row of the parking field, and she was searching her purse for her keys when he asked, "Why my father?"

Vanessa looked up sharply, not quite sure she'd heard him correctly. If she had, then she didn't understand the question. Intense blue eyes collided with hers for a heart-jolting moment before he looked away.

Before he waved a hand at the field still littered with Bentleys and Porsches and Mercedes. "You wanted this life, you could have had it with any man you wanted. Why my father?"

For a second she stared back at him, stunned by the question and then by its subtext. She'd set out to trap a rich man because of a childhood Cinderella fantasy. Then she kicked herself hard for her stupidity.

She'd known he held that opinion right from the first

time she spoke to him, so why should the question shock her now?

"I hope to God I'm reading you wrong," she said tightly, "and that you're not suggesting I could have done better than Stuart."

"Not better. Younger."

"Because a *younger* man could have given me what?" She huffed out a contemptuous breath. "For the life of me I cannot think of any man—younger, older, whatever—as kind and generous and concerned for others as Stuart Thorpe."

"What about your other needs, Vanessa?"

His meaning was clear in the dark burning light in his eyes, in the way he closed down the distance between them, in the sexual energy that seemed to pulse in the air as his gaze trailed slowly over her face and lingered on her mouth.

She shook her head slowly. This part of her marriage she discussed with no one. Not Gloria, not Andy, not Emma or Lily or any of her girlfriends. She'd promised to keep the platonic nature of their relationship a secret, to protect Stuart's pride as a man and to prevent the scuttlebutt of gossip.

"You're young," he persisted. "Didn't you want a family?"

"No."

It wasn't a lie, despite her recent pangs of baby envy. She'd already brought up her brother, taking over his care when she was little more than a child herself. She'd used up all her nurturing spirit. She had no emotional energy left for babies of her own. None whatsoever.

"No," she repeated, more adamantly. "I didn't want a family and I didn't need a lover. Your father gave me everything I wanted, everything I ever dreamed of wanting, and more. And he chose to leave his estate to me. Why can't you accept those truths? Why can't you go back to Australia and let me be?"

Seven

*G*o *home to Australia and let her be?*

No, Tristan couldn't do that. He could never quit a task half-done.

He still needed to know everything about Vanessa, but before he even approached her in the parking lot after the polo match he'd accepted that his motivation had shifted focus.

That's what drove him to ask why she'd chosen his father.

Frustration. Self-defense. Finding that full-bodied smile trained on him for the very first time, he'd felt a primal rush of possessiveness, a *she-should-be-mine* kick that transcended desire. He'd needed a reminder, damn fast, of why he couldn't get in that car and drive her back to his hotel and claim her as his own.

Her fervent response had done the trick. It had also convinced him of one of two things: either Vanessa had genuinely cared for her husband or she was one bloody fine actress.

And if he was out-of-the-ballpark wrong about her relationship with his father, was he wrong about other things?

Questions and conflicting answers chased through his mind all night long. At dawn he plunged his restless body into the hotel pool and slugged out a hundred laps. Afterward he'd intended returning to his suite and to his regular, controllable Monday morning of work, where questions had answers, where decisions triggered action, where results ensued.

Where he never backed down from the tough issues…or from digging too deeply because of a woman's heartfelt appeal. *I'm asking that you respect the privacy of others. Think about it, please. Think about doing the right thing.*

That plea still had his conscience tied in knots a week later.

Instead of working, he found himself driving out of town and into the sprawling midcountry estates, heading for White Birch Lane and a score of knotted intangibles. He needed facts. He needed truths.

Not only about Vanessa, but about the father he'd not spoken to since he left Eastwick as a twelve-year-old.

Focused on that result, he didn't consider the early hour until he was driving up to the closed and silent mansion. It was too early for her to be gone for the day but not too early, he discovered, to find her in the garden.

The morning sun was less than an hour old, its light as pale as her hair. As diaphanous as the shell-pink sweep of nothing that shaped her body. The image was soft and ethereal, an artist's rendition of *Girl with Flowers*, and Tristan stood transfixed by her beauty for a minute too long. Twenty yards of lawn and several bays of massed rose bushes away, he sensed her sudden stillness and the shock in her eyes when his presence registered.

The polite thing to do was acknowledge her, maybe with a teasing remark about wandering the grounds in her negligée, then retreat so she could dress in something more…substantial. The sensible thing was to turn on his heel and get the hell out of there without taking any more notice about what she was wearing or not wearing.

But he had noticed. His body ached with its impolite and not-sensible response to noticing.

The best he could do was keep a bed of rose bushes between them as he approached, an extra thorny-branched barrier to the one he was busy erecting in his mind.

She's out of bounds. She loved your father. She was his wife for five years.

No matter what resulted from their legal wrangle, from the letter's allegations, from his investigations, she could never be his.

The massed shrubs shielded much of her body from view, but it didn't help. He could still see her face, her throat, the skin framed by lace at her shoulders and breasts. And he could see what had brought her out of doors so early.

One of her gloved hands held a bunch of long-stemmed blooms; the other wielded a pair of lethal-looking shears. The part of his body that had noticed the diaphanous nightdress and the shape of her body beneath took due note.

"I hope I didn't startle you too much. Those things—" he inclined his head to indicate the shears "—look like they could do serious damage."

"I heard you drive up, so no."

"Yet you looked surprised."

"I thought you were Gloria, arriving early."

Her accompanying shrug caused her negligee's deep neckline to dip, and Tristan's hand itched to reach out and slide it back into place. With a silent curse he shoved both hands in his pockets, out of temptation's way. "I'm not Gloria."

"No," she said, as soft as the morning. "You're not."

Their gazes meshed for what felt like a long time. He could feel the pulse of attraction between them, a silent energy that hummed in the summer's morning. She felt it too—he could see it in her eyes and in the slight flush of her cheeks.

Hell. She felt it too.

He buried his hands deeper in his shorts. "I should have called first."

"It's fine, really."

"Really?"

"You saved me a phone call." A frown of concentration formed between her brows and turned her eyes serious. "I wanted to talk to you about what I said yesterday…or what I didn't say."

"About?"

"Your father. The will. I'm not backing down on anything I said, but on my way home yesterday and last night and this morning I was thinking—" She paused and although her eyes were clear, the dark smudges beneath flagged her lack of sleep. "I may have given the impression that Stuart didn't want you to have anything. That is not true."

"He left me a thousand bucks. To show he hadn't forgotten me."

"That was the lawyers' doing and not what I meant. He would have made you a beneficiary, Tristan, if you'd come to see him when he asked."

"Guess I must have missed that."

"I guess so," she said with a damn-you note to her voice. With great care she snipped off another pink bud and added it to her collection. The petals quavered—because her hands were shaking?—and when she looked up again, her eyes glistened with moisture. "Ignoring his letter, not even bothering to reply—that was just plain cruel, Tristan. He was your father and he was dying. Would it have hurt to swallow your pride and pick up the phone?"

Hit hard by the husky edge to her voice and the sheen of emotion in her eyes, it took a moment for the words and the message to register. Then everything inside him went still. "What letter?"

"He wanted to see you or at least to speak to you, to explain his side of the story. I suggested he write—that he might find that easier than trying to explain over the phone."

"And he sent it?"

"I posted it myself." She stared back at him, at first with that same hard edge as earlier and then with slowly dawning comprehension. "You really didn't receive it, did you? And when I tried to call…"

He'd deliberately stonewalled her, not taking the calls and then not returning her increasingly insistent messages until it was too late. His father had passed away an hour before.

What-might-have-been frustration swelled inside him, tightening his chest, his throat, his expression. "If he wanted to talk to me so badly, why the hell did he leave it so late?"

"Because he was as proud and as stubborn as you! He poured his heart and his soul into that letter and when you didn't reply, when he got nothing but stony silence, he gave up."

"But you didn't."

In her eyes, he saw that truth. She'd pushed Stuart to write the letter. And she'd made those calls when his father was hospitalized, a last ditch effort to reconcile them: the husband she'd loved and his only child.

"That's when he made up his mind about the will." Carefully she closed the shears and clicked the safety lock into place. The metallic snick punctuated the finality of his father's decision. Closed, done, ended. "He said you'd made your own life in Australia. You were a success. You didn't need his money and you didn't need him."

She was right. At thirty his time of needing a father had long passed into a faded, bitter memory of the years when he'd silently yearned for that support. Even if he had read the letter or if he'd taken her calls, he doubted it would have led to anything but cold, hard words. "Too little, too late."

For a moment he thought she might dispute that, but then she changed tack—he saw the switch in her expression and the set of her mouth as she gathered up her bunch of cut roses and started to move off. "You might not believe this," she said, "but he never forgot you were his son. He told me once how glad he was that your football career took off, because that made it so easy to keep up the connection. The more your star rose, the more stories he found in the press."

"His son, the famous footballer."

A vehement spark lit her eyes. "It wasn't like that, Tristan! Of course he was proud of your success—what parent wouldn't be? But this was about knowing some part of you, about having that connection. He learned all about your Aussie Rules game and he read all the match reports and stats. He watched the games on cable.

"One night I found him sitting in the dark, in the theater room where he watched the games. And the television was showing, I don't know, ice-skating or rhythmic gymnastics or something I knew he wouldn't watch. I thought he'd gone to sleep so I turned on the light to rouse him and send him back to bed."

She paused in a gap between two heavily-laden bushes, her expression as soft as the mass of creamy-pink roses that framed her slender curves. And, damn it her eyes had gone all dewy again. He braced himself, against the punch-to-the-heart sensation the sight of her caused and against whatever she was about to tell him.

"He didn't turn around because he didn't want me to see his tears, but I heard them in his voice. I knew he was sitting there in the dark crying. He told me later that you'd been playing your two hundredth game and they'd run a special on you during the halftime break. He was so proud and I was so damn mad at you both for not doing something about your rift."

Rift? The gap between him and his father had been more in the scope of a canyon. If there'd ever been any chance of bridging it… "That was up to him."

"Would you have listened?"

For several seconds they stood, gazes locked, the atmosphere taut with that one telling question. And when he didn't answer, she shook her head sadly. "I didn't think so."

"It makes no difference."

"You're that callous?"

"I am what I am."

She nodded slowly. And the disappointment in her eyes hit him like a full-throttle shoulder charge. "You are also more like your father than you know."

"Kind. Generous. Concerned," he quoted back at her.

"Proud. Stubborn. Unprepared to step back from your line in the sand." Her eyes narrowed with a mixture of challenge and speculation. "Why is the inheritance so important to you? Your success at football carried on into business. You just sold your company, advantageously, I gather. You can't need the money."

"Money isn't everything, duchess."

"Is it the house you want?" she persisted, ignoring his gibe. "Does it have special meaning?"

"Not any more. Does it to you?"

"It meant a lot to Stuart, so, yes."

"I'm asking about you." And even as he asked the question, he felt its significance tighten in his chest. "Is this your idea of home, Vanessa?"

"It's the only place I've ever felt happy to call home."

"You're happy here, living this life?"

She looked him square in the eye. "Yes, I am. I work hard on fund-raising committees. I love the volunteering work I do."

"A regular philanthropist, are you?"

It was a cheap shot but she took it on the chin without flinching. He sensed, in the briefest of pauses before she responded, that she'd taken a lot of hits in her life. That she was a lot less delicate than she looked. "I do what I can. And just so there are no misconceptions—I like most everything about my life. I like the security of money, of knowing all my needs are taken care of."

"Not to mention the things that money can buy."

"I don't care about the things."

Really? "You told me you love your car. Your clothes aren't from Wal-Mart. And what about the trinkets?" Forgetting the self-defensive caution that had driven him to keep a garden's width between them, he rounded the end of the bay and closed down that separation. "If *things* don't matter, then why were you so upset when the figurine smashed?"

"It was a gift."

"From Stuart?"

A shadow flitted across her expression but her gaze remained clear and unwavering and disarmingly honest.

"A New York socialite my mother worked for gave me that figurine for my twelfth birthday."

"Generous of her."

"Yes and no. It was nothing to her but a kind gesture to the housemaid's poor daughter. But to me…that little statue became my talisman. I kept it as a reminder of where it came from and where I came from. But, you know, it doesn't matter that it broke." She gave a little shrug. "I don't need it anymore."

Maybe not, but there was something about her explanation's matter-of-fact tone that belied the lingering shadows in her eyes. She could shrug it off all she wanted now, but he'd been there. He'd witnessed the extent of her distress.

Damn it all to blazes, he'd caused it by backing her into the corner and shocking her with his kiss.

And here he was, forgetting himself again. Standing too close, infiltrating her personal space, breathing the sweet scent of roses and aching with the need to take her in his arms, to touch her petal-soft skin, to kiss every shadowed memory from her eyes and every other man from her rose-pink lips.

The physical desire he understood and could handle. It had been there from the outset, crackling in the air whenever they got too close. But this was more—dangerously, insidiously more—when he needed less.

"You mightn't need it," he said gruffly, "but it matters."

"No. What matters is how Stuart wanted his wealth distributed. We talked about this—about which charities and the best way to help—but everything is tied up because of your legal challenge. Why are you doing this?" Her eyes darkened with determination. "Why, Tristan? Is it only about winning? Is it only about defeating me?"

"This isn't about you."

"Then what is it about?"

The first time she'd asked about his motivation, Tristan had turned it into a cross-examination. And she'd answered every one of his questions with honesty. The least he could do was offer equal candor. "It's about justice, Vanessa."

"Justice for whom?"

"My mother." He met her puzzled eyes. "Did you know she got nothing from my parents' divorce?"

"You can't be serious."

"Deadly. After fifteen years of marriage…nothing."

"Is that how you count yourself, Tristan? As nothing?" Her voice rose with abject disbelief. "Is that how your mother counted what she took from Stuart?"

He'd heard the same message from Liz Kramer. *She took you, Tristan, the most valuable thing.*

But the other side to that equation set his jaw and his voice with hard-edged conviction. "She counted herself lucky to gain full custody." Except to do so, to prevent an ugly court battle and a possible injunction preventing her move to Australia, she'd ceded her claim on a property settlement. "I guess that kind of payoff made me worth a hell of a lot."

For a long moment his words hung between them, a cynically-edged statement that conveyed more of his past hurt than he'd intended. He could see that by her reaction, by the softening in her expression and the husky note in her voice. "He thought Andrea would reject that offer. He thought they would negotiate and reach an agreement of shared property and shared custody. He didn't want to lose you, Tristan."

"Then why didn't he fight to keep me?"

She shook her head sadly. "He didn't want to take you from your mother. It broke his heart to lose his whole family like that."

"*He* kicked us out. *He* divorced my mother. *His* choices, Vanessa."

"I was under the impression that Andrea was at fault," she said after a moment's hesitation. "That she had an affair…which Stuart found out about and forgave. The first time."

Tristan went still. "What do you mean, the first time?"

"I mean…" She paused, her face wreathed in uneasiness. "How much of this do you know? I'm not sure it's my place—"

"You don't think I need to hear this?"

She nodded once, a brief concession to his point, and moistened her lips. "He took her back because he still loved her and because she promised it was a once-only thing, because she was lonely, he was working too hard. He took her back and when she announced she was pregnant, he was ecstatic."

"I know the twins aren't Stuart's," he reassured her grimly. "I know they're only my half sisters."

"And that's what broke his heart, don't you see? She never told him. She let him believe they were his and she kept seeing the father before they were born and afterward. When he caught her out again, when he did the paternity test and discovered the truth…that's why the marriage ended, Tristan. And that's why Stuart felt so strongly about adultery."

He didn't have to believe her but he did. It made too much sense not to. It tied everything together in a neat bow…and brought them looping back to his reason for being here in Eastwick. His reason for wanting, so vehemently, to defeat her.

"That's why he added that clause to his will," he said slowly. Not a question, but a statement.

Not because he suspected Vanessa of cheating, as Tristan had believed, but because of his own mother's infidelity. Not one mistake, as she'd led Tristan to believe, but repeated betrayals. Which put her subsequent choices into perspective, too.

Her acceptance of the divorce settlement.

Her flight to Australia, in pursuit of the twins' father.

Her objection to his challenge of Stuart's will.

"Does Andrea know why you're doing this? Is it what she wants?"

Vanessa's soft voice cut straight into his thought process, as if she'd read his mind.

And when he didn't answer, she added, "I thought as much."

That jolted him hard. The initial questions, the way she'd read him so accurately, the knowledge that she'd turned his beliefs inside out.

Yet this had been his pursuit for two years, his conviction for longer. He would not toss it without hearing the truth from his mother. Not without considering all he'd learned this morning, away from the influence of steady green eyes and rose-scented skin.

Resolve tightened his features as he nodded to her bundle of flowers. "Shouldn't you be putting those in water?"

She blinked with surprise, as if she'd been so intent on their discussion that she'd forgotten her morning's purpose. "I…yes."

"I need to go. I have some decisions to make."

Hope fluttered like a bird's wing in her eyes. "You'll let me know…once you've decided."

"You'll be the first."

He nodded goodbye and had gone maybe ten strides before she called his name. He paused. Turned to look over his shoulder and was floored again by the picture she made with the sunlight silhouetting her body and legs through that filmy pink robe.

Like the roses, he figured she'd forgotten her state of dress. Or undress. For both their sakes, he wasn't about to point out what was clearly defined by the unforgiving light.

"The letter I told you about, from your father—I kept a copy. It's yours, Tristan. If you like, I can go and get it for you."

Eight

After Vanessa offered him the letter, Tristan had stood staring at her down the paved path, face and body both set hard and still as a Grecian statue. There'd been a dizzy moment when her imagination played memory tricks, stripping away his clothes to reveal sun-gilded skin and rippling pool-wet muscles. When he pointed out—his voice dark and quietly dangerous—that if she were going to fetch anything, it should be more clothes, she'd shaken her head with confusion.

How did he know she was picturing him near-naked? Was she that transparent?

One slow sweep of his shuttered gaze and she realized that, yes, courtesy of the sun's backlighting, she *was* pretty darn transparent.

Oh, she'd played down her discomfiture. Ignoring

any reference to clothing, she'd lifted her chin and invited him to wait in the foyer while she located the letter and a file box of photos and clippings and other memorabilia Stuart had kept.

At first she'd thought he wouldn't bother taking them. Later she'd decided that his lack of response as she pushed them into his hands was all a crock. Vanessa understood the pretense. She, too, was a master at hiding her heart.

With an offhand shrug and a polite thanks he took them, presumably back to his hotel.

Vanessa should have been overjoyed to see the back of him and that morning's intense emotional drama. She should have been thrilled that they'd finally talked through some of the misunderstandings and misinformation, and that he might now reconsider his stance on the will. But, no, his departure had left her feeling hollow and restless and anxious, her mind buzzing with more questions.

Twice she picked up the phone, once her car keys and purse, with a view to pressing him for answers. Did he have any ideas on who had written the letter that brought him to Eastwick? Would he continue to investigate its allegations? Or was his challenge of the will now over?

But she forced herself to wait. He needed time to digest Stuart's heartfelt words, to come to grips with the truth of his split from Andrea and their subsequent custody settlement.

The hollowness in her middle grew into a raw ache when she thought about what he'd believed and what his mother had let him believe. From experience, Vanessa knew that twelve was a vulnerable age to have a parent cut from your life. To go through that in a new country, in a new school, without your friends, believing you'd been traded like a chattel in your parents' divorce…

She hadn't looked at this from Tristan's side before. So much about the man now made sense. Those hard edges, his drive to succeed, this pursuit of an inheritance he didn't need. It wasn't all about doing the right thing by his mother; it was also about himself and the father he'd believed didn't want him.

She could almost forgive him his resentment. If only he'd returned her calls or given her a chance to explain earlier, they could have avoided all this. And that thought added to her turmoil while she waited to discover what would happen next.

Tuesday morning she forced herself to push aside another restless night and her frustrating angst as she set about her usual routine…although she did take care to dress this time, before venturing out into the garden. Tuesday was one of her regular days at Twelve Oaks, and she cut enough blooms for several arrangements at the grand house and put them in water.

Next, she headed to the kitchen and mixed a double batch of chocolate cherry muffins. The precise processes involved in baking always calmed her. Picturing her brother's blissed-out grin when he opened the container and discovered his favorite treat always brought a smile to her face. It still hovered—a happy curve of affection—when the timer chimed and she pulled the baking trays from the oven.

They'd turned out perfectly. Her smile broadened

with satisfaction. Then she turned and looked up, and everything—her smile, her brain, her legs—froze.

But only for a split second. The instant their gazes connected she felt an ungoverned rush of heat all the way from her quick fix ponytail to her freshly painted toes.

"Where did you spring from?" she asked, her voice husky with astonishment. And, yes, a note of pleasure because of the way Tristan was looking at her and because, well, simply because he was here.

"Gloria let me in. I followed her up the drive."

Vanessa had been so absorbed in her task she hadn't heard the housekeeper's arrival. After depositing the trays on cooling racks, she put a hand to her rapidly beating heart. "This is two mornings in a row you've sneaked up on me. You have to stop doing that."

"Just evening up the score. You surprise me all the time." He paused, taking in the sunshine yellow dress she'd chosen to empower her mood, before his gaze returned to her face. "Although at least today you're dressed."

Which did nothing to hide her reaction to the appreciation in his eyes or the satisfaction of knowing she surprised him. She felt the flush rolling through her skin and the tightening of her nipples against the lace of her bra. Today she might be dressed, but she had no bouquet of roses to hide behind.

"Where's Gloria?" she asked, shifting the conversation to neutral ground.

"Putting away the…things…you loaned me."

The letter and photos? Her eyes widened. "Oh, no. You didn't have to return them. They are yours to keep."

"I don't need them."

"Maybe, but I want you to have them. Stuart would have wanted that."

Something quickened in his eyes, a flash of emotion, of sorrow or regret, but he lifted a shoulder and it was gone. Shed like a stray leaf.

He strolled farther into the room and inclined his head toward the marble island. "You bake?"

So. He didn't want to talk about the letter or his father. Vanessa's stomach dipped with disappointment. But what could she do? Perhaps if he stayed a while, perhaps if she went along with the teasing note to his question and kept it light, she could steer the conversation back.

"Yes, I bake." She arched her eyebrows at the racks of cooling muffins. "Behold the evidence."

Palms flattened on the countertop, he leaned over to breathe the rich aroma. His eyes rose up to hers, and the look of sybaritic pleasure on his face turned her knees to jelly. "Chocolate chip?"

"Chocolate cherry. With coconut."

"Are they as good as they smell?"

Showing off a bit, she deftly loosened the first batch of muffins and turned them onto the cooling rack. A dozen, each one perfectly formed. She looked up and smiled. "Better."

"Do you cook anything else?"

"I know my way around a kitchen."

He chuckled, and that unexpected appreciation did nothing to help strengthen Vanessa's jelly-knees. "Maybe I should have taken Frank's prompt and angled to come stay here instead of the Marabella."

"Oh, I don't think that would have been a good idea," she countered. "The two of us trying to share a house."

It was only banter, deliberately lighthearted as they danced around the reason for his visit and the topic she desperately wanted to address. But in the short hesitation before he answered, Vanessa caught the glimmer of heat in his eyes and the mood changed. An unspoken acknowledgment of their attraction stretched between them, as palpable as the rich scent of oven-warm chocolate.

"No," he said, much too seriously. "Not a good idea."

To break the tension, she offered him coffee. Perhaps, then, she could broach the question of what next.

"Do I get anything with the coffee?"

Muffins, Ms. Pragmatist muttered in her ear. *He's talking about muffins.* "I guess I can spare you one."

"The rest being for...?"

Fussing with the coffee making, she answered automatically. "The guys at Twelve Oaks."

"This is the place where you volunteer? Where your friend Andy works?"

"Yes."

"Interesting name. Twelve Oaks."

Vanessa looked up sharply. Nothing showed in his expression beyond curiosity but, still, she was so used to *not* talking about Twelve Oaks, to protecting this part of her life from scrutiny. "That's the name of the estate," she explained carefully. "A grand old Georgian home with separate servants' quarters and stables and a small farm. The owner willed it to a foundation that worked with the developmentally disabled and they developed it into a residential facility."

"What do you do there?"

"I help the therapists. Tuesdays it's with arts and crafts. On Thursdays we cook." She rolled her eyes. "Chick stuff."

He didn't counter with a teasing quip as she'd imagined, and she felt him looking at her differently, with a new respect or admiration that she did not deserve. If not for Lew, she would never have known about Twelve Oaks. She would never have gotten involved.

"I don't do very much, as it happens, and what I do is not exactly selfless."

"How long is your session this morning?"

Frowning at his question—where had that come from?—she looked up and got tangled in the intentness of his blue, blue eyes. "Does it matter?"

"I had this idea of going with you." He let go a huff of breath. "Bad idea."

"Why?"

"I have a plane to catch this afternoon."

Although this only half answered Vanessa's *why,* it snagged her attention in a whole new way. Her pulse started to beat faster. "Where are you going?"

"To see my mother."

"You're going back to Australia?" she asked in a rising rush of alarm.

"Florida. My mother moved to the States last year."

"I did not know that," she murmured, barely audible above the *thump thump thump* of her heartbeat.

"That's what I came to tell you. In case I don't come back."

Only a few days ago she'd begged him to go home, to leave her alone, but now…. Vanessa drew a breath and blew it out in a rush. "Does this mean you're finished here?"

"Not quite."

She barely had time to absorb that enigmatic reply before he circled the island and offered his hand. Vanessa's mouth turned dry as she stared at the long, lean fingers, the strong knuckles, the thick male wrist. Moistening her lips, she asked, "Is this a peace offering? An apology? Or just goodbye?"

"Maybe it's all three." He took her hand, engulfing it in heat, in rough-textured sensation, and in the notion that a truce might send their relationship veering into new, uncharted territory. "And maybe I'm doing what I have to do. To set things right."

"That's important to you, isn't it? Setting things right?"

"Yes."

"And doing things right?"

"Always."

Butterfly nerves beat a tattoo in her stomach as she met his steadfast gaze. "So now you know your father's thoughts and feelings and wishes, you will do the right thing? You will set matters right?"

"That has always been my intention, Vanessa." His grip on her hand altered, a minute easing of pressure, a realignment of palms. And just as smoothly he redirected the conversation. "You remember the night you came to see me, at the Marabella?"

"Which part, exactly?"

"The part where you maligned my…expertise."

He was talking about his kissing expertise. The certainty skimmed through her in a quicksilver flash and, wow, she had not seen it coming. Not even when he suggested he wanted to set things right; and that he always did things right.

"If my memory serves me—" which it did, word for word, beat for beat "—I said you wouldn't ever get a second chance."

"And I thought I'd give you a chance to reconsider."

Intense curiosity tingled in a dozen places, in her accelerated pulse. He was saying goodbye, leaving and possibly not coming back. Would it hurt to succumb to temptation, to feel his mouth on hers without the blaze of antagonism that fired their first kiss?

Not if she approached it with eyes wide open, as an experiment, a new experience...

"Five seconds." She straightened her shoulders and met his eyes. "You have five seconds to prove your expertise."

He stared at her a moment.

Vanessa shrugged. "Take it or leave it."

Something shifted in his expression, a slight flare of his nostrils, a subtle tightening of the lines at the corners of his eyes. *Challenge accepted. Game on.* Vanessa had half a second to think *I am so out of my league* before he tugged on her hand, bringing her infinitesimally closer.

Eyes holding hers, he lifted that hand to his mouth.

He kissed her fingertips first, one after the other, and then he pressed his mouth to the center of her palm. It was unexpectedly subtle, dangerously seductive, and when he gently nipped the flesh at the base of her thumb, intensely erotic. Heat bloomed in her skin, in her blood, in her breasts and her thighs.

She wanted more, a real kiss, the touch of his hands, but he let her go. Just like that.

He left without a word, but she got the message. His goodbye kiss was an apology for the other and a sign that he could do things right. So very, very right.

He'd reached the front door before she remembered the other reason for this visit. "Wait," she called after him. "Stuart's letter. I want you to have it."

She didn't know if he heard her or not. He kept on walking and didn't turn back.

Emma Dearborn had wanted an intimate fuss-free wedding with just family and closest friends, partly because of the short time frame she had in which to finalize her vows with fiancé, Garratt Keating, but mostly because that's the way Emma liked things. But then she let her parents get involved and, well, the lavish event took over the Eastwick Country Club ballroom and gardens and anyone who was anyone in Eastwick society made the guest list for the evening affair.

In the end it didn't matter. Emma only had eyes for her new husband.

After the ceremony, the Debs gravitated together to share their relief that it had gone so beautifully and their praise of Felicity's wedding planning magic. Somehow she'd pulled it all off while also taking her place as Emma's maid of honor.

"I don't know how you did it, Felicity." Abby Talbot shook her head. "You are a genius."

Felicity smiled and said, "I know."

But then ever since falling for Reed Kelly her smile had been a constant, as big and bright and sparkly as the monster pink diamond on her engagement finger.

"Look at her." Lily directed their attention to the dance floor. "Could she be any happier?"

Emma and Garrett waltzed by, lost in each other, and Vanessa felt her heart squeeze with a mixture of joy for her friend and good old-fashioned bride-envy. But she kept on smiling. Between weddings, babies and engagements, she needed to get used to this feeling.

The smile faded when she saw Delia making a beeline for their group, a look of predatory purpose painted on her face. Vanessa didn't have time to issue a warning before the woman swept up in a cloud of Valentino chiffon and her signature perfume, made exclusively for her in France.

Caroline Keating-Spence once suggested that Poison would have worked just as well as her signature scent. Delia had not been amused.

"Are we all having fun?" she asked with an inclusive smile. Her wide-eyed gaze came to rest on Lily's pregnant belly. "Oh, dear, you are getting huge. Should you be standing?"

Lily assured her she was fine.

Delia, being Delia, ignored her. "Where is that darling husband of yours? Surely he isn't neglecting you…. Is that him over there? Talking to *your* beau." She placed a solicitous hand on Felicity's arm and lowered her voice. "I do hope today hasn't been too awkward for you both."

Felicity's fiancé, Reed, had been engaged to Emma but she'd broken it off when Garrett resurfaced in her life. Then Reed and Felicity got together and, well, it had been awkward for a little while, but that was history.

"How sweet of you to be concerned, Delia." Felicity batted her lashes. "But why should there be any awkwardness?"

Delia gave her a poor-dear look. Then her attention shifted to her next victim. Abby. "And where is your gorgeous man, Abigail? I haven't seen him once tonight."

"Luke couldn't be here, unfortunately."

"Really? He's missing the wedding of one of your dearest friends? And so soon after your poor mother's passing."

"He's away on business," Abby supplied tightly.

"He spends a lot of time away, doesn't he? Are you sure it's business? You know how these men can be…."

Reacting to her pointed barbs only incited Delia and they'd decided long ago not to play her game. But after the stress of recent months Abby was a vulnerable target. Vanessa could see the gleam of moisture in her eyes. She needed rescuing, fast.

"We probably don't know as much about men as you, Delia," she said with a gracious smile. "I doubt many women do."

Delia laughed it off but her eyes glittered with malice. However she was fixing to respond, it would not be pretty. Vanessa braced herself.

But it was Mary Duvall's voice that broached the sudden tension. "Oh, look. I believe Emma is preparing to throw the bouquet. We mustn't miss this!"

Of course, Mary was mistaken but they all kept moving, intent on getting as far away as possible from the razor-sharp slice of Delia's tongue. With talk of rustling up a dance, Felicity went in search of Reed. Lily hooked her arm through Abby's and suggested they quench their thirst with cold drinks, which left Vanessa and Mary.

"Is this how it feels to escape the firing squad?" Vanessa's smile echoed the wry tone of her voice. "Nice diversion, by the way."

"I needed to do something. I was next in line."

"I think you were pretty safe. You haven't been back in Eastwick long enough for Delia to select the most damaging weapon."

Mary didn't reply. In fact she looked pale and un-easy—enough that Vanessa felt badly about her blithe comment. But before she could apologize, Mary excused herself and hurried off to the bathroom.

Vanessa frowned after her. She didn't know Mary Duvall well. An old schoolfriend of Emma and Abby and Felicity, she'd lived in Europe ever since graduating from college but had recently returned to Eastwick at the behest of her dying grandfather. There was defi-nitely something going on with her, and Vanessa couldn't help wondering if it was connected to Bunny and the diaries.

Perhaps Mary, too, was the victim of an extortion attempt.

They knew of two thwarted attempts but what if other letters had been sent and not reported? Other victims could have agreed to buy the blackmailer's silence. As for the letter to Tristan—its lack of an extortion demand didn't make sense. Unless it was just a random, unconnected piece of mischief-making…

Her gaze shifted back to where they'd left Delia. Could she be responsible? One part of Vanessa screamed, *Hell, yes*, because Delia thrived on making strife. On the other hand, she seemed to get her kicks from delivering pointed barbs face-to-face, watching for a reaction, and then driving another dart into the wound.

Letter writing was not Delia's weapon of choice.

And the note alleging Vanessa's adultery wasn't written in Delia's bitchy style.

Off to her right Vanessa detected the rapid swish of apricot Valentino and she turned to track the woman's progress. It seemed Delia had her sights on someone over by the entrance. As much as Vanessa—and all the Debs—would have loved to peg Delia as the villain, the current Mrs. Forrester had no need to blackmail. Not with a doting husband to keep her in designer dresses and plastic surgery.

Vanessa turned away and saw Lily beckoning, Jack at her side. Perfect. Vanessa wanted to get them alone, to quiz Jack on any recent developments with the extortion letters and to ask if he'd heard anything from Tristan's lawyers.

Three days had passed since he'd walked out of her kitchen. There'd been a note of finality to his parting words that suggested he wouldn't be back, and Vanessa discerned that any news would be relayed via their legal counsels.

The three days had crawled by, not in edgy anticipation of an end to her legal struggle, but under a heavy pall of disappointment. For two years she'd wanted nothing more fervently than to end her feud with Tristan Thorpe. Now she had her wish and it felt like a giant anticlimax.

All because of that damn kiss.

You are a sad case. Ms. Pragmatist shook her head in disgust. *What does a twenty-nine-year-old virgin know about kissing anyway? We both know he was only proving a point, settling a score, taking the points from one challenge because he was on the brink of losing another.*

She started toward Lily and Jack's table but had only taken half a dozen steps when she sensed a disturbance back by the door…where she'd last seen Delia. She paused, swung her head to look across her shoulder, and her gaze collided with the cause of every disturbance in her recent life.

Tristan Thorpe. Here. His expression filled with purpose as he shouldered aside whoever held him back.

He looked dark and forbidding and gorgeous.

And he was heading her way.

Nine

What was Tristan doing here? What had happened to bring him back so soon? What could be so important that he would crash Emma's wedding?

Vanessa's mind raced with questions while her heart raced with an insane desire to fly across the ballroom and fling herself into his arms. She'd taken half a dozen—sedate, controlled, nonflying—steps in that direction when Jack Cartwright cut into her path.

"You aren't leaving?" he asked, when she frowned at her blocked view of the door.

"No. I was just going to…see someone."

"Is this someone a better dancer than me?" Jack shifted, turning to look in the direction she'd been headed and revealing that *this someone* had also been intercepted.

By Delia.

Her arm was hooked through his. Her voluptuous body angled in close. Her perfectly coiffed head tilted back as she made some kind of appeal. And when she led him onto the dance floor, jealousy sliced through Vanessa, swift and sharp.

Appalled by her response, she looked away…but not quickly enough. Jack's eagle-eyed gaze trained on the couple. "What is Thorpe doing here?"

"Dancing with Delia, it would appear."

Jack made a scoffing noise. "Let's hope it's only dancing."

His meaning sat all kinds of uncomfortable in Vanessa's stomach, but as she watched the couple circling the floor she couldn't impugn his comment. They danced close enough that Delia's filmy skirt swirled around Tristan's legs. Her head was tilted, allowing her to look intently into his face. Her fingers lifted to touch the back of his hair and Vanessa swallowed hard to stem the rising pall of red-hot anger and disgust.

How dare she paw him like that, here at Emma's wedding, in view of half of Eastwick and her own husband. How dare he let her. When Frank had been the one local gracious enough to welcome him home and invite him into their social circle.

"About the dancing…" Jack drew her attention back to him. "My wife suggested you might like to do me the honor. She being somewhat incapacitated in the waltzing department."

Vanessa glanced across at Lily, who patted her middle and grimaced. She supposed her friend had caught her looking alone and forlorn. That was Lily, always looking out for others. She made a shooing gesture with her hand and mouthed, "Go on."

Vanessa sighed. As much as didn't want to be anywhere near the Delia-Tristan floor show, she knew she wouldn't be able to stop watching from the sidelines. Like a horror movie, she'd be drawn and repelled and disgusted and completely unable to look away.

At least dancing with Jack she could pretend to be unaffected.

"I'd love to dance." She offered him a smile and her hand. "Thank you."

Dancing with Delia gave Tristan a new appreciation of the term *grin and bear it*. She'd rescued him from the pair of doormen who'd followed him inside, so he owed her. Not that he couldn't have dealt with them, but that would have gotten him kicked out on his backside. He'd already drawn attention when he plowed right past the lightweight security, all because he'd caught sight of Vanessa and suffered a momentary brain snap.

But Delia had stepped in and forestalled a large-scale disturbance. "He's my guest, darlings. There's no need to check the list. Unless you want to trouble the Dearborns in the middle of their only daughter's wedding…"

How could he refuse her invitation to dance? He figured that one more turn of the floor should be enough gratitude, although if she touched his neck again or made another heavily-suggestive sexual remark, he was walking away. If they threw him out, so be it. He'd grow some patience and wait outside—as he should have done all along—to confront Vanessa with the new hard evidence.

No smoke screens this time. No turning him inside out with her tear-filled eyes and husky-voiced stories of his father's last wishes and years of regret. No more playing him for a fool with her protestations of innocence.

Either this bloke from Twelve Oaks was her lover or he wasn't. In which case, Tristan needed to know who the hell the guy was and why she insisted on hiding him away like a guilty secret.

He'd noticed the second she joined the dancing. Hell, how could he not notice? Even in a ballroom dripping with diamonds and designer one-offs, Vanessa's classic beauty shone. It wasn't her dress—an understated glimmer of silvery-blue—or the cool sparkle of her jewelry when it caught the light of the ballroom's massed chandeliers.

It was her; and it was him. The awareness he'd felt from the moment they met had strengthened into a living, breathing devil with teeth. He couldn't stop himself wanting her; he couldn't stop himself watching her.

And before tonight was out, he would make good his promise to know her every secret.

"Ah. So that's what brings you here."

Tristan concentrated his focus on Delia, and found hers zeroed in on Vanessa. There was something in her tone and in the set of her face that raised his protective hackles. But he kept his own expression impassive as he used the waltz's natural moves to turn her away from the object of her scrutiny. "I have no idea what you're talking about."

Delia laughed, a crystalline tinkle that grated over every raised hackle. "It's all right, darling." She leaned even closer and employed a stage whisper. "Your secret's safe with me."

"There is no secret, Delia."

"No?" She widened her eyes, all fake credulousness. "Have I read those long, lingering looks all wrong then?"

Damn. Was he so obvious?

"Married all those years to an old, ailing man," Delia continued, low and confiding. "No offense to your father, darling, but I can understand why she's mooning after you. I know I miss sex with a young, fit man."

Whoa. Tristan went still inside. Vanessa was watching him? That's what Delia was referencing?

"We're very alike, she and I. Not that Ms. High-and-Mighty would ever admit it. She belongs to the Debs Club." Delia sniffed. "As if she was ever a debutante!"

"Were you, Delia?"

She blinked. Then, as if realizing she'd gone a step too far, she laughed it off. "Of course I wasn't a deb. I never went in for all that snooty WASP stuff back then. I was too busy having a good time."

"But you like it well enough now?"

"Of course I do, darling. I love this lifestyle and everything it offers, just like our Vanessa. Pretty clothes, pretty jewels, pretty men." She caressed his shoulder and the ends of his hair with an overly-familiar hand and her voice dropped an octave. "I especially love the men."

Delia wasn't as easy to shed as the doormen. Fortified by French champagne and his acquiescence during their dance, her advances grew even bolder. When she suggested they adjourn to his hotel room, Tristan drew the line. He delivered her back to her husband—poor sod—and suggested he take her home.

Then he went hunting for Vanessa.

She was still dancing, but with an older man he didn't recognize or care to meet. Although he approached with an aim of taking her somewhere private to talk, keeping Delia's busy hands above the belt had stretched his patience to a thin twanging cord. Suddenly he didn't want more friction—unless it was the kind created by this woman against his body.

The only way that was going to happen was under the guise of dancing.

But after he sent her partner packing, she ignored his proffered hand. "I've had enough dancing."

"I haven't," he said shortly, taking her into his arms.

"I need a break."

Tristan stood firm. "You looked like you were enjoying yourself with your other partners."

"Not half as much as you."

Ah. So this was about Delia. She *had* been watching. Primal satisfaction roared through his veins and pooled low in his body. He pulled her closer and despite the resistance resonating through her stiffly-held body, she felt right.

The perfect warm-blooded, sweet-scented antidote to Delia's venom.

And, what the hell, Vanessa felt so right that he drew their joined hands to his lips and kissed her knuckles.

She recoiled as if he'd bitten her. Which he might

have done, with the same lazy eroticism as in her kitchen, if she'd let him. Judging by the wariness in her eyes, that wasn't happening any time soon. "What was that for?" she asked.

"Just trying to relax you." He tugged her nearer again. "At the moment you're dancing with all the suppleness of a tackle-dummy."

"Did you consider that might be because I'd rather be dancing with the tackle-dummy?"

Smiling at the image, he swept her into an exaggerated turn. She had to relax to keep up and once she was dancing again, he asked, "Because of Delia?"

She didn't have to answer. He felt the response in her grip and the falter of her step. He stopped teasing and took pity. If Jack Cartwright had pulled Delia-like moves on Vanessa, Tristan would have laid the bastard out cold in the middle of the dance floor.

Tristan didn't bother debating the wisdom of such fierce possessiveness. He tucked her under his chin and bent to speak near her ear. "For your information, I wasn't enjoying myself."

"Then why did you dance with her?"

"She saved me getting kicked out of here."

Finally she relaxed a little, although Tristan fancied he could hear her brain ticking. He figured she'd want to know why he'd crashed the wedding reception and he'd have to tell her. End of warm, relaxed perfect woman in his arms. Resurgence of hostilities. Damn.

When she tipped her head back to look up into his face, he contemplated kissing her. To silence the inevitable question, to buy some more time, and because he'd spent the last three days regretting the lost opportunity in her kitchen. When she hit him with the five-second challenge, he'd wanted to shock her in return and knew he'd done so by ignoring her lips.

Talk about outsmarting himself.

But she didn't ask the expected; she surprised him again. "I hope you don't take anything Delia says too seriously."

Tristan didn't carry tales or repeat rumors. He had to consider what he said carefully. "I gather you two aren't buddies."

"No. I think…" Her brow puckered, thoughtful, worried, and his whole body tightened with the urge to kiss it smooth. To take that anxiety from her and make it better. "I think she imagined we were kindred spirits because of…superficial similarities." She cut him a fierce look. "We're not alike. At all. She likes to play games."

"And make mischief?"

Their eyes met, no clash, no surprise.

But she shook her head.

"You don't think she could have sent the letters to me?" Because as far as Tristan could tell, Delia was the only person in Eastwick society with a gripe against Vanessa.

"The thought did cross my mind, but she likes hand-delivering those verbal gems. She lives for reaction. The letters don't seem li—" She stopped midword. Sucked in a breath, her eyes wide. "You said letters, plural. *Letters* to you."

Intent on each other and the conversation they'd

danced to a halt on the edge of the floor. Another couple bumped Tristan's back and he turned Vanessa in his arms, shielding her from their curious gazes. "We should take this somewhere private."

"You did say letters?" she persisted.

"There's a second. Delivered Tuesday."

He ushered her out into the gardens, much too far and too slowly for Vanessa's impatient imagination. By the time they'd cleared the perimeter of the pool area and the clusters of wedding guests spilled from the ballroom into gardens festooned with lights, scores of questions clamored for answers.

Barely knowing where to begin, she spun around to face him. "You went to Florida. How did this person know where to find you?"

"It was delivered to the Marabella before I left. I thought it was Stuart's letter—the one you loaned me and said I should have. I thought you'd sent it in. You seemed so insistent."

"I am."

A corner of his mouth kicked up, acknowledging that.

"And when did you discover it wasn't from me?"

"After talking to my mother last night." He gave a tight shrug. "I couldn't sleep. I'd put the envelope in my pocket and I decided to read it again."

The letter he'd returned because he thought he'd never read it again. *Right.*

But that was another story, for another time. Right now she needed to know about this second letter of Tristan's. "This letter…is it from the same person?"

His eyes met hers, dark and unreadable. "It appears so."

"The same allegations?"

"Dates. Times. Places."

That she'd met an imaginary lover? Vanessa shook her head. Apparently this last week had proved nothing. Instead of anger she felt a choking wave of disappointment. "And you believe this piece of fiction?"

"There's more." He reached into the inside pocket of his suit jacket, and in that second's pause her heart stalled with a prescient sense of doom. "A photo."

She stared at the enlarged print but she didn't take it from his hand. Even upside down, in the shadows of a dimly lit garden, she could see enough.

"Who is he, Vanessa? If he's not your lover, then who?" He asked quietly, without accusation or antagonism, and her heart started to beat with a strong, thick pulse of hope. This week *had* meant something. He was prepared to listen.

She lifted her chin and met his eyes and the words came easily.

"His name is Lew Kotzur. He's my brother."

"Why didn't you tell me about your brother before?"

They'd left the wedding after her revelation, seeking privacy from the chance of interruption. He drove and Vanessa talked, at first in fractured snippets and then with growing fluency. She discovered a cathartic release in finally sharing about Lew and his autism and the wonders Twelve Oaks had wrought on his behavior and esteem.

Except for an occasional prompt, Tristan didn't interrupt. He let her talk until she was done and she realized they'd arrived at the shore. The beach would be packed with sightseers during the day, but at night they were alone with the moonlight and his opening question.

"I wanted to," she answered candidly, aware of all the times she'd prevaricated and danced around the full truth. "That night I came to the restaurant, after I talked to Andy down at Poynton, I intended telling you."

"But you didn't."

"There was too much anger and resentment still hovering from our first meeting. And then Frank came over to visit." And she was making excuses when there wasn't any excuse. She'd chickened out or frozen up or let her temper get the better of her logic. "It seems that every time we get together, there is some emotional drama or other and I get sidetracked."

"The other morning in your kitchen you told me about Twelve Oaks. That was the perfect opportunity."

"It was. I know. A missed opportunity."

When he didn't respond, she turned and found him angled in the driver's seat, his fingers drumming against the steering wheel, a slight frown drawing his brows together as he watched her with silent intensity.

Was he watching her mouth? And thinking of another missed opportunity?

She shook that thought aside and stared ahead, through the windshield. *Concentrate*, Ms. Pragmatist scolded. *This is your chance to clear away the final misunderstandings. Do not get sidetracked.*

"Does anyone know about Lew?"

"Gloria. Andy. Jack and some other professionals. But no one else in Eastwick. None of my friends."

"Why not?"

Expecting the question, she'd already grown tense and wary. She didn't expect her way of thinking would make sense to a man like Tristan, who charged after his goals and damn the consequences. She didn't want to open herself and her background up to his judgment. "That's not an easy question," she prevaricated. "I'm not sure you will understand."

"Try me."

She exhaled a shaky breath. "Lew has been my responsibility since I was a teenager."

"What happened to your parents?"

"A long story, another time." *Hopefully, never.* "But even when they were around, they weren't around much. They were working or—" she shrugged "—whatever. I'm eight years older, so it fell on me to look after my little brother from when he was in diapers."

"You were just a kid yourself."

His voice was tight with anger and, pity help her, this was exactly what she'd feared. "Please, do not give me that poor-Vanessa look because I never minded. Not for one second. I wanted to look out for him," she said fiercely. "He needed someone to."

"Because of the autism."

Vanessa nodded. "He was always…different. And you know how kids can be with that."

"Not in the same league, but yes."

She cut him a look. "When you moved at Australia?"

"A long story, another time."

For a second their connection held the warm strength of understanding, and that sensation helped her shuck some of her tense reservations. *It might be okay to share. He may understand more than I'd imagined.*

"Anyway," she continued with more confidence, "I grew up protecting Lew from ugly insults and neighborhood bullies, and I had to fight tooth and nail to get anyone to acknowledge he had a serious problem. His well-being was my responsibility years before my mother passed away and I became his guardian."

"How old were you?"

"Twenty-one."

In the brief pause that followed, he must have done the math. Two years a widow. Five years married. Not much left over. "And along came Stuart Thorpe."

"The answer to my prayers," she said.

"How did you meet?"

"Oh, I'm pretty sure you know I was a waitress."

"That's not what I asked."

Vanessa lifted a shoulder and let it drop, shifting uneasily under his watchful gaze. *Tell him*, Ms. P. whispered. *Tell him everything and the slate will be clean.*

"One of my jobs was in the city, in a restaurant near Stuart's office. He was a regular, a lovely man who was always friendly and who remembered what we'd talked about a week before." When she paused to moisten her dry mouth, she tensed, anticipating his dig about Stuart's tips or about her scheming to snag a millionaire. But he remained silent, watchful, waiting for the rest. "One day he came in when I'd just had a call from Lew's school. He was on a last warning for his violent behavior and I was at wit's end. I told Stuart and he offered to come to the school with me."

On the wheel, his long fingers clenched and straightened. A reflexive action? In response to Stuart's visit to the school?

"I didn't accept his offer."

"Why not?"

"Lew was my responsibility and to be honest—" she looked up at him through her lashes "—I wondered what he would want in return."

Even in the tricky moonlight, she could see the harsh lines of cynicism etched in his expression. She hated that look and its cause, but he'd requested the true story not a rose-colored adaptation.

"The next week," she continued, "he brought all the information about Twelve Oaks."

"The answer to your prayers."

His murmured aside made a mockery of her earlier comment and that stung deeply. Damn him and all this rotten history. She felt as if she'd started a swift slide back to the start, to that day when he'd appeared at her door with his scorn and derision riding shotgun alongside.

"I didn't have the money for a place like Twelve Oaks," she told him. "And the very thought of entrusting Lew into the care of strangers made me sick. I threw the brochures in the trash, but Stuart persisted. He sent a car the next weekend, to take me and Lew up there for a look around. I saw these young men, so content and confident, and I saw all the possibilities for Lew."

"So he offered you marriage, and everything that goes with it, in return for Twelve Oaks."

He could have used more brutal language. He could have come right out and accused her of selling herself into marriage. It was no less than the truth. A deal, a trade, and a regular bargain from her side.

Except she hadn't accepted everything.

She lifted her chin and met his eyes. "Stuart and I had a contract, a private handshake deal. I wanted Lew taken care of, for his entire life. In return I became Stuart's friend, companion, hostess. A trophy wife, yes, and he loved to play on that, buying me all the pretty things you mock. Taking me places I'd be photographed on his arm.

"But we kept separate bedrooms. I was his wife in name only. I was never his lover."

Ten

"That's why I laughed so hard at your adultery allegation. Not because it was funny but because it shocked me with its utter implausibility. And there you were standing in my keeping room vowing to prove my guilt—" she released a breath of laughter, soft and self-effacing "—when it would have been easier to prove I couldn't have had a lover!"

Tristan almost choked on his next breath. His head whipped around to stare at her. "Are you implying you've never had a lover?"

For a moment she studied her hands, and he wondered if she was reconsidering her provocative claim. *It would have been easier to prove I couldn't have had a lover*. By sleeping with her? By discovering that she was untouched?

That notion turned visual, sensual, carnal, a sweet thick rush of desire that settled between his thighs.

"You're a virgin?"

"Is that so hard to believe?"

"You're thirty years—"

"Not quite," she interrupted.

"About to turn thirty and a widow. You're so damn beautiful you could have any man you wanted. Yes, it's hard to swallow."

Slowly she raised her eyes to his. "You think I'm beautiful?"

She didn't know? He shook his head in disbelief. Women. "I knew you were beautiful before I hit your doorstep and then you opened the door…" He lifted a hand and let it fall, lost for words to describe that impact.

"How did you know?"

I knew when I found myself lifting my jaw off the mat. But he didn't think that's what she meant.

"You said you knew, before…" she prompted.

"I'd seen your photo. On that society Web site."

Her eyes narrowed a fraction, but that didn't conceal the glimmer of surprise. Or pleasure. "You were checking me out?"

"I like to know what I'm up against."

"Did that help?"

"No."

They sat a minute in silence. The car and the night created a cocoon of intimacy, but the mood was not exactly comfortable, not really relaxed. Not a big surprise given her disclosure. He felt he needed to say something—something other than "This changes everything" and "Come back to my hotel room." Both seemed premature but the longer the silence stretched, the harder that notion hammered through his body.

She had never slept with his father.

She had never slept with any man.

He shifted in his seat, turning to look at her. "Thank you for telling me. I appreciate your honesty."

"It's a weight off." When she gave her trademark little shrug, her silvery dress glistened in the moonlight. She waited for his eyes to drift back up to her face. "Can I ask something of you in return?"

"As long as it's not another five-second challenge."

A hint of a smile teased her lips, drawing his attention and reminding him how he'd outsmarted himself in her kitchen.

"I'd like to know how you got on in Florida," she said. "When you went to visit your mother."

Tristan found it easier to talk about than he'd imagined. Perhaps because of her honesty, perhaps because of the soothing backdrop of beach and water and velvet-dark night, perhaps because they'd already shared so much that he felt Vanessa knew him better than anyone outside his immediate family.

She suggested they walk and he agreed. As they strolled along the boulevard, he told her how his mother had eventually confirmed what he'd learned from Vanessa and from Stuart's letter about the adulterous affair with the twins' father and the subsequent fallout. He didn't tell Vanessa how his mother had attempted to justify her deception or how she'd wept buckets as she begged his forgiveness.

Not wanting to think about that emotional mael-
strom, he kept on talking about the twins—his half-
sisters—and his hometown of Perth where he'd lived
until his career took off. Prompted by Vanessa's perceptive comments and questions, he divulged the culture
shock of landing in a new country in the middle of a
school year. The Yankee kid with a strange accent, who
didn't know a thing about any of the local sports.

"Is that why you took up Australian football?" she
asked. "To fit in?"

"It was easier than cricket. At least I knew how to
kick a football."

"And so the Yankee kid mastered the Aussie game
and showed those locals."

"It sure didn't do me any harm." In fact, the market-
ers had used that unique spin to turn him into a house-
hold name and that high profile hadn't hurt him in the
world of business. "It put me where I am today. I'm not
sorry about that."

He felt her gaze on him, sharp with contemplation.
Already he'd revealed more than he'd intended, more
than he was comfortable sharing with anyone. He sure
as hell didn't want to defend that last statement.

He didn't have to because she suddenly tripped
and might have fallen if he hadn't caught her. "All
right?" he asked.

"My heel is stuck." Steadying herself on his arm, she
tried to pull her shoe free and failed.

Tristan hunkered down to take a look and found the
stiletto wedged tightly in the gap between two paving
stones. If not for a delicate lacing of straps around her

ankle, her foot would have come free and left the shoe behind.

But there were the straps. And a delicate foot and ankle and toes with their nails painted a pearly pink. And something about that sight turned his fingers into thumbs and hazed his vision.

"Put your hands on my shoulders," he instructed, his voice deep and gruff with that sudden rush of desire. "This might take a while."

"There's a buckle at the side, Can't you see it?"

Yeah, he could see it. Just. But he was enjoying this unique perspective, with her weight resting on him and his hand cradling her foot. He felt no way inclined to give it up too soon.

The strap came loose and he traced his thumb over the imprint left in her skin. Through her sheer stockings he could feel the warmth of her skin and the scent of roses twined through him, enticing him, when he palmed the backs of her calves, he thought he heard her draw a shudder of breath and her hands flexed and tightened on his shoulders.

He came to his feet in a long, slow slide of body against body and she tilted her face to meet his kiss with a soft sigh of relief. This was the kiss he'd wanted that morning in the kitchen; it felt like a kiss he'd been wanting all his life. A sensuous giving and taking as they learned each other's lips and mouths and tongues with a heat that threatened to engulf them both.

Eventually they came apart, their breathing an elevated rasp in the stillness.

"What now?" she asked.

Everything inside Tristan was still and hard. "That's up to you."

"What are my choices?'

"I can take you home," he said. "Or I can take you back to my hotel. Your choice, Vanessa."

Vanessa chose his hotel because she wanted this between them. No third parties. No history, just them and this night and the latent promise of that kiss.

But after he'd parked his car and turned off the engine, her insides jumped with misgivings. "What are we doing?" she asked. "What is this about?"

"That's up to you," he repeated. And the way he looked at her with all that contained male intensity did nothing to calm her nerves. "Do you want to go upstairs? Yes or no?"

For the entire ten-minute drive from the shore, her pragmatic side had screeched an increasingly strident *no*. But there was a *yes,* as well, a whispered temptation of a voice that beat in her accelerated pulse and in a dozen places she'd barely known existed before this man strode into her life.

Perhaps knowing he would stride back out again influenced her choice. She could have this night, she could savor the experience, she could say goodbye and get on with real life. All before she turned thirty at midnight.

She sucked in a quick breath and nodded. "Yes."

He took her by the hand and led her to the elevators. Keeping her knees from shaking took all her concentration. She'd made her decision. She was pretty sure she would go through with this…experience.

Upstairs in his top-floor suite, she wasn't so sure. When the door clicked shut behind them, her nerves shot through the roof. She bought some time pretending interest in her surroundings, ambling a slow investigative circle of the living room and keeping her eyes averted from the turned-back bed she glimpsed through the half-open door to his bedroom.

Eventually she'd seen the entire suite, balcony and bathroom included. She strolled back into the living room and pulled up short. Bare from the waist up, Tristan was hunkered down at the silent stereo. Soft light spilled from a standing lamp and played over the long muscles of his back. Perhaps she made a sound, because he looked up sharply and came to his feet. And in that instant his face looked so tense and hard and untouchable, she felt an urgent need to bolt.

Her mouth went dry. Her heart raced. But her feet remained glued to the spot.

A muscle jumped in his cheek and she realized, with a startled sense of discovery, that he looked nervous, too. She found that oddly reassuring.

"Would you like a drink?" he asked.

"If I were ever to start, tonight would be the night. But…no."

He stood, silently watching her for another second. Butterflies flapped in her stomach. She couldn't stand the tension any longer. "What now?"

"Take off your jewelry," he said in a low controlled voice.

She lifted a hand to touch the delicate diamond and sapphire necklace. "You don't like it?"

"No."

"And the dress?"

Slowly he started to cross the room toward her. She saw the flare of his nostrils, the unwavering intensity of his eyes, the clench and flex of his hand, and all her senses sharpened with anticipation. He stopped in front of her, his gaze a long, slow slide of approval. "I like the dress."

"I'm glad," she said simply.

An unexpected tenderness lurked deep in his eyes as he took one of her hands and tugged her closer. His kiss started gentle, a brush of lips, a teasing shift of pressure from top lip to bottom and back again. A kiss that was everything his look had promised. Vanessa spread her hands over his chest, exploring the heady contrast of coarse hair and hot, smooth skin. He nipped at her bottom lip and dragged it between his teeth, a move so unexpected and incredibly sensual, it curled her toes.

Warm and dizzy with desire, she swayed nearer and closed her eyes.

Her hands slid over his shoulders, her fingers laced in his hair, and she made a muted sound of discovery at its softness. He took the invitation to deepen the kiss, opening her mouth with the pressure of his and sliding his tongue inside. The kiss exploded with heat in the beat of a second, and she surrendered to the unrestrained pleasure.

When he retreated, she followed, sliding tongue against tongue and learning his dark male flavor. Desire sang in her veins as she sank into his mouth and discovered a new angle to the kiss.

She could have lapped this up forever but he slowly eased her back to earth with a luscious series of kisses that trailed from her lips to her chin and along the edge of her jaw. He pulled back far enough to look into her eyes and murmur, "Better?"

She smiled and something primal beat in his eyes.

"Turn around."

Dipping one shoulder, she turned within his arms. Her heart raced like a bird in flight while she waited in anticipation of what came next. His hands skimmed up her arms and cupped her shoulders in rough-textured heat. When he leaned forward and spoke at her ear, the deep resonance of his voice pulsed through her body.

Her breasts grew tight and heavy. Heat bloomed all through her skin. And she had to ask him to repeat his request because no words registered, only sensation.

"Hold your hair up out of the way."

With both hands she lifted the long tresses high. She felt his hands at her nape and then the necklace fell free. He caught it in one hand and added the matching earrings. When he nuzzled the side of her exposed throat, Vanessa's knees all but gave way.

But his hands curled around her hips and held her steady, captive to the hot kisses he peppered along one shoulder and then the other.

She couldn't contain the low needy sound that escaped her throat. The same need shuddered through her, an aching desire to press herself against him, soft to hard. As if he'd heard her silent plea, he pulled her back into his body. She felt the hard jut of his arousal, heard the rough growl rumble in his chest.

Arching her back she pressed closer and his hands slid up to span her rib cage. The tips of his thumbs brushed the underside of her breasts and she shivered with expectancy. She'd never experienced anything like this intensity of sensations. And she was still fully clothed.

The thought of doing this naked brought a flush of heat to her throat and face, and when he turned her in his arms she found the same raw need reflected in his eyes.

"Okay?" he asked.

"Oh, yeah."

He kissed that satisfied sound from her mouth, a long, deep extended kiss that left her breathless and panting. Then he took her hand and led her into the bedroom. He kissed her again and looked down into her eyes. "Shall we lose the dress?"

Her nerves skittered and her breath caught on her whispered, "Yes."

"Nervous?"

"A little."

"Yeah," he said, but his fingers seemed sure and steady on her dress fastening. "I know."

The loosened bodice fell forward and she caught it in her hands. "What do you have to be nervous about?"

He paused, eyes serious on hers. "Doing it right."

Well, sure, but at least he had experience on his side. She, on the other hand, was acting on impulse. And the sensations he aroused with the sure touch of his hands and the heat of his mouth and the erotic wet slide of his tongue.

Before she could think, *I'm not quite ready to be seen in my underwear*, her dress lay in a silken pool at her feet and she was being seen in her underwear. With high heeled sandals. She felt gauche and exposed, but when she saw the primitive desire on his face she lifted her chin and forced her hands to rest at her sides.

He stepped in and cupped her breasts, his thumbs stroking over her aroused nipples until pleasure pierced her body and stretched straight to her core. When he removed her bra, an arrow of fear immobilized her for the first exposed moment but the touch of his bare hands brought her zinging back to life. The pad of his thumb circled her areola and grazed her nipple.

"Easy," he murmured when her knees dipped and wobbled. "I've got you."

He eased her to the bed and followed her down.

His mouth found her breast. Sliding her fingers through his hair, she sifted the strands in a fretful echo of the pull of his mouth. *Oh, yes,* Ms. P. whispered, *he definitely has you.* Then his hot tongue swirled over her nipple and her back arched from the bed. She cried out, a ragged appeal for release.

He left her breasts to slide lower, hooking his fingers into her underwear and peeling them away. A restless fire licked through her body. His hands were on her legs, his mouth on her thighs, his fingers finding her wet and ready.

Then he left her alone and she felt the abandonment in every turned-on cell. Her eyes fluttered open to find him beside the bed. Shoes already gone, he stood to unzip his trousers and her mouth went dry. She'd known he was a big man, hard and uncompromising, and that had never been more apparent than when he straightened, naked and very, very aroused.

Apprehension flickered through her and she swallowed.

Perhaps this wasn't such a good idea after all.

Perhaps she could have remained a virgin for life.

But then he finished donning protection and returned to her side, kissing the worry from her lips, reassuring her that he'd look after her, touching her supersensitive flesh with a delicious pressure that spiraled low in her belly.

"Please," she whispered, catching at his body and pulling him close. She wanted this now, while she felt like this, ready to go up in flames. "Please, can we do it?"

Heat blazed in his eyes as he moved over her, spreading her thighs and pressing a slow, deep kiss to her open mouth as he eased into her body. Restraint tightened his face. "Are you sure?"

In answer, she lifted her hips into the insistent press of his sex.

Eyes fixed on hers, he eased his way with the measured rock of his hips. Sweat broke out on his forehead when he stopped, and she felt a momentary panic.

"Don't stop." Her hands slid down his back and her nails found purchase in the taut muscles of his buttocks. "Please. Don't stop."

"I'm just," he said tightly, "going slow."

He pressed a little deeper and a tremor quivered through the long sweat-dampened muscles of his back. In that moment she recognized the effort in his restraint and knew it was for her, in deference to her first time, and she felt an overwhelming wave of tenderness.

She lifted a trembling hand to touch his mouth, and he muttered something low and fierce, an oath or a promise, and then he was inside her all the way, filling her to the brink with his heat and with the enormity of the moment.

She rocked her hips, adjusting to the unfamiliar, surprised by the lack of pain, and wanting it to never end. But he'd started to move with a slow, smooth cadence, rising over her with a look of burning intensity that caused her heart to stall out. She picked up the rhythm and held his gaze through each rolling thrust, moving with him as he drove toward his completion.

He didn't leave her behind. He reached between them, finding her and stroking her until her world narrowed and converged on one wildly spinning pleasure point. She heard him call her name as he followed, a hoarse shout of release that hung in the cooling air and wound its way around her heart.

Tristan watched Vanessa sleep, at last seeing her with her guard completely down. No clothes, no makeup, no facade of sophistication. Just Vanessa, her delicate beauty incandescent in the soft lamplight. So beautiful and proud and complex and fierce, she made him ache in a dozen ways and a dozen places.

Propped on an elbow he watched her and he willed her to wake, impatient to start over. He wasn't proud of how he'd judged and treated her so harshly and he intended making it up to her every way he could. Thinking about what she'd revealed in the car, about her childhood and her care and protection of her brother when she'd been too young for such responsibility, fuelled his resolve.

He'd got it so wrong. This time he intended getting it right and he couldn't wait to start.

Leaning close he kissed the soft sleepiness of her mouth and the sexy dent in her chin and traced a fine blue vein across the near-translucent skin of her breast.

The nipple peaked and she came awake instantly. It took another second for her memory to catch up and the flush to rise from her throat. She met his eyes but a note of shyness kept her expression wary.

He couldn't halt the surge of possessive male pride that gripped him. He wasn't sure he wanted to. He smiled and shook his head. "A virgin."

"You didn't believe me?"

Trick question. Something in her tone warned him to take care with his answer. "I didn't understand how that could be possible."

"I think lack of opportunity sums it up."

"You didn't have boyfriends?"

"No. I was either working or looking after Lew. And the boys I knew weren't interested in having him tag along." She rolled a shoulder dismissively. He sensed she didn't care that she'd missed the teen-dating scene. "And then I was married at twenty-two."

For a moment he said nothing, his need to know warring with his need to leave the past behind.

But he did need to know. That was his problem—he was greedy to know everything about her, even the bits better left buried. "This contract you made when you married. Didn't you ever want to break it?"

"No. I never looked at Stuart that way. He was more like a…"

In her hesitation he sensed what she was reluctant to admit. "A father?"

"Like the father I wished I'd had. I'm sorry, but that's the truth. And, you know, I think that was why Stuart suggested this arrangement in the first place. He never got over losing his family. He was desperately lonely, especially when he got older and his health problems caused him to cut right back on his work."

"He was semiretired?"

"Yes. That's when he started coming into the restaurant more often. He was a bit lost." She smiled, a wistful little curve of her lips that fisted around his heart. "At first he just wanted to help. Then he got invested in me and Lew. I think he saw us as a substitute family."

It hurt, but not as much as before he'd read the apology in Stuart's letter. And she'd needed the support of a father figure, it seemed. Desperately.

"Your parents—you said they weren't around much."

"No. And when they were...I often wished they weren't." Sadness, dark and profound, shadowed her expression. "They didn't handle Lew's difficulties. They didn't know how to handle him. My father had a violent temper."

"Against you and your brother?"

"Only my mom. And she drank to counter it. We were the classic dysfunctional family."

"And no one saw this?" he demanded, angry at the injustice of everything she'd told him and his impotence to change it. "Nobody helped?"

"My parents were working, too, providing in their own modest way. And if the authorities had gotten involved, Lew and I might have been fostered out and split up. We coped, okay? Much better than if a kid like

Lew had landed in the foster system. And I ended up here, living in Eastwick, with everything I ever wanted."

"Except a family."

She looked up sharply. "Lew is my family. I don't want it any other way, Tristan. I have no regrets over marrying Stuart. He knew it was for the money and we were both happy with that choice."

"And me," he asked. "Do you have any regrets about me?"

She studied him a long while and a myriad of emotions darkened her silvery gaze. "That would depend."

"On?"

"On how this ends up."

"At the moment I was wondering about so far." He lifted a hand and touched a mark on her throat. *His* mark on her throat. His body tightened in response. "Do you regret this?"

"Not yet."

It was a start. And she was still here, in his bed, which had to count for something.

"Will you stay?" He tugged at the sheet she'd pulled up to cover her nakedness until she relented and let it go. Then he turned her into his arms and looked deep into her eyes. "I want to make it up to you, Vanessa. Will you let me?"

Eleven

Vanessa stayed. A fitful sleeper even in her own bed, she hadn't counted on sleeping soundly and waking to the sound of running water. Jackknifing upright, she discovered Tristan lounging in the doorway to the bathroom. He was naked, which she noticed straight away, and looking cat-got-the-cream satisfied and very much at ease.

She frowned at the thought. How long had he been standing there, watching her sleep?

Disconcerted, she pulled the sheet up beneath her chin.

He arched his eyebrow in a way that reminded her he'd seen it all already, from much closer. "I'm glad you're awake."

"Oh?" she asked, immediately suspicious.

"I'm running a bath for you. If you hadn't roused soon, I was going to have to take drastic action."

"Such as?"

He straightened off the doorjamb and sauntered to the bed. With each approaching stride her heart kicked up another beat. He didn't say a word. Eyes locked on hers, he bent down and swung her into his arms as if she weighed nothing.

She gasped in shock and because, well, she wasn't used to being manhandled. But as he carted her back to the bathroom, she discovered she liked the manhandling too much to fight it. She made a token protest as he held her over the brimming three-cornered spa tub, but instead of dropping her into the bubbles he stepped over the rim and sank down with her in his arms.

Then he kissed her and murmured, "I'm glad you stayed," and she decided to stay a little longer.

Breakfast arrived on the heels of the bath and Vanessa felt extremely spoiled.

When she finished dressing and walked into the living room, she discovered a pancake stack lit with candles and sparklers in the center of the dining table. Her eyes widened with disbelief and her heart did a crazy painful lurch.

"Happy birthday, darling."

Not duchess. Darling.

Hot tears ached at the back of her throat and she took an age to compose herself enough to say, "Thank you." She cleared her throat. "How did you know?"

"I just took a wild stab in the dark."

Of course he knows your birth date, Ms. Pragmatist mocked. *And probably a whole lot more that he's not letting on. He was investigating you. Digging up your secrets. Remember?*

The mood nose-dived after that. Oh, she sat at the table and blew out the candles and pretended to make a wish. She was hungry enough to appreciate the fabulous breakfast spread and he'd even remembered her specialty coffee—or he'd known enough to check with the restaurant staff.

But she couldn't get past the sinking feeling that however wonderful the night, however enjoyable his company, however seductive his intent, the specter of their past conflict would rise between them.

"So." He leaned back in his chair and studied her across the table. "What have you got planned for your special day?"

"I have a date with Lew."

"Lunch?"

She nodded. "A picnic at the shore."

"You might want to rethink that." He tilted his head toward the balcony and outdoors. "Storms are forecast."

Bother. She put down her cutlery, frowning.

"We could do something else. Go somewhere else. Maybe the rain will fizzle out and we can still picnic—" He stopped. Frowned back at her. "What's the problem?"

The initial problem was the storms, which Lew loathed and feared. But the second problem superseded the first, and was now jittering around in her stomach. "You said *we*. I'm not sure that's a good idea."

"Which part? Me spending the day with you? Or me spending the day with Lew?"

Vanessa's stomach twisted into a pretzel knot. There were so many concerns, so many not-a-good-ideas she did not know where to start. "It's difficult," she said carefully. "He can be difficult."

"He's autistic. You mentioned that."

She shook her head. "I don't think you understand. He needs routine. Anything out of the ordinary— changed plans, new people, storms—makes him fret. Difficult with Lew can be sudden and violent."

"I would like to meet your brother," he said with quiet insistence.

"I'm afraid that's out of the question."

"For today? Or forever?"

She should not have to explain her decision—it was hers alone to make. But his obdurate expression demanded an answer and she knew he would push and push until she ended up losing her temper. It was better to explain while her head was cool and clear. "This isn't personal, Tristan. I don't take anyone to see Lew because his reaction to people is so extreme. He either ignores you altogether or he takes an instant shine."

"And which do you think I can't handle?"

Damn him, she had one difficult male in her life. She did not need another.

And wasn't that the crux of this whole issue? Tristan did not have a future in her life. So why introduce him into Lew's? Why set up the potential for disappointment?

Instinctively she knew that Lew would adore Tristan. They would talk sports and throw a football and swap the kind of guy-talk she couldn't even fake. And tomorrow or next week or whenever, Tristan would return to his own life and she'd be left with the constant hammering of, *Where's Tristan? Can we go visit? He said we'd go to the Yankees. Can we go today?*

Even worse, there'd come a day when Lew would finally accept that Tristan wasn't taking him to a ballgame. And she was the lucky one who would have to deal with his why-doesn't-he-want-to-be-my-friend moping.

She shook her head firmly. "My answer is still no."

"What about Stuart? Did you take him to visit Lew?"

"They met. But he didn't have an active role in Lew's life."

His gaze narrowed. "I thought you two were his surrogate family."

Damn him, did he ever let up? "I said he *thought* we might be, but it turned out to be too painful. He tried, but he didn't want a constant reminder of the son he didn't get to see and toss a ball with. That substitute didn't work."

Finally, he had no comeback. His silence was not satisfying, however. It banded tight around Vanessa's chest, an aching reminder that this father-son conflict would always come between them, driving one of them to speak out of turn and hurt the other.

An aching reminder that she needed to protect her own heart as well as Lew's.

She lifted her chin with a new determination. "I'm not debating this anymore. I am spending the day with Lew. Alone." She pushed to her feet. "I'll just get my purse and shoes."

"All right," he said with great reluctance. "But I am taking you to dinner tonight."

"No, Tristan."

Something darkened in his narrowed eyes. "Are you suggesting that this is it?"

"You told me last night, that *this* was whatever I wanted it to be."

"That was before you came upstairs and took off your clothes." He, too, came to his feet. They faced off across the discarded birthday breakfast. "This is not over, Vanessa."

"Because you say so? We can't have a relationship, Tristan. Even if I wanted to, even if we didn't have all this angst and conflict and history between us, I couldn't. I have priorities and they're all about Lew. I can't do a relationship!"

"Then why did you sleep with me? What was last night about?"

"You tell me," she fired back, instantly defensive. "Maybe I just wanted to prove my innocence!"

"You didn't think I believed you?" A muscle jumped in his jaw. His voice went very low, gruff with intensity. "I hope you are kidding."

Vanessa walked away from the table. Her heart was thundering, anxiety chased through her veins. At the French doors leading onto the balcony she whirled back around. "Look at us! We can't go a day without one of these confrontations. This is what I grew up with, Tristan. This is why I love my life with all its calm and order. That's why my marriage was so perfect."

Her impassioned little speech crackled between them a long time before he spoke. "You're pushing me away because you're scared."

"I'm pushing you away because you are so damn stubborn you won't take no for an answer!"

"I'm trying to work out what's going on with you. Last night was…" He let out a frustrated huff and shook his head. "Maybe you don't realize it, but that was amazing. I want that again, Vanessa, but I'm not going to beg. I won't go down on one knee. I won't promise you a perfect life of calm and order, because I'd rather have you with the heat and the passion and, yeah, even the fights."

Heart knocking hard against her ribs, she stared back at him. "I didn't ask for any promises. And I hate the fights."

"Yeah, I figured."

She didn't know what else to say. She'd made up her mind and she needed to get out of there. At the door she turned and found him standing in the same place, motionless but for that muscle jumping in his jaw.

She swallowed a large ache in her throat and met his shuttered gaze. There was one last thing to broach. "I can't go without asking about that letter. The second one."

"I'll hand it over to the police."

"And the will challenge?"

"You proved your point," he said flatly after a long beat of pause. "I'll talk to my lawyers tomorrow. It's all yours. Just as Stuart wanted."

Tears welled in her eyes before the door shut behind her. She dashed them away with her wrist as she strode to the elevators, eager to be somewhere private before the emotional storm erupted. She pressed the button and fixated on the floor indicator. More tears threatened and she swallowed against the harsh throb in her throat.

At least she could be thankful for one thing. He hadn't insisted on driving her to collect her car from the country club where she'd left it last night. She would take a taxi. And if the tears came, it wouldn't matter.

The elevator arrived and she stepped forward as the door opened.

"Wait." Tristan's voice called after her, from back at his suite.

Heart racing, Vanessa pressed the ground floor button. She couldn't take any more of this emotion and she was afraid that one kind word, one softening of his hard-set expression, would send her sobbing into his arms.

Counterproductive, Ms. P. decided.

The doors started to close. Vanessa breathed again.

But at the last possible moment, a large, familiar hand blocked their slide. She remembered it on her breasts, between her legs, drawing her to an exquisite climax. And the ache in her throat grew unbearable.

She straightened her shoulders and sucked in a fortifying breath. *Please don't cry. Please don't cry.*

"You forgot this."

She forced herself to focus on what he held in that extended hand.

The jewelry he'd asked her to take off before they made love. She stared at the glittering pieces in his hand, a symbol of the bought-and-paid-for wife. A symbol of the conflicted history that would always come between them.

She took them and put them in her purse and gamely met his guarded eyes. "Thank you, Tristan. For everything." The doors started to slide, and she hurried to finish. "I will never forget last night. You're right—it was amazing."

When he returned to his suite, Tristan packed his bags. There wasn't a lot to do; he'd packed for Florida never meaning to return. And now, he didn't know if he was glad or sorry that he'd come back.

He didn't dwell on working out an answer. Vanessa had made her mind up and he'd come closer to swallowing his pride and begging than he'd ever wanted to try. And for what? To buy another week in her bed? To instigate a long-distance relationship with no future, because she didn't want anything that might threaten her secure world.

She might have her priorities all screwed. She might be living at delusion-central when it came to her happiness. But she'd been right about one thing: they could never go one day without a fiery confrontation.

That's what he loved most about her: that fierce commitment that made her stand to her convictions and made a mockery of her desire for a calm, orderly existence.

He understood her reasons. After that hellish childhood, who wouldn't want security? But courtesy of Stuart's estate she had truckloads of prime greenback security.

She needed more. He hoped someday she would come to that realization, even though he'd be long gone. But before he left, he had three loose ends to tie.

First, he phoned his lawyer with orders to drop his challenge of the will. Then he called the detectives on the Bunny Baldwin case and made arrangements for an officer to collect the second nuisance letter.

The third task was all about setting things right and he didn't expect it to be easy. He figured it might take several days to track down the exact model and he was going to do everything in his power to make sure he did.

If he found it, well, it would serve as an apology and a thank-you and a goodbye.

To set his search in motion, he lifted the phone and called the number he knew by heart.

Vanessa's thirtieth birthday was hardly an unqualified success. The squally storms missed Lexford, but it only took the threat of dark clouds and thunder to put Lew on edge. She transferred the picnic to the recreation room at Twelve Oaks and spent the afternoon watching DVDs with Lew and several of his friends.

Which wouldn't have been all bad if their taste in movies didn't run to gross-out humor.

Still, the time spent with her brother reassured her that she'd made the right choice. Watching him nudge his buddies and guffaw over the lame jokes brought a poignant ache to her heart. He couldn't be happier or in a better place. And his laughter was her happiness.

"Watch this bit, Ness," he called over his shoulder. "It's a crack-up."

The boys all thought so but Vanessa rolled her eyes. She'd set her cell phone to vibrate, and when it started to hum she fought the temptation to answer.

What if it's important?
What if it's Tristan?

That made no sense after they'd ended on such a blaring note of finality. There was no reason for him to call and nothing left to say. That didn't stop her heart plummeting with disappointment when she picked up and heard Jack Cartwright's deep voice.

"I don't know what you got up to with Thorpe last night and, frankly, I don't want to know. But you pulled it off. His lawyer just called to let me know. He's dropped the contest."

There was a huge moment's hollowness. Then Jack saying, "Hello? Are you there? Vanessa?"

"No, no. I'm here."

"I don't hear you screaming with jubilation. I must say I'm disappointed in you."

"I think I'm just numb," she said honestly. "Maybe the joy beans will kick in later."

Although she doubted it. She could hardly confess that she'd known his decision earlier that morning. Not without admitting she'd possibly influenced the result between the Egyptian cotton sheets of the Marabella's Columbus suite.

Her cheeks grew hot, her body restive with remembering. Driving home from Twelve Oaks she talked herself into calling Tristan. To thank him for following through on his promise so promptly.

But the receptionist informed her that Mr. Thorpe had checked out that morning.

He was gone and it was over. Two years of torment and trouble at his hands were finally finished, and all Vanessa felt was a gaping chasm of aloneness.

Twelve

"Did you hear that David Duvall passed away last night?"

Abby shared the news of Mary's grandfather's death as soon as Vanessa and Felicity joined her on the country club terrace the following Wednesday. They had all just attended a social committee meeting, finalizing details for the Eastwick Ball. Abby had asked them to stay and have a drink with her as she had some news.

Vanessa had expected an update on the investigation into Bunny's death so this came as something of a shock. "How is Mary?" she asked. "She seemed very strained at the wedding. Maybe it was because of her grandfather…"

"He's been sick a long time, but a family death is never

easy." As soon as she finished speaking, Felicity winced and put her hand over Abby's on the table. "Me and my mouth. I'm sorry."

"Please, you don't have to cosset me." Abby smiled gamely. "I actually asked you to stay because I have some news about Mother. I wanted to tell you before you read it in tomorrow's newspaper."

"Has there been an arrest?"

"No." The corners of Abby's mouth tightened. "But the police have finally acknowledged that they're treating this as a murder investigation."

"Oh, Abby." Felicity squeezed her friend's hand. "Are you okay with this?"

"I'm pleased they appear to be doing something about my suspicions."

"Has there been new evidence?" Vanessa asked.

Abby nodded. "The police recovered a single pill near Mom. The tests show it's a placebo made to look like digitalis. I couldn't work out why no medication showed up in Mom when I'd *seen* her taking her pills!"

"Someone had swapped them for these placebos?"

"That would also explain the disappearance of her pill case."

"If the murderer took it."

Felicity and Vanessa swapped shocked looks. Up until now they'd known of Abby's suspicions, but this sounded like hard evidence. And whoever did this had to have access to Bunny's pill case and Bunny's home. They'd also known where to find the journals.

"It has to be someone we know," Vanessa mused. "Someone close to Bunny."

"The police are still trying to locate the woman Edith heard arguing with Mom that day."

"It is odd that no one saw this mystery woman."

They all agreed. Vanessa cleared her throat. "There's something odd about the letters, too."

She felt the other women's eyes on her, waiting for her to explain.

"You know the letter I mentioned, addressed to Tristan but not demanding any money....well, he received a second one."

"When did this happen?" Felicity asked.

"Last week. That's why he crashed the wedding."

"I wondered what was going on between you two. When Lily said you left with him, I thought we should report your abduction."

Vanessa felt heat in her throat and her face. "It wasn't an abduction." *It was more of a seduction, really.* "We worked out a few misunderstandings, and he's dropped the will contest."

"Are you for real?"

"That's wonderful, Vanessa. You must be thrilled!"

"I'm relieved, mainly."

Felicity was studying her with curiosity. "Those must have been some misunderstandings. Were they connected with the letters?"

"Yes, actually. The second letter was supposed to prove my adultery. There was a photo and a list of dates and places where I met this man."

"Someone followed you? And wrote all that down? How sick."

Vanessa nodded. She felt sick thinking about that

level of surveillance, all unnoticed. "Anyway, Tristan has given both letters to the police," she assured Abby. "In case they're connected to the missing diaries."

"But you don't think they are?"

Vanessa shrugged. "I don't know. There's no demand for money. They're just…odd."

The other women considered this for a long moment before Felicity spoke. "And the photo? Who did this creep think you were seeing on the sly?"

Felicity's phrasing was particularly apt and made it easier than Vanessa had anticipated to swallow her resistance to sharing this part of her life. "My brother."

"You have a brother?" Abby asked. "I don't think you've ever mentioned him."

"I haven't. That's the thing."

That hadn't been so hard, Vanessa decided afterward. Felicity and Abby had been supportive and understanding and nonjudgmental. Driving home from the country club she felt her whole body sigh with relief.

Finally.

Maybe now she could muster some enthusiasm for the rest of her life. With the lifting of conservation orders on Stuart's estate, she could start executing his wishes for distributing his wealth. She had her friends, her committee work, Lew and Twelve Oaks. Everything would soon fall back into a routine and life would resume its calm, orderly pattern.

By the time she walked in her front door, Vanessa was feeling a renewed serenity. She paused in the foyer and called for Gloria. The sound of her voice echoed through the downstairs rooms, unanswered.

She crossed to the library and opened the door to peer inside. No Gloria and she almost missed the parcel sitting in the center of her desk.

A belated birthday present?

She had no idea who it could be from.

Intrigued, she crossed the room and picked up the unmarked gift box. She was still turning it over in her hands, a frown between her brows, when Gloria appeared.

"Ah, you found it," she said.

"Yes, but what is it?" Vanessa asked. "And where did it come from?"

"A delivery man brought it. Just an hour or so ago."

"Who's it from?"

"I don't have X-ray vision. Why don't you open it and see?"

Of course she should open it. Ms. Pragmatist would have had the sucker unstuck and unwrapped and the thank-you card written by now.

She drew a quick breath and started on the box. She had a strange sensation in her belly, a feeling of momentousness that made Ms. P. shake her head in despair.

Inside the box was a tissue-wrapped…something. She peeled away the layers with shaky fingers to reveal a Lladro figurine.

"It's your *Girl with Flowers*," Gloria said unnecessarily. "Who could have sent that?"

She almost missed the card tucked inside the box. Three lines in a bold hand.

Setting things right.

A peace offering, an apology,

A goodbye.

The words he'd offered in the kitchen, the day he turned a simple kiss on the hand into sensual bliss. Gently her thumb stroked over the illegible scrawl of a signature that swam before her eyes.

"Are you all right, Nessa?"

She turned the delicate little girl over in her hands and the memory of him doing the same, that first day in the keeping room, washed through her in a debilitating wave. No, she was not all right. She was trembling with emotion, inside and out, so much so that she had to sit down.

"How on earth did he find her?" she murmured. It couldn't have been easy to locate a piece cast seventeen years ago, especially in less than a week. How had he even known which figurine to look for? Someone must have helped. Her gaze settled on Gloria. "Did you have anything to do with it?"

"All I did was point him in the right direction. It'd be just like him to hare off on a wild goose chase."

"I didn't want him chasing after anything!"

"After all he put you through?" Gloria retorted. "It was the least he could do."

Vanessa tried to summon up the same righteous indignation as her loyal housekeeper. Then she might be able to repack the gift and send it back. Hadn't she told him that the figurine itself meant nothing? Its symbolism was indelibly imprinted on her life. She didn't need a place-keeper anymore and certainly not this…substitute.

Except her heart—poor, foolish, smitten creature—recognized this gesture as much more than replacing a broken ornament. The figurine itself didn't matter; his act in sending the gift did. It represented an apology for the discord of the last two years and for the way he'd confronted her in her home and for every misconception and accusation and altercation.

Setting things right mattered to him—he'd told her so.

She should accept that, send a prettily worded—and sincere—thank-you note, and get on with her life.

That is what she wanted, right? That's what she'd told him that morning in his hotel suite. In the days since, she'd even reconciled her wretched romantic side with that reality. She'd put Tristan Thorpe behind her, she'd moved on with her own life, concentrating on her true priorities.

But her gaze kept returning to the little note.

Goodbye.

Was that what she really wanted? Now, like this, when she'd been less than truthful? Or was it her turn to set one last thing straight...?

Tristan was in a cab en route to the airport when his phone buzzed. He knew it was her by the telltale little sound of her inhalation when he answered. His body did the complete *it's-Vanessa* rattle and hum before she got anywhere near saying those words.

"It's Vanessa. I'm glad I caught you. The hotel told me you'd checked out and I was afraid—" She paused, sucked in an audible breath, slowed the headlong rush of her voice "I thought I might have missed you."

"I'm still in the city. Stuck in traffic."

"I suppose the rain isn't helping. Not at this time of morning."

"Wet up there, too?"

"It's just started to close in."

Tristan shut his eyes and shook his head. Had it come down to this? Stilted small talk about the weather interspersed by awkward seconds of silence?

Yes, he answered himself in the next cumbersome pause. *It had.*

"What do you want, Vanessa?" he asked on a sigh.

"I want to thank you for the figurine. I can't imagine how you found the *Girl with Flowers.* You must have gone to a lot of trouble and that wasn't necessary but… thank you. It's lovely and I…" He pictured the hitch of her shoulders she'd give as her voice trailed off, and in those last husky words he also heard the threat of tears. The image—of that distinctive Vanessa gesture, of her beautiful eyes misty green with moisture, of her dimpled chin lifting as she struggled for control—squeezed all the air from his lungs.

For a long beat of time he couldn't speak. Couldn't do anything but sit there, fighting the urge to offer up sentiments she didn't want to hear and which his battered pride wouldn't allow him to utter. He felt like one big, harsh, frustrated bundle of regret.

Finally, he managed to shrug and say, "It's the least I could do."

She gave an odd little laugh. "Funnily enough, Gloria said the exact same thing."

Funnily enough, that didn't surprise him. "And what about you, Vanessa?"

"Oh, I think it's a start."

"Didn't you read the note? I thought it was more of an end."

"And your way of setting things right."

Yeah, except nothing felt right. Not about leaving, not about the way things were between them. Not about this whole agonizing goodbye conversation from the back of a cab. That was all kinds of wrong.

"Before you go—" her voice, soft and resolute, cut through the rough storm of his thoughts "—there is something I need to set right."

"I'm listening."

"That morning in your hotel suite, you suggested I was running scared but I wasn't so much scared as full-out terrified." She proffered that with another rueful laugh. "I hadn't had the time—or perhaps the courage—to work out what I was doing there with you or what should happen next. It was too much, too intense, and then you hit me with wanting to meet Lew. I'm not used to sharing that part of my life. I'm not used to sharing anything quite like I did with you that night."

"Yet you did. To prove a point."

"No. I didn't sleep with you to prove anything."

That admission hit Tristan with sledgehammer force, somewhere in the region of his heart. He rolled his head back and pinched the bridge of his nose, as if that might contain the giant ball of ache inside him. "Are you sure about that?"

"Yes," she said with a quiet conviction that resonated right through the phone.

"Why did you sleep with me? Because I've been thinking about it and your explanation is the only one that makes any sense."

"Does it have to make sense? When it seems like there was no choice."

What the hell? "I gave you the chance to back out. There was no force."

"I'm not talking about force, Tristan, I'm talking about desire. At the beach…the way you touched me, the way you kissed me, the way you looked at me. You didn't have to take me back to your hotel room. You could have done anything you wanted, any way you wanted, right there."

"Beach sex is overrated."

"While making love," she countered, "isn't. At least not in my limited experience."

"Why are you telling me this?" he asked roughly, because, hell, in two hours he'd be in the air, heading back to Australia. He didn't want to think about the passion of that night, the sweet taste of her mouth, the hot silk of her body. He couldn't afford to ponder her choice of words. Not sex but *making love*. "Why now, when I'm about to leave?"

"Do you have to go?"

He couldn't have heard her right. Probably because of the rush of blood in his ears, the roar of hope racing to fill every raw aching hollow in his body. "Why would I want to stay?"

"I'm going to Twelve Oaks this afternoon. If you are still interested, I would like you to come with me." She paused, as if to gather breath or courage or both. And when she spoke again, her voice was strong and steady and blessedly sure. "I would like you to meet my brother."

He wasn't coming.

Vanessa waited an hour longer than the usual travel time from the city before resigning herself to that fact. She should have expected as much by his silence after her invitation, a silence she'd filled by blabbering about the rain and the traffic and how long the drive may take and how much Lew would enjoy meeting him and how much she looked forward to seeing him. Then she realized that his cell had dropped out.

He'd heard her invitation, though, she was sure of that. He hadn't come because he was going home. He had meant the goodbye on the note and there would be no other.

Still she waited another half hour after the extra hour, and then she sucked back the useless tears and drove up to Lexford alone. Sure, the bottom had fallen out of her world but she'd promised Lew. She would keep on doing what she had always done—looking out for him, building her days around his care, using Stuart's estate to help others in the same situation she'd found herself in before his timely intervention.

Except with every passing mile the ache of wanting what she'd witnessed between Lily and Jack, Emma and Garrett, Felicity and Reed—that devoted connection which she'd thought she could live without in her own life—grew thicker in her chest. She attempted to summon up the voice of pragmatism, to remind herself that this yearning was for a chimera of a relationship. They barely knew each other. A couple of weeks, a series of clashes, a belated understanding and one long, hot night of passion.

"This is not a relationship," she said out loud. "Will you please back me up here?"

But Ms. P. remained ominously silent while the rain continued to fall, enclosing Vanessa in a bleak gray curtain to match her mood.

Lost in her desolate musing, she didn't notice the car tailing her until its headlights flicked on and off, on and off, catching her attention in the rearview mirror. Thinking *police,* she instantly slowed and started to pull over. She hadn't been speeding, but did she miss a yield sign or…

Her heart gave a huge stutter as she glanced into her mirror again. Not a police car. No siren or flashing lights, just the warm yellow-tinged beam of headlights from a silvery gray sedan following her onto the shoulder, and a matching bright glow in the center of her chest as a tall, broad, familiar figure stepped from the driver's seat.

Fingers quaking with a nervous blend of hope and relief, Vanessa fumbled to release her seatbelt. Her door opened and somehow she spilled from the seat and straight into the hard wall of Tristan's body. For a moment that was enough: the familiar breadth of his chest, the shelter of his large frame, the sweet scent of rain on his skin. Then his arms folded around her, holding her close against the drumming beat of his heart, and she knew that nothing would be enough again, not without the comforting strength of those arms.

Despite the cool drizzle of rain neither moved for a long time, except to burrow closer, to stroke the wet strands of hair from her face, to wrap her closer into the hard heat of his body. This might not be a relationship, Vanessa thought, but it felt so perfectly right and so full of promise.

She closed her eyes and for several seconds imagined that it could be this simple; that walking into his arms might magically fix everything she'd feared would come between them. It wouldn't. After those precious few seconds, she raised her face from his chest. "When you hadn't arrived after all those hours, I thought you'd gone home."

"I thought I was home," he said with heart-stopping simplicity. A frown creased his brow. "Are you crying?"

"No."

It wasn't quite a lie, since the tears were part of the smile that formed on her lips and arrowed to her heart…or perhaps it was the other way around. When he thumbed the betraying moisture from her cheek, the smile swelled to fill her chest. "It must be the rain."

He turned his intense-eyed focus from her face to survey the sky. "I need to get you out of this."

"We're already wet," she countered, not ready to relinquish her position. "Besides, this isn't cold rain."

At least it didn't feel that way to her, not with his body heat seeping into her flesh.

When he looked set to argue the point, Vanessa held a hand up to his lips. Her expression turned serious. "You said you were home—do you mean to stay?"

"If you want me to."

Her heart started to pound. Of course she wanted him…but could it be that simple?

After another second she felt a change in his posture and his gaze narrowed on her face. "That is why you called me? Or did I read that message wrong, too."

"No, oh, no. I called because I wanted you to stay." She drew a quick breath, suddenly more nervous than she had ever been in her life. "I want you to stay, Tristan. I want to take this chance at…at whatever it is we might have together."

"What do you think that might be?"

Vanessa frowned, not understanding what he was getting at. "I don't know."

"I didn't walk away from that airport today for nothing."

"The morning in your hotel room, you said no promises."

"That morning in my hotel room, you said you had everything you wanted," he countered. "Do you want what you've got…or do you want that and more?"

A week ago the notion of *more* had terrified her. She hadn't wanted the intensity and emotional roller coaster. She hadn't wanted to open herself up to the possibility of a love this powerful and breathtaking.

Now, looking up into the intense blue of Tristan's eyes, she saw every vestige of her quiet, restful, ordered life slide away. A frisson of fear chased in its wake but she lifted her chin and moistened her lips. "I would very much like the more," she said. "If it's with you."

He kissed her, possibly because he'd been waiting too long to do so, and possibly because the magnitude of this step had tightened her expression. He kissed the rain from her lips and then from her lashes, her cheeks, the point of her chin. Then he kissed her mouth with a tenderness that sang through her blood. Everything else, every worry and every anxiety, melted in the restrained promise of that kiss.

"There will be a lot more, Vanessa. And there will be promises."

"You said no p—"

"I lied."

She swallowed. "In what way?"

"I promise to be here for you and your brother, in whatever capacity you want. I promise to support you and protect you." He stroked a thumb across her lips and the look on his face almost caused her knees to buckle. "I'd also promise to love you, but I'm afraid that might terrify you."

Strangely, it didn't…and that worried her just a little. "We don't know each other well enough for promises. What if this doesn't work out? What if we keep on clashing the way we have always done? What if this is just—"

He kissed her again, this time for a very long while. It silenced Vanessa's worries once more and she could have gone on kissing him for days, weeks, months, but the rain started to fall more heavily and he lifted his head to glare at the sky again.

"I need to get you out of this rain before you drown." He drew her back to her car, but before opening the door he paused. "We mightn't have known each other long, but I know you well enough."

Well enough that he'd stayed, to support her, to protect her, to be her rock. To love her.

The notion wasn't half as terrifying as she'd imagined. It rolled through her and settled somewhere deep and vital. *So this is love*, she thought on a note of wonder.

It felt like something she would like to get used to.

She went up on her toes to press a kiss to his mouth.

"What was that for?"

"Just something I'd like to get used to," she said with a smile. She had a feeling it wouldn't take too long to work up to more. "Would you like to meet my brother now?"

"I thought you'd never ask."

It was the perfect answer and the perfect start to a new happiness she didn't bother trying to hide. She had earned this happiness—it was hers, bought and paid for, and delivered from Australia, with love.

* * * * *

Don't miss the next book in the
SECRET LIVES OF SOCIETY WIVES
series!
Look for
The Once-a-Mistress Wife
by Katherine Garbera
Coming in October 2007
from Mills & Boon® Desire™.

New York Times bestselling author
Linda Lael Miller
is back with a new romance featuring
the heartwarming McKettrick family
from Mills & Boon® Special Edition.

Sierra's Homecoming
by Linda Lael Miller

On sale December 2007,
wherever books are sold.

Turn the page for a sneak preview!

Sierra's Homecoming

by

Linda Lael Miller

Soft, smoky music poured into the room.

The next thing she knew, Sierra was in Travis's arms, close against that chest she'd admired earlier, and they were slow dancing.

Why didn't she pull away?

"Relax," he said. His breath was warm in her hair.

She giggled, more nervous than amused. What was the matter with her? She was attracted to Travis, had been from the first, and he was clearly attracted to her. They were both adults. Why not enjoy a little slow dancing in a ranch-house kitchen?

Because slow dancing led to other things. She took a step back and felt the counter flush against her lower back. Travis naturally came with her, since they were holding hands and he had one arm around her waist.

Simple physics.

Then he kissed her.

Physics again—this time, not so simple.

"Yikes," she said, when their mouths parted.

He grinned. "Nobody's ever said that after I kissed them."

She felt the heat and substance of his body pressed against hers. "It's going to happen, isn't it?" she heard herself whisper.

"Yep," Travis answered.

"But not tonight," Sierra said on a sigh.

"Probably not," Travis agreed.

"When, then?"

He chuckled, gave her a slow, nibbling kiss. "Tomorrow morning," he said. "After you drop Liam off at school."

"Isn't that…a little…soon?"

"Not soon enough," Travis answered, his voice husky. "Not nearly soon enough."

MILLS & BOON
Desire 2-in-1
On sale 17th August 2007

Heartbreaker by *Diana Palmer*

JB Hammock was a bachelor through and through...but could sweet, caring Tellie Maddox be the one woman who could finally hook this heartbreaker?

Scandals from the Third Bride by *Sara Orwig*

Katherine Ransome had never expected the man who jilted her to try to woo her a second time. Would she trust Cade Logan with her heart...again?

❦

The Intern Affair by *Roxanne St Claire*

Executive Cade McMann had his eye on his intern, Jessie Clayton, but seducing her could expose a secret that could unravel their relationship...and the family dynasty.

Forbidden Merger by *Emilie Rose*

When tycoon Liam Elliot falls for Aubrey Holt, the one woman he can't have, their secret affair sends more than the bed sheets up in flames.

Mini-series – The Elliotts

❦

The Morning-After Proposal by *Sheri WhiteFeather*

Dylan Trueno vows to protect Julia Alcott, on one condition – she becomes his wife. Will she succumb to her desires and his dutiful proposal?

Executive Seduction by *Kristi Gold*

Corri Harris' steamy affair with her boss was everything she'd hoped. But as things got hotter, would Aidan O'Brien toss her aside or was he in it for keeps?

Mediterranean Men

Let them sweep you off your feet!

Gorgeous Greeks

The Greek Bridegroom by Helen Bianchin
The Greek Tycoon's Mistress by Julia James
Available 20th July 2007

Seductive Spaniards

At the Spaniard's Pleasure by Jacqueline Baird
The Spaniard's Woman by Diana Hamilton
Available 17th August 2007

Irresistible Italians

The Italian's Wife by Lynne Graham
The Italian's Passionate Proposal by Sarah Morgan
Available 21st September 2007

www.millsandboon.co.uk

M&B

*Romancipation

ro·man–ci–pa–tion *noun*

The freedom for women to love whom they choose whilst retaining their own space and identity

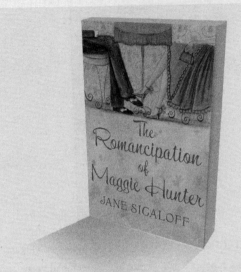

Maggie is living the life she's always wanted. Her career is taking off and, thanks to Japanese straightening technology, her hair is lying down. Maggie even has a funny, caring boyfriend – but there's one problem: he wants Maggie to move in.

Maggie's not sure she's ready to move from "me" to "we"… As she examines the relationships around her, Maggie has to decide: is she ready to face her fears and embrace her own romancipation?

Available 17th August 2007

In the heat of the desert, two women find love in the arms of their Arabian princes

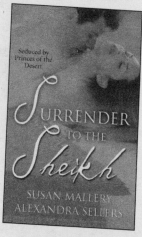

THE SHEIKH'S SECRET BRIDE by *Susan Mallery*

Malik Khan, Crown Prince of El Bahar, had been determined to possess Liana Archer from the moment that he saw her. But should Liana trust the man who could give her anything – everything – but love?

SHEIKH'S TEMPTATION by *Alexandra Sellers*

Sheikh Arash Khosrari was the only man who had ever touched Lana Holding in one night of unbridled and electrifying passion. But would the obstacles in their path be enough to take the heat out of their white-hot desire?

Available 7th September 2007

www.millsandboon.co.uk

FREE

2 BOOKS AND A SURPRISE GIFT!

We would like to take this opportunity to thank you for reading this Mills & Boon® book by offering you the chance to take TWO more specially selected 2-in-1 volumes from the Desire™ series absolutely FREE! We're also making this offer to introduce you to the benefits of the Mills & Boon® Reader Service™—

- ★ **FREE home delivery**
- ★ **FREE gifts and competitions**
- ★ **FREE monthly Newsletter**
- ★ **Books available before they're in the shops**
- ★ **Exclusive Reader Service offers**

Accepting these FREE books and gift places you under no obligation to buy; you may cancel at any time, even after receiving your free shipment. Simply complete your details below and return the entire page to the address below. You don't even need a stamp!

YES! Please send me 2 free Desire volumes and a surprise gift. I understand that unless you hear from me, I will receive 3 superb new volumes every month for just £4.99 each, postage and packing free. I am under no obligation to purchase any books and may cancel my subscription at any time. The free books and gift will be mine to keep in any case.

D7ZEE

Ms/Mrs/Miss/Mr...Initials ....

BLOCK CAPITALS PLEASE

Surname ....

Address ....

....

....Postcode ....

Send this whole page to:

The Reader Service, FREEPOST CN81, Croydon, CR9 3WZ